PRAISE FOR THE NOVELS
OF JILL SHALVIS

"Clever, steamy, fun, Jill Shalvis will make you laugh and fall in love." —Rachel Gibson, *New York Times* bestselling author

"Shalvis writes with humor, heart, and sizzling heat." —Carly Phillips, *New York Times* bestselling author

"Fall in love with Jill Shalvis! She's my go-to read for humor and heart." —Susan Mallery, *New York Times* bestselling author

"A fun, sexy story of the redemptive powers of love. Jill Shalvis sizzles!" —JoAnn Ross, *New York Times* bestselling author

"Witty, fun, and sexy—the perfect romance!" —Lori Foster, *New York Times* and *USA Today* bestselling author

"Fast-paced and deliciously fun . . . Jill Shalvis sweeps you away." —Cheri Adair, *USA Today* bestselling author

"A Jill Shalvis hero is the stuff naughty dreams are made of." —Vicki Lewis Thompson, *New York Times* bestselling author

"Shalvis makes me laugh, makes me cry, makes me sigh with pure pleasure." —Susan Andersen, *New York Times* bestselling author

"Delightful . . . Jill Shalvis rules." —*Midwest Book Review*

Animal
ATTRACTION

Jill Shalvis

BERKLEY SENSATION, NEW YORK

THE BERKLEY PUBLISHING GROUP
Published by the Penguin Group
Penguin Group (USA) Inc.
375 Hudson Street, New York, New York 10014, USA

USA | Canada | UK | Ireland | Australia | New Zealand | India | South Africa | China

Penguin Books Ltd., Registered Offices: 80 Strand, London WC2R 0RL, England
For more information about the Penguin Group, visit penguin.com.

ANIMAL ATTRACTION

A Berkley Sensation Book / published by arrangement with the author

Berkley Sensation Books are published by The Berkley Publishing Group.
BERKLEY SENSATION® is a registered trademark of Penguin Group (USA) Inc.
The "B" design is a trademark of Penguin Group (USA) Inc.

For information, address: The Berkley Publishing Group,
a division of Penguin Group (USA) Inc.,
375 Hudson Street, New York, New York 10014.

ISBN: 978-0-425-26837-7

PUBLISHING HISTORY
First Berkley Sensation mass-market paperback edition / October 2011

PRINTED IN THE UNITED STATES OF AMERICA

10 9 8 7 6 5 4 3 2 1

Cover photo of couple by Shutterstock/eyedear; porch by Shutterstock/Robin Keefe;
kitten by Shutterstock/OKSun; dog by Shutterstock/Erik Lam.
Cover design by Annette Fiore DeFex.
Interior text design by Kristin del Rosario.

ALWAYS LEARNING   **PEARSON**

Animal
ATTRACTION

One

C ome on, baby," he murmured. "Give it up for me. You
  know you want to."

Jade Bennett did her best to ignore the way the low, sexy
voice made her shiver. Besides, it wasn't aimed at her. Dr.
Dell Connelly—dog whisperer, cat whisperer, horse whisperer, and known woman whisperer—was talking to a stray
kitten.

The feline in question huddled miserably beneath the
bench seat in Dell's vet center waiting room, staring at him
from narrowed eyes, clearly having none of the sweet talk.
She was a scruffy, mangy grayish brown with sharp green
eyes, and, like Jade, *not* swayed by sweet talkers.

"Huh," Jade said from behind the reception counter.
"Most females leap right into your arms at the slightest en-
couragement."

Dell craned his neck and regarded her from eyes as dark
as his secrets. "Not all."

There was a beat of silence during which she did her

best not to break eye contact. He was right. Not all females—otherwise she'd have made the leap.

You're leaving in one month; it's far too late now . . .

As if suddenly realizing Dell was in the room, the huge St. Bernard snoring behind Jade's chair snorted awake and lifted her head. Seeing her beloved, Gertie lumbered up to her huge paws with a joyous bark of welcome before barreling toward Dell, skidding a little on the smooth linoleum as she scrambled around the corner of the desk and . . . launched herself into Dell's arms.

It was a good thing the guy wasn't a lightweight because Gertie moved with the velocity of a freight train. Dell braced himself, but all that delicious warm mocha skin of his—courtesy of his Native American mother—covered an impressive amount of tough testosterone and muscle. Still, even a six-foot-two, 180-pound veterinarian extraordinaire could be leveled by the freight-train force of a chunky St. Bernard, and at impact Dell landed on his ass. He merely laughed and gathered the dog in close, not appearing to mind either the floor or the sloppy kiss on the jaw.

He was wearing dark blue scrubs that looked annoyingly good on him, the bottoms of which had slipped low in the scuffle, revealing a inch or two of forest green knit boxers and a strip of smooth, slightly paler skin, not to mention the hint of prime male ass.

Unconcerned about the display, Dell gave Gertie a full body rub, then pushed her off of him.

The stray kitten, which looked to be three to four months old, old enough to have gathered plenty of wariness, did *not* approve of Gertie's exuberance. Beneath the chair, she pressed herself closer to the wall and hissed.

"Aw, you're fine," Dell told her, rubbing his jaw as he studied her. He had a hint of stubble, like maybe he'd slept too long to spare the time to shave that morning.

It shouldn't have been so damn sexy.

Neither should the way Gertie was sidling back up to him, trying to love him from not so far.

Animals always loved Dell. Little kids, too.

And women. Let's not forget how many women loved him.

He was bending low to whisper to the kitten, using that low, undeniably authoritative but oh-so-mesmerizing voice, the one that could melt the panties off a female at five paces.

Good thing, then, that Jade was at least seven paces away.

"Gertie here's just a big hunk of love," he was assuring the kitten. "Emphasis on the big hunk. Sit, Gert," he commanded with soft demand over his shoulder.

Gertie wriggled with barely contained joy but sat. Then grinned.

"There," Dell said to the kitten. "See? We're all harmless."

Harmless? Please. Dangerously smooth, maybe. Effortlessly charming, yes. A walking orgasm . . . without a doubt.

But harmless? Hell no, and at just the thought, Jade snorted.

"Ignore her, too," Dell said to the kitten. "She's the smartest one here, but she never learned how to chill. In fact, she's a lot like you, all tough and wary and grumpy, but I'm betting you're both just big softies deep down inside."

"I can hear you, you know," Jade said.

"Way deep *deep* inside . . ."

Jade worked at ignoring his alluringly boyish smile—which she didn't buy for a second because there was *nothing* boyish about him—and went back to loading the schedule for tomorrow's patients.

You want him . . .

She worked at avoiding that little voice as well. Lots of things to avoid. But she was leaving, going back home to Chicago at month's end. Plans had been made, notice had been given. It was as good as done.

The kitten went back to being pissed off at the world.

And Dell laughed softly. "So now I've got *two* women completely ignoring me. I'm going to get a complex."

As if. Dr. Dell Connelly knew the meaning of the word. He was sure and confident, always. Steady as a rock. Never second-guessed himself.

It was really annoying.

"Come on, kitty," Dell said. "Trust me."

Jade could have told her not to bother resisting, that she'd cave eventually. They always did. It was because Dell was the genuine deal, and animals could see that. Animals meant everything to him. While women flocked to him like bees to honey, she'd never seen him put his personal life ahead of his work. It was really a fascinating paradox. The gorgeous man could have anyone he wanted, and yet he didn't seem to want much more than what he had. A successful animal center, a few close friends, and speed-dial to the pizza joint.

Jade knew that she tended to shut people out and keep them at a distance. Dell did, too, but he went about it differently, making himself available to everything and everyone . . . while keeping it all shallow.

He didn't take anything too seriously, especially women.

But the kitten continued to stare at Dell with a heartbreaking defiance that Jade recognized from every time she looked into the mirror.

Gertie whined and wagged her tail, sweeping the floor with each pass, hopeful to make a new friend.

Wasn't going to happen.

"Okay, how about this," Dell said. "Come out and I'll buy you dinner."

The kitten didn't blink.

"Losing your touch," Jade murmured, sorting files.

Dell flashed her a smile that said *As if*, and her nipples hardened. Which meant he was right—he wasn't losing his touch. Not even close.

*   *   *

Dell eyed the unhappy kitten and wished she could talk to him. He wished the same thing about his enigmatic receptionist behind him.

Jade was working her computer with her usual slightly OCD efficiency, which was in complete opposition to her eye-popping green fuzzy angora sweater that reminded him of a lollipop. A lollipop with really great breasts. Peanut the parrot was perched on the printer at her right. Both Peanut and Gertie were part of Belle Haven, and since Belle Haven was Dell's large animal clinic, the animals and everything in the place belonged to him. Well, except Jade.

Jade belonged to no one.

"From what I can gather," she said, eyes still on her keyboard, "the kitten was deserted at some point during the mob of the free vaccine clinic this afternoon. And," she added in the same conversational tone, "if I figure out who did such a thing, I'm going to shoot them."

Nothing reached Dell's hard-shelled, softhearted receptionist faster than a neglected or abused animal.

Something they had in common.

"We'll find her a home," he assured her, looking the kitten in the eyes. "Promise. Now how about it, you, ready to come out yet?"

"Ready to come out!" Peanut chirped, doing her best imitation of Dell's low-pitched voice.

Dell didn't take his eyes from the kitten. "I know, you've had a majorly sucky day. Come tell me all your troubles."

"Does that actually ever work for you?" Jade asked.

"Shh, you," he said, and keeping his movements light and easy, he reached beneath the chair. "Come on, beautiful."

"Mew," said the kitten.

"Mew," said Peanut.

"It's all going to be okay," Dell assured the cat. "No one's going to hurt you."

When the kitten just stared at him, Dell slowly slid his hand beneath her belly, which was nearly concave. Her ribs were so prominent he could have counted them, which pissed him off, but though she growled and let out one last protesting "mew," she let him pull her from beneath the chair without slicing him raw with her claws. "Good girl," he murmured, holding her against his chest and scratching her beneath the chin.

She watched him very carefully, but it was as if she knew that he knew. Hell, maybe abandoned souls recognized abandoned souls, he wasn't sure, but she slowly relaxed until finally, unable to resist the gentle scratching, she even closed her eyes and rested her head against his chest.

"Yeah, there you go," he said quietly. "Lifting his head, he flashed a grin at Jade. "If only *your* species were as easy."

"We both know that for you they are." She shook her head. "And that should be illegal."

"What?" he asked innocently. "Sweet-talking a p—"

"If you say pussy," she warned. "I'll make sure that tomorrow you'll be up to your eyeballs in vaccines and well-puppy checkups from sunup until sundown."

"I like puppies."

"Scratch the puppies. Did I say puppies? I meant anal-gland expressing. I'll find every large animal in Sunshine who needs it done and book them, just for you."

Dell laughed. She did that a lot, his stalwart, snarky, razor-tongued receptionist. Made him laugh.

As well as threaten him.

He was used to it. Hell, he even liked it, which made him all kinds of sick, he knew. Maybe it was the fact that she ran the front desk of his vet clinic in those runway clothes, never so much as blinking when she got covered in dog and kitten hair. Or worse.

Maybe it was her ability to handle his patients and their owners with equal aplomb or that she never took any of his shit. Or that she had a way of uncomplicating his life for him—a miracle considering that she'd come here with virtually no references whatsoever. Dell still no had no idea what had possessed him to hire her, but he had, putting her into a position that had supposedly been only temporary while he looked for someone more qualified.

And yet he'd never looked for anyone else.

It had been eighteen months, but that ship had sailed. She was going back to her old life, whatever that was—she'd been frustratingly stingy with details—and leaving them.

Him.

He had no idea what he'd do without her sitting at the helm of his world, running it with cool, distant efficiency. Not to mention, she was a nice view. She kept her silky strawberry blond hair perfectly twisted on top of her head, except for the few errant strands that had slipped out and were brushing across her shoulders. Her eyes were green, shot through with streaks of amber, and saw everything. She had a mouth, too. Smart, cynical, and made for a man's fantasy.

And since he should absolutely not be going down that road, thinking about that mouth with the vanilla gloss that he always wanted to lick off, he shook his head to clear it. He usually had more sense, but there was something about Jade and her whole don't-touch attitude that made him want to rise to the challenge.

And he meant rise.

Her fingers were clicking on her keyboard, her screen revealing her beloved spreadsheet program, which he knew held her notes on anything and everything from which patient he was going to see tomorrow to what color her fingernails would be next.

His favorite was the bright fuck-me red.

"Adam's checked in from Boise," she said, referring to his brother. "His class went late, he's staying over." She stood. She was average height and average build, but there was nothing else average about her.

Ever.

She coaxed Peanut onto her arm, easily transferring the parrot from the printer to the bird's night cage.

"Night-night?" Peanut asked her.

"Yes, Peanut go night-night," Jade said with a sweetness that Dell never got directed at him. He watched her blow a kiss to the bird, receiving one in return, along with a soft mimicking "mew," and with a low laugh, Jade covered the cage with a blanket.

Her black trousers had pleats, Dell noted, and were snug on the best ass he'd ever seen. All business in front, party in the back . . .

That eye-straining sweater that matched her eyes and name seemed to shimmer beneath the overhead lights. He'd once asked about her name and she'd told him it was for her grandmother, who'd ruled her family with the strength and elegance of the jade gemstone.

Clearly she took the name seriously. Dell had the feeling that when it came to the family she didn't often talk about, she took everything seriously.

She wore tiny sparkling earrings up one earlobe, matching the myriad bracelets on her wrist, and heels that he wasn't sure how she managed to balance on, though he enjoyed listening to them click, click, click across his floors all day. His patients enjoyed it, too, especially their owners. The male owners. How many times had he seen a guy come through here and attempt to pick her up? Exactly the same number of times he'd seen Jade politely and firmly shut them down.

There was a little part of him that enjoyed that very much. Okay, a big part, but he'd never made a move on her. Like the government, he preferred to keep his state and church separated; never the two shall meet. Not that *that* stopped him from wondering what secrets his sexy receptionist had that kept her celibate.

Or hell, maybe she merely left Sunshine and whooped it up on the weekends somewhere else, out of the limelight of their small Idaho ranching town.

She was moving around the room, shutting down for the night. Belle Haven was a full-service clinic. Behind this main building was also a large barn housing their horses and additional equipment, both his own and his brother's. Adam was a local trainer, breeder and search-and-rescue specialist.

Their reception area was large and airy, with wide-planked wood floors lined with comfortable benches for waiting. At one end was a long counter—Jade's—and behind it was the hub of the entire place.

Jade's jurisdiction.

She ran this front room like a drill sergeant, and half the time Dell wanted to put his hands around her neck and squeeze.

The other half of the time he wanted to put his hands on her for something else entirely. Since he was fond of living, he kept both these urges to himself.

"What are we going to do with the poor thing?" Jade asked. "Take her home? Oh, wait. You never take any of your women home."

This was true. He didn't bring women home.

He went to their place. He gave the kitten a cursory look over. Other than being far too skinny, she seemed healthy enough. "She'll need to be spayed and vaccinated."

"Want me to call Lilah for tonight?" Jade asked.

Lilah ran the kennel next to Belle Haven, and she was also the Humane Society as well as one of Dell's closest friends. Lilah would take the kitten and keep her until she could be placed in a good home. "That'd be best," he said. "Because I have a—"

"Date," she said, swiveling her chair to give him her back. "Shock." She went back to closing up.

Everything had its place with her. Files were always meticulously filed; the copier, fax, and computer were carefully covered to protect from dust. Pencils, pens, and assorted other equipment placed into their spots in drawers. Dell never got tired of watching her, and never failed to smile when the last thing she did was consult her various to-do spreadsheets to make sure everything had been done, even though she knew damn well it had been.

She never forgot a thing.

"It's not a date," he said. Or not *exactly*. "I'm heading into Coeur d'Alene for a friend of a friend's birthday party."

"Yeah, I know. I get the messages on the machine, remember?" She clicked over to another of her spreadsheets on the computer. "Your friend of a friend left a message reminding you that he wants to introduce you to—and let me give a direct quote here"—she read from her screen—*"Mandy, a stacked blonde who's hoping to play dirty doctor with a doctor."* Jade swiveled back to arch a brow in his direction.

He shrugged. "You can't believe all of what Kenny says."

"What percentage?"

"What?"

Her expression was classic *don't mess with me*. "What percentage of what Kenny says can we believe?"

"Half." He lifted a shoulder. "Maybe forty percent."

"Okay, so by sheer odds, you're either meeting a stacked blonde, or playing dirty doctor."

Dell laughed and came around the counter. Good Christ, had she smelled that delicious all day long? He leaned over her chair and took another whiff.

"What are you doing?" she asked.

"Seeing what's left on your spreadsheet."

"Hey." She pushed him with her shoulder. "Personal space intrusion." She pushed him again as she dialed Lilah. She had to leave a message, which she did while keeping a narrowed eye on him at the same time. The same sort of narrowed eye the kitten still had on him.

Two females, both suspicious. Both wary.

Both having been hurt.

Dell would have laid money down that Jade had no idea how much of herself she gave away when she looked at him like that. And to be fair, she was good at hiding.

But he was better. The skill had been hard earned from his growing-up years, further honed by the nature of his job. There were no words when it came to animals, and out of necessity he'd become the master at reading anyone and anything. He could see past Jade's dazzling clothes and tough-girl exterior, past the uptight perfectionist to the vulnerable woman beneath.

Yeah, the woman was definitely hiding.

What he didn't know was why. He had a few ideas, none of which he liked, but whatever the reason, it made him a little heartsick for her, it the same way he felt for the kitten, sitting quiet but not compliant in the crook of his arm. Unfortunately, he knew without a shadow of a doubt that only the kitten was going to allow him to help her. He smiled down at her as he stroked her beneath the chin, which seemed to be the magic ticket because she let out a rumbling, rusty purr. "You're sweet," he murmured, rubbing his jaw along the top of her little head.

"Aw thanks," Jade said. "I try."

Dell smiled because that was a lie and they both knew it. Then she surprised him.

"I'll take the kitten," she said, and in her usual efficient way stepped back from her desk and critically eyed the clean surface as she slung her purse over her shoulder. Heels clicking, she moved to the wall of storage cabinets. Without hesitation, she opened one and pulled out a kitten carrier. Then she went to another cabinet, bending low to grab a bed liner, expertly lining the kitten carrier. "Grab me some food? And a litter box, too," she said over her shoulder.

He didn't move. "*You're* going to take the kitten overnight," he repeated dubiously.

"Yes." Her hand and arm brushed his chest as she relieved him of the kitten. "Why do you look so flummoxed?"

"Well, maybe because you've never done such a thing before. Hell, Jade, you've never even let any of us come to your place."

Ignoring that, Jade carefully slid the kitten into the carrier and turned her back on him, heading to the door.

They were the last two in the building. Keith, his animal tech, and Mike, his vet nurse, had both already left. Jade hit all the lights except one interior, casting them in a soft glow. "Look," she said. "My job is running this front reception room like a well-oiled machine, right? That includes any loose ends."

He stepped between her and the door. "And the stray is a loose end?"

"At this point, Doctor, *you're* a loose end. Everything in the back handled?"

The "back" consisted of two exam rooms, a surgical suite, an x-ray and ultrasonic suite, and his and Adam's offices. "Closed up tighter than a drum," he assured her.

"Hmm." She didn't look impressed. She liked it better when she made the last walk through. And with good reason. He'd been known to be distracted enough to forget to turn something off or to even lock himself out. He opened the front door for her, then put a hand on her arm, waiting until she met his gaze. "I owe you. Lunch tomorrow?"

"We can never agree on a place."

"Name it, then," he said. "Name your price."

This appeared to interest her given how she cocked her head. "That's a lot of power."

She had no idea how much power she already had. "Anything."

She considered this so seriously he smiled. Then she flashed him a rare one of her own and his heart actually stuttered. "You're not going to like it," she warned.

Oh, how wrong she was. "There's not much I don't like, Jade."

She poked a finger in his chest. "Okay, what did I tell you about flirting with me, about using my name in that sex-on-a-stick voice?"

Now this interested *him*. "You think my voice is sex on a stick?"

She poked him again. He liked to think it was because she had a secret thing for touching him, but then again, he was a realist. If she'd wanted him that way, she'd have let him know by now.

"I want you to let me take care of the stack of bills on your desk," she said. "The one that's threatening to fall over and hit the floor."

They both knew that the state of his desk, which looked like it had been napalmed, drove her organized, anal heart absolutely nuts. As did how he could be counted on to lose his keys, wallet, or hell, his own brain in the mess at least once a week. But though he hated paperwork with the same passion that he hated vegetables, he wasn't going to hand over the reins of his admittedly sloppy accounting. He realized that meant that he trusted the animals in his care more than he did the humans, but hell, everyone had their faults. "If you took care of the mess on my desk," he said, "that would be you doing *me* the favor."

"Not really. I *need* to organize that desk, Dell. And you hate handling the bills, I heard you swearing at them just this morning."

"I was swearing at the news. Another vet clinic was robbed last night." There'd been a series of vet robberies between here and Spokane in the past week. The threat of it happening here, at his place, the one he'd built with his own sweat and blood, pissed him off. "Just after closing time. This time a tech was still in the building, working late, and was knocked out."

"Oh my God," she said, covering her mouth. "What did they take?"

"Ketamine."

"Ketamine." She frowned. "Horse tranq?"

"Turns out it's a good human narcotic as well." Not to mention an effective date rape drug but she'd gone very still, very pale. "Hey. You okay?"

"That's why you stayed tonight," she said. "You wanted to walk me out to make sure I was safe."

"And the kitten. I wanted the kitten to be safe, too." He smiled, but Jade didn't. Instead, she looked out the window into the dark parking lot with obvious unease, making him doubly glad he'd stayed.

Belle Haven was just outside of their small town of Sunshine, five miles down a narrow, winding road. Their closest neighbor—Lilah's kennels—was a quarter mile away. They were surrounded by the rugged, majestic Idaho Bitterroot mountain range, the peaks looming high. To say that they were isolated out here was an understatement.

Since Jade was still just standing there looking out the window, Dell took the kitten carrier and litter from her and nudged her out the door.

It was early autumn and the chill on the night air cut to the bone, reminding him that winter would be here before they knew it.

At her car, Jade took the kitten back and set the carrier on the backseat, making him smile when she carefully pulled the seat belt across it. Straightening, she faced him again. "See you and your disastrous desk tomorrow."

The cell phone in his back pocket was vibrating. He was late and knew it, so he ignored the call. "Forget about my desk. It's a mess, it'll take you days."

"My greatest fantasy," she said.

"That's just sad, Jade."

"Don't distract me with your perverted mind. I was made for this."

"What, were you born with the need to organize?"

"No, I was born with a silver spoon in my mouth. The need to organize is just a freak of nature, one of life's mysteries."

Infamously private, Jade didn't talk about herself often. She'd been born and raised in Chicago, he knew that much. And that she had family there, family she'd promised that she'd come back to.

Fairly private himself, Dell had never pushed her for more, but every time she doled out a little tidbit about her past and gave him a tiny glimpse inside, he found himself all the more fascinated by her.

A silver spoon . . . If that was true, they'd grown up just about as different as two people could get.

"So, what do you say?" she asked. "You going to let me in or what?"

Actually, the question was—would she ever let *him* in . . . "You're a nut," he said. "You know that, right?"

"When I clean your office, you'll be calling me a goddess."

"I'll call you whatever you'd like, but forget about the—"

His phone was going off again. Reaching around him, Jade slid her hand into his scrubs back pocket. Through the thin cotton, her fingers stroked his ass cheek, and his brain clicked off. Just completely clicked off. This condition was not improved when her breast brushed his arm as she lifted his phone.

"Dr. Connelly's phone," she answered professionally, her face so close to his he could have turned his face and captured her lips with his.

It was her scent, he decided; it drugged him. Made him stupid. Maybe it was her skin, too, so pale compared to his, so soft and deceptively fragile-looking.

Hell. It was her. Everything about her.

The night around them was so quiet he had no problem hearing the feminine voice coming out of his phone, inquiring of his whereabouts.

"Let me check for you," Jade said, eyes back on his. "Please hold." She muted the phone and looked at him, affecting a sex kitten voice to match the one on the phone. "Are you . . . *available*?"

Having some problems accessing working brain cells, it took him a minute to answer. "Last I checked."

She pushed a button on his phone, working it better than he did. "Yes, Dr. Connelly is still here. Who's calling?" Jade listened with careful politeness, contrasted by the long look she slid his way just before she rolled her eyes.

Not at the woman.

At him.

She slapped the phone against his chest. "She says you're late." She slid behind the wheel and drove off into the night, leaving him in her dust.

Literally.

Still he watched until her taillights vanished before he lifted his phone to his ear.

Two

At her place, Jade deactivated her alarm and flipped a switch. As they'd been programmed to do, four different lights came on, one in each corner of the living area, kitchen nook, bedroom area, and entry to the bathroom.

Instant visual access.

Expensive, and worth every penny. Everything was neat as a pin and just the way she'd left it. In order.

Order meant safety, and Jade depended on both. She set the kitten carrier on the foyer floor and opened the little door. The kitten tentatively poked her nose out, definitely not quite as sure of herself without Dell's warm arms.

Jade supposed she couldn't blame her. Dell had a way of making a woman feel safe. "Get comfortable," she said as her cell rang.

Dr. Doolittle himself.

"Don't tell me," she said. "You lost your wallet and/or your car keys."

"Okay, now that hurts," Dell said, sounding anything but wounded.

"Uh-huh. Why else would you be calling after hours when you're supposed to be playing doctor?"

"If you think you know me so well, why don't you guess?"

"You've forgotten the code for the alarm," she said. "Again."

"Hey," he said. "Once."

"Yeah, once. Once a week."

"I'm calling to make sure you got home okay."

His words were a direct hit to her carefully built defenses. She'd gotten used to being on her own. But Dell was a true pack leader and took care of his own. Whether she liked it or not.

She didn't. It gave her a false sense of security. She'd been working on that, on letting people in. On trying to loosen up. She'd even put it on her to-do spreadsheets to remind herself. *Live. Open up. Have fun.*

Wasn't she driving into Coeur d'Alene every Wednesday night to take a line-dancing class? Skiing here and there on the weekends?

So she needed to not be charmed by him. She was leaving, and now was not the time to get involved, not when her time here was nearly up. "I'm home safe and sound, thanks," she said, then paused. "Good night, Dell."

"Night, Goddess Jade."

She hit the End button and looked down in surprise at the soft "Mew." She'd almost forgotten about her house guest. "That was our boss," she said, and shook her head. "Making sure we're okay."

"Mew," the kitten said, sounding . . . lonely.

Common ground, Jade thought. Loneliness. And something she could understand that Dell could not. He wouldn't know lonely if it bit him on his very fine ass.

The kitten had stepped outside of the carrier but not a foot farther.

"It's okay," Jade told her. "It's all about baby steps."

The kitten sniffed the floor.

"Really. *Mi casa es su casa*," Jade assured her. "Well, for the night, anyway." She walked through her living room area. She'd rented this place the day she'd come to town eighteen months ago now. It was an older building, built in the 1950s, and beautifully renovated. Jade was on the top of three floors. The loft was large, the ceilings high, lined with intricately carved crown molding. It had come furnished and cost an arm and a leg.

But far more important to Jade, she could see everything in one sweeping glance.

She flipped through her mail, separating it into three piles: junk, bills, letters. The junk mail she dropped directly into the shredder under her small desk in the corner. The bills she set next to her laptop to be promptly paid. The letter she set on the mantel and then stared at for a few minutes.

It was from her mother. Everyone else in her life called, texted, or e-mailed, but her mother had never gotten the hang of modern technology.

Jade had a pretty pothos plant whose abundant leaves had worked their way in front of the few pictures she had on the mantle. Nudging them aside, she looked into the eyes of her family. Her well-meaning retired physician parents were arm in arm in front of their large successful medical center, which until eighteen months ago, Jade had overseen for them. The job had been her life, which was no wonder given that the center had five major departments to oversee; urgent care, ob-gyn, family practice, pediatrics, and orthopedics.

Then there was the picture of Jade and her cousin, Sam Bennett, a doctor as well, the two of them on skies and mugging for the camera.

Both pictures had been taken two years ago now and represented a time when Jade had known exactly who and what she was, and the path of her future.

They'd been a happy, loving, successful family.

She ran a finger over her father's face and heard his

voice in her head, shaking slightly with the Parkinson's disease that was slowly killing him. *Nothing can scare you, princess. You're a natural, you were born to be strong and do anything you want.*

How often had he told her that?

Every day.

Her mother, too.

Sam had been fond of the mantra as well, and it had meant even more coming from him. Only two years older than Jade, Sam was far more a brother than a cousin. He called weekly and texted daily, checking on her, bugging her to come home.

Something she'd promised to do the day she'd left Chicago. She'd told them she'd be back within the year. But that year had come and gone and she'd had to ask for an extension because she hadn't been ready.

Now it had been eighteen months and her grace period was gone. But as it turned out, she could get her pencils and her lists and her clothes just the way she wanted, she could expect her world to fall into place just the way she wanted, but healing . . . healing couldn't be ordered.

Healing had to come from the inside.

It had to come from the "strength" her family had constantly told her she had, strength she'd blindly accepted as fact.

That had been the fatal flaw.

Because she'd never had to actually *be* strong. And as it turned out, being told you're strong and actually *being* strong were two very different things.

Which she discovered the night she'd been tested beyond endurance.

After the attack, she realized the truth—that everyone had been wrong, *very* wrong. She hadn't been strong at all. Once that had sunk in, her foundation had cracked and fallen away from beneath her feet.

And she'd run. She'd run hard and fast, from family, from

well-meaning friends, from work, from everything. She'd come here to Sunshine and ordered herself to feel safe. But the attack had showed her that even ordering something to happen couldn't stop the unexpected. So even as she worked hard at creating structure to Dell's life, she wasn't facing her own weakness—dealing with the unexpected.

Her cell phone rang again, and still staring at the un-opened letter, she answered without looking at the ID. "Dell, I'm going to start to think you'd rather be playing doctor with me."

There was a startled beat of silence. "You and Dell are playing doctor?"

Jade winced. "Hey, Lilah."

"Don't 'Hey, Lilah' me. You got some 'splaining to do, Lucy. You're playing doctor with Dell?"

"No! I just thought you were him again, and—"

"Again?" Jade was sounding excited now, a *big* mistake on Jade's part. Lilah had the nose of a bloodhound, and she was on the scent.

"Is there something going on that I need to be informed of pronto?" Lilah asked.

"No!" Jade drew a calming breath. Like Dell, Lilah worked with animals and could read a lie a mile away. "Okay, let's focus here. Where are you?"

"In Boise with Brady."

Damn. "Are you at least getting some action from the hottest pilot in all of Idaho?"

"In all the *land*," Lilah corrected. "Not just Idaho. And don't think I didn't spot the subject change. Nicely done. What did you do with the stray?"

"I took her."

There was a prolonged silence at this. *"You?"*

Jade sighed. "It's not that weird. You were gone and there was no one else."

"So . . . you have the stray at your place?"

"It's just for the night, Lilah."

Another pause. "Can I talk to her?" Lilah joked. "And get the secret admittance handshake?"

"Ha," Jade said at the subtle knock at the fact that she never invited any of them over. She had no idea why Lilah liked her, but she was glad. Lilah was open and welcoming and inspired trust. And she got the same feelings from Sunshine itself. "I'll bring you the kitten tomorrow."

"Sounds good. But I'm actually calling about tomorrow night. I want to get everyone together at Crystal's."

Everyone meant Lilah and her boyfriend Brady—an ex–army ranger, now a pilot for hire—and Brady's brothers, Dell and Adam. They were a tight group, and considered themselves family.

By some miracle, they'd included Jade in that group. "Sounds good."

"Tell Dell for me?"

"Okay."

"Aha!" Lilah cried triumphantly. "So there *is* something going on with you two."

"Lilah, we work together. I meant I'd tell him tomorrow at work."

"Or when you play doctor . . ."

There was no doubt Dell could show Jade a good time. But she'd seen his patterns over the past year and a half, and they didn't involve being friends with the women he slept with. And they were friends. So she could squelch the occasional yearning for more. Especially since . . . "He's on a date."

"Oh." Lilah sighed. "You got my hopes up there for a minute. I know, stupid."

Yes. Yes, Jade and Dell together would be stupid. He was her boss. He had an allergy to relationships. And she wasn't made for quickie affairs, not to mention that she was going back to Chicago soon.

All good, solid reasons to avoid said stupidity.

"Bringing this back to me," Lilah said. "Put tomorrow night at Crystal's on your fancy spreadsheet calendar thingie and send it to Dell. Wait—are you still forbidden from sending him any more spreadsheets?"

This had happened a few months back after Jade had accidentally (on purpose) mixed up his social calendar, causing him to pick up the wrong woman on the wrong night. "Nah, he got over it." Dell got over everything, it was part of his easy charm. Nothing much got to him.

"Make it seven o'clock tomorrow night," Lilah said.

"I'll be there."

"Want me to come by and get you?"

"Sure."

"I'll honk for you."

The usual routine. Jade looked around her loft. Eighteen months, and though Lilah had picked her up numerous times for a girls' night out or dinner or any of a hundred other things, Jade had never invited Lilah inside.

Or anyone.

At first it was because she'd been protective of her privacy. And then as she'd made friends, it had been a way of keeping her heart protected from becoming too attached.

Which, of course, was far too late. She drew in a breath. "Don't honk," she said.

"What?"

"Tomorrow night. When you get here, just come up."

"You mean you're finally finished painting?" Lilah asked, sounding excited.

Jade bit her lip, feeling a flush hit her cheeks at the shame of the little white lies she'd told everyone to protect herself. "Yeah. I finally finished painting."

"Well, it's about damn time, considering you're leaving next month, sheesh! Can't wait. See you tomorrow."

Jade hung up the phone and looked at the kitten sitting in the doorway of the foyer, watching her with those narrowed feline eyes. "Baby steps," she reminded the both of them.

* * *

When Lilah picked Jade up the next night, she was grinning as Jade opened the front door. "Lemme in, lemme in," she said, pressing past Jade.

Jade held her breath as Lilah walked through the place. "It's—"

"Nice," Lilah finally said, turning in a circle. "It's . . . wow nice." Lilah lived in a tiny cabin, one that was both adorable and ancient. At any given moment either the plumbing or electricity were threatening to go out and stay out. But the place had been purposely, carefully, lovingly furnished by Lilah herself, and every inch of it was . . . well, Lilah.

Jade looked around now, trying to see her loft as if for the first time to decide what these furnishings said about her. Smooth lines, glass, mostly white or pale earth tone colors.

Clean.

Neat.

They said *expensive lease*.

"So neat," Lilah said, sounding amused. "I shouldn't be surprised at that."

There was very little clutter. Jade had always been proud of that, and the clean lines. It said she was on top of things. Successful. Smart.

An illusion, and one easily shattered at that.

"It's so light and airy," Lilah said. "Fancy."

And costly. The word went unspoken, but it was true. She paid for the tight security and a good neighborhood, made all the more pricey because she was on a month-to-month, not an annual lease. The owner charged her more to give him the security he needed in case she bailed.

And she did plan on bailing.

Sooner or later . . .

Or so she'd been saying every month for over a year now.

"Mew," said the stray kitten that Jade hadn't given to Lilah this morning.

Lilah scooped the kitten up for a hug. "Aw. You're what, four months old? You're precious." She looked at Jade. "I thought you were going to bring her to the kennels for adoption."

"I am. Tomorrow."

She's meant to do it today, but there was just something about those green eyes that said the little thing had seen too much for her few months. And the way her little ribs stuck out, it grabbed Jade by the heart and wouldn't let go. She wanted to fatten her up first, is all, give her a day off from the cruel realities of the big, bad world out there.

"You have beautiful taste," Lilah said, something new and a little different in her voice now, and Jade paused. She understood Lilah's confusion. Jade had once told her that she'd come to Sunshine for the good winter skiing and a break from her life.

Obviously the receptionist job and ski-bum premise didn't quite add up to being able to afford a place like this. "I lease it furnished."

Lilah looked at her as if she was speaking another language. "Really? Why?"

Jade hesitated. She could tell Lilah the whole sordid story. That's what friends, *real* friends, did.

But she couldn't tell. She couldn't tell anyone, not without falling apart, and falling apart was not on today's to-do spreadsheet.

But she could be honest about something, at least. "I leased it furnished, because as you know, I never intended to stay in Sunshine long."

Lilah nodded. "So the whole 'I'm painting my place' thing . . ."

"I've never painted anything in my entire life," Jade admitted. "I'm sorry. I—"

Lilah set the kitten down and squeezed Jade's hand, her

eyes warm with understanding. "You don't have to explain yourself to me, Jade. Not until you're ready."

It was the first time that Lilah had ever let on that she knew that Jade hadn't been honest with her, and the knowledge made Jade's throat burn. "Thanks," she whispered.

"But you can tell me something else."

"Anything," Jade said, relieved.

Lilah watched the kitten jump up on the couch and make herself at home. "Why did you keep her?"

They both looked at the kitten now daintily licking her Lady Town.

Jade bit her lower lip. "I don't know. Anyone claim her?"

"Nope. And she's going to leave hair all over that pretty couch."

"I didn't want her to be put down," Jade said.

"I don't put animals down. Ever. And you know that."

Jade sighed. "Look, she acclimated. I can't kick her out now."

Lilah grinned. "You are so full of shit tonight. All the way around. Why can't you just admit you've fallen for her?"

"I don't fall."

At that, Lilah laughed outright. "Oh, honey. Haven't you learned yet? You can control a lot of things—work, what you watch on TV, how much ice cream you inhale—but you can't control what your heart does."

Jade brooded over that for a moment. "You can control how much ice cream you inhale?"

Lilah laughed again. "Come on, Brady's meeting us at the bar. He told me I had to be on time tonight or he wouldn't put out later." She took one last look around and sighed wistfully. "Someday," she murmured. "I'm going to have a place like this."

Jade followed Lilah out and carefully set her alarm. Maybe she had the more expensive place and bigger savings account, but out of the two of them, Lilah with her tiny cabin, kennels, and adoring boyfriend was by far the richer.

*   *   *

Jade accepted her small glass of wine from the bartender and lifted a brow at the *huge* margarita he placed in front of Lilah.

"I have big plans for tonight," Lilah said with a grin, licking the salt off the edge of the glass.

"Does it involve being flat on your ass?" Jade asked.

Lilah laughed and took a healthy sip of her drink. "Flat on my *back* maybe." She grinned stupidly at the man who walked into the bar and headed directly for her.

Brady Miller.

The big, badass ex–army ranger didn't look any less big and bad as he returned Lilah's goofy smile and bodily plucked her out of her chair and squeezed her tight.

Lilah sighed sweetly, cupped his face, and kissed him long and hard, like maybe she hadn't seen him in a year instead of that morning before she'd left for work.

Jade turned away to give them a moment, and herself, too. Had a man ever looked at her in the way Brady looked at Lilah? If so, she couldn't remember it.

She'd dated in Chicago, usually with men she met through her connections at work or at the charity events she'd often run for her family. Similar minded as she, these men had professional lives that took up much of their time, and for whatever reason, not a one of them had sparked a long-term interest.

They'd been wrong for her.

She was good at that, meeting men who were wrong for her.

Still, she'd managed to have relationships, some that had even hung on for a few months at a time, often longer than they should have. What hadn't happened was the magic that made her want to take the next step. Magic she would have said didn't exist.

Except it did.

She was looking at it between Brady and Lilah. Then she locked eyes on another man entirely, Dr. Dell Connelly. She felt a little quiver, which was ridiculous because out of all the men in the land, he was the most wrong for her of them all.

Three

Dell and Adam walked toward the bar, side by side, looking like the brothers they were from head to toe. Of the two, Adam was two years older but they almost could have passed for twins. Dark disheveled hair, dark eyes, features as strong and beautiful as fallen angels. Mix that with his dark skin and six feet plus of solid muscle and testosterone, and there wasn't a woman in the place not wishing they were going home with one of them.

Or both.

There were subtle differences though, if you knew them, and after working for them, Jade knew them well.

Adam was his usual unsmiling, serious self. Dell was much more open, already looking like he was having a good time, but the truth was that Dell could have a good time anywhere.

He was out of the surgical scrubs that so defined him at work, wearing a pair of jeans and a snug black T-shirt that made a woman want to drop at his knees and give him whatever he wanted.

But not her.

At least not in her waking hours. And what she fantasized about in the dark of the night was just that—fantasy.

He was smiling and would have looked younger than his thirty-two years—except for his eyes. His eyes said that he'd seen far more than his affable smile showed, and it had been those eyes to tell her eighteen months ago that she could work for him and be safe.

But safe was relative. And the fact was, she'd never seen so much male perfection grouped so closely together, and if you added Brady into the mix, it was a wonder that any woman in the place could put a thought together. These were rugged guys, built for stamina and the tough life out here that they all led. Not a single one of them were "city." They'd never had a pedicure or worried about wrinkles or the cut of their clothes. They were real, as real as they came.

These qualities had a universal appeal, proven when Dell and Adam passed a table of three women, one of whom reached out and snagged Dell's arm.

Jade recognized her as Cassie, a local rancher. Dell stopped and set a friendly hand on Cassie's shoulder and she beamed up at him. So did the others at the table. This was because Dell could make ninety-year-old women preen and get infant girls to bat their eyelashes in his sleep.

He was the heart and soul of Belle Haven, and the rock of all of them.

This morning when she'd shown back up with the kitten in her carrier and informed him she was keeping her for a few days, he'd just smiled and said, "I know." He'd known before Jade that she'd look into the strong, independent but down-on-her-luck kitten's eyes and not be able to let her go.

Yet.

Lilah finally removed her lips from Brady and waved at Adam and Dell. "Over here!"

Since Dell was currently being hugged by another woman at the table, Adam got to them first.

"'Bout time," Lilah said.

Adam looked at his watch. "We late?"

"Nope, I'm just on time for once," Lilah said. "All my pretties got picked up on time today."

These "pretties" could be anything from dogs and cats to the more exotic. Jade had seen her driving around with a duck, a pig, and a lamb, stuck on babysitting detail. The woman had more patience than anyone Jade had ever met.

Adam nudged Jade and she obliged him, moving over in the booth, making room. He looked back to where his brother was attempting to extract himself from the woman's arms and shook his head. "I told him, keep your head down and keep moving, but does he listen?" He glanced at Brady and Lilah and grimaced when he found them lip-locked again. "Ah, man, come on."

Brady lifted his head and smiled into Lilah's eyes. "Been wanting to do that all day."

"You flew me around all day," Adam said, helping himself to Jade's wine. "We've been flying S&R in Eagle Canyon searching for a lost hiker."

Brady smiled at Lilah. "I can multitask."

Adam shook his head.

Dell finally appeared, his hair looking like it'd just been tousled by a hungry female. Kicking Brady's legs out of his way, he stepped around Adam and pushed his way into the booth on Lilah's other side.

Jade knew he'd spent much of his day in surgery but you couldn't have told that by looking at him. Or smelling him. He smelled like undiluted amazingness as he bumped a broad shoulder to hers.

"Show-off," he said.

She'd organized his inventory before he'd gotten out of his second surgery. "Just trying to help," she said demurely.

His dark warm eyes held hers for a minute. "Bullshit," he said, letting the smile in his voice break through. "You couldn't help yourself, Jade."

"That's Goddess Jade to you."

He laughed, and as always, the sound did something funny low in her belly. Which was really annoying considering the fact that every other woman who came in close proximity to him felt the same way.

"So, what is it you did in your previous life again? Run the world?" he asked.

"Close enough." Running her family's medical center had been much like running a small country, complete with the politics that went with it. "I have skills. Got 'em from my grandmother Jade. I got lots of things from her."

"Such as?"

"Well, she, too, was always right."

Dell fought a smile and lost. With his warm eyes on hers and his hard thigh pressing to her own, Jade felt a silly little flutter.

No doubt this was how the women at the other table had felt when he'd focused his attention on them. At least she wasn't simpering. She refused to simper.

"Are you always right?" Adam asked. "Or do we just let you think it because it's easier?"

Jade took her wine back from him.

"Oh, and after you left," Dell told her. "I took a few phone calls and squished a few more patients in for tomorrow." He stopped to smile at someone waving to him from across the bar.

Jade poked him to get his attention back. Right in the biceps. Her finger bounced off him. "You didn't have room in your schedule. It's packed."

"Yeah, but Mrs. Kyle's cat is feeling 'peakish.'" He shrugged. "Doesn't tell me much, but Miss Kitty's like a hundred, so it could be anything. She needs to be seen."

Jade didn't bother to sigh. It wouldn't help. If there was an animal in need, Dell would work around the clock. "Tell me you did not even attempt to update the computer yourself."

"Okay, I won't tell you."

"Man," Adam muttered beneath his breath. "You never learn."

Dell's eyes were lit and Jade relaxed. "You're just messing with me."

A small smile crossed his face as he studied her. "How can you be sure?"

"Because if you'd messed anything up, you'd have brought me flowers, or you'd be kissing my ass like last time."

"I'll cop to the flowers, because you are one scary woman when you're mad at me. But I've *never* kissed your ass." He cocked his head and pretended to study said ass, even though she was sitting on it. "I'd be happy to do so, though. Anytime."

She reached out to shove him, but he had lightning reflexes and grabbed her hand in his much bigger, darker one. His was calloused and work-roughed, and because that gave her an odd flutter, she pulled free. "Save it for someone that those moo-moo eyes actually work on."

The band kicked into high gear. Lilah had pulled a reluctant Brady onto the dance floor.

"Better Fly Boy than me," Adam muttered, and headed to the bar for a pitcher of beer.

Dell nudged Jade.

"In your dreams," she said.

"What, is Goddess Jade afraid of something as innocuous as a dance?"

No, what she was afraid of was getting too close and getting sucked into his Hotness Vortex. She wasn't afraid he'd ask anything of her she wasn't willing to give.

She was afraid of what she was willing to give.

But you're leaving, said the little devil on her shoulder. Her inner slut. *You're going back, you're better now, what would it hurt to have him, just once?*

Before Jade could thoroughly process this thought and take any action, Cassie appeared at their table. "Dell," she said, tugging him up. "You owe me a dance."

His smile was light. Flirty. But he shook his head. "Actually, I was just going to dance with Jade."

"Go ahead," Jade said. This was the little angel on her other shoulder. She wasn't an inner slut.

Beaming, Cassie pulled Dell out of his chair. Jade shook her head at herself and headed to the bar.

Adam was there. He eyed Dell on the dance floor and he gave her a long look.

"What?" she asked, maybe a little snappish.

He just shook his head.

When Dell finally escaped the dance floor, he turned back to their table. Jade was back from the bar, and there was a guy trying to pick her up.

Poor sucker, he thought with a good amount of sympathy, watching as Jade shook her head. As Dell moved closer, he heard the guy say, "Aw, come on, Red. I've seen you swing your sweet thang in class, let's take it to the dance floor."

"I'm with someone," Jade said.

The guy admitted defeat and moved off. Dell dropped into the coveted spot right next to her, sprawling out. "Hey, Red?"

She sipped her drink.

"Class?"

She shrugged.

"Oh come on. Tell me about swinging your sweet thang." He accepted her eat-shit-and-die look and laughed.

She rolled her eyes. "So I take a line-dancing class once a week in the city."

"Which clearly you're not doing so that you'll get picked up by guys in bars."

"It's for exercise." She blew out a breath. "And because I sort of promised myself I'd do things for me. For fun. It's the year of the fun for Jade."

"Well, I'm all for that."

At that, she cocked her head and looked at him. "You don't think it's silly?"

"Everyone deserves fun, Jade." He smiled at her and reached for his drink. "Their own brand of fun."

Jade's eyes cut to Brady and Lilah, plastered up against each other on the dance floor. "What do you think of their brand?"

Dell took in the expression on Brady's face, which held warmth and love and a whole hell of a lot of lust, and shrugged. It would be nice to know there was a woman waiting on him at the end of the day. He wouldn't mind that. It was the emotional depth and level of attachment that bothered him. The love part. Love would take trust and blind faith. It would take allowing access to parts of him that he didn't allow himself access to. "I'm not really cut out for it."

"So you've tried it, then?"

"Not so much. You? I'm betting you have a spreadsheet for this, for meeting the right guy to give you a white picket fence and two point four kids."

"Some things even my spreadsheets can't do," she said, and he laughed softly just as Brady and Lilah came back looking flushed and happy as they slid into the booth.

"Okay," Lilah said. "It's been an hour and no one has said one freaking word about the bling." She spread her hands on the table. "Seriously?"

Jade's eyes went directly to Lilah's left ring finger, and the fat diamond there. "Holy shit!"

Lilah grinned. "I know, right?" She flashed the ring in each of their faces. "Brady had it made for me. It's the most sparkly thing I've ever owned." Turning to Brady, she clapped her hands to either side of his face and kissed him on the mouth. "I've never been all that sparkly, but I am now, cuz of you."

Brady smiled up at her. "Sparkly, *and* you smell like a strawberry."

"It's the margaritas."

Adam toasted to Brady and Lilah, and Dell added his congratulations, genuinely thrilled for them. Lilah felt like as much a sibling to him as Brady was. And though he might not quite get why two of his favorite people in the world wanted to tie themselves to each other and give up all the other possible options, it meant that Brady would be sticking around Sunshine. And Dell was all for that, so he grinned and topped off their glasses from the pitcher, giving Lilah the last of it and the most.

Brady slid him a look.

"What, you're already going to have to pour her into your truck to take her home," Dell told him. "Might as well make it a night to remember."

Lilah laughed and slapped Brady's shoulder, as if he'd been the one to say it. "It *will* be a night to remember." Indeed, two sheets to the wind, she blew a strand of her hair from her face and waggled a finger at her new fiancé. "But just so we're clear—we're still not crossing that one last thing off the taboo list. I'm not *that* far gone."

Adam looked pained.

Brady didn't look concerned. He was smiling affectionately at Lilah, looking content and confident that he could talk her into anything he wanted, wasted or not.

"You have a taboo list?" Jade asked.

"You don't?" Lilah asked.

Jade bit her lower lip and Adam laughed. "Jade has a list for *everything*."

"True," Dell said, studying her, getting nothing from her expression. She had quite the game face, his Jade. "You do, you have lists for everything."

"Not *everything*."

"Jade, you have a list for every situation, big or small, from when to brush your teeth, to how to handle every potential patient to cross my door. Hell, you've got a list on what's in your purse and my office fridge and—"

"And don't forget the list on how many different ways I could kill you," she said, sipping her drink.

"Now that's one I'd like to see," Brady said.

Adam looked intrigued. "How many ways are there really to do that?"

"You have no idea . . ." she murmured serenely.

Dell laughed. "Come on. There's no doubt in my mind, you have a list of sexual taboos. Tell us."

"Yeah," Lilah said, leaning forward. "Tell us! I might need to add to my list."

"Why are we still talking about this?" Jade wanted to know.

"The question is," Dell said, "why are you avoiding talking about this?" He smiled at her and though she blushed a little, she held his gaze evenly.

He didn't have a hard time imagining Jade as a sexual creature. She was beautiful, innately sensual, from that full bottom lip, to her glorious curves, to the way she moaned while eating her hidden stash of chocolate from her bottom desk drawer.

What he had a hard time imagining was her having a one-night stand. Which meant that she'd have to let someone in close enough to have a relationship with before she had sex. And she wasn't any better at that than . . . well, him. He got her, he really did. Because other than the people right here at this table, he never felt the overwhelming need to let anyone in, either. "Come on," he coaxed, teasing. "Give us something from your taboo list."

She smiled at him. "You should be far more concerned with what's on tomorrow's to-do list."

"Ha," Adam said to his brother. "You have a to-do list."

"So do you," Jade said, and Brady laughed.

"Nice deflection," Lilah said to Jade. "You're good at that."

It was a definite talent, Dell thought, and let her have the deflection. They all hung out for another hour before Brady stood and grabbed Lilah's hand. "We're out," he said.

Lilah smiled wickedly. "'Bout time." She looked at Jade. "Can we drop you off?"

"No, that's okay," Jade said, shaking her head. "Go home with Brady."

"You sure?"

"Very."

Lilah hugged her and then she and Brady made tracks. Adam's cell vibrated, and he excused himself out into the night as well. Dell looked at Jade, who was scrolling through her contacts. "Looks like it's you and me. Come on, I'll give you a ride."

"No, it's out of your way. I'll call . . ."

"That guy from your line-dancing class?"

She sighed. "Okay, so I could use a ride."

He walked her out to his truck and then had to clear her a spot in the passenger's seat because he had a stack of work files, his hockey gear from the weekend league he played on, and some other shit he'd shoved into the truck and forgotten about. "There," he said, tossing everything to the back.

"Thanks," she murmured, and got in. "Your truck looks like your desk."

True statement. "I have a little organizational problem." Her gaze met his. "I could help you with that."

"Sure, if you'll let me help you with your taboos list."

"How do you know that you don't have the same taboos?"

"I don't have any."

That shocked her into silence, and the rest of the drive to her place stayed quiet, though she was thinking so loud he could almost hear her thoughts.

The minute he pulled into her lot, her hand was on the door. She was in a hurry. He wondered which of them she didn't trust.

"Thanks for the ride," she said.

"Anytime, Jade."

She glanced back at him, and in a purely feminine move, bit her lower lip, her teeth pressing into the plump curve. "So, tomorrow I thought I'd tackle your office."

There was a light in her eyes. *Lust,* he thought, dazed. He nearly groaned. But the lust wasn't for him, it was for his damn desk. She looked practically orgasmic at the thought of getting her hands on his messy office. "If only I could get you to look at *me* like that."

They both smiled because they each recognized the lie. If she looked at him like that, he'd run like hell. He didn't have anything against a good old-fashioned love affair. It was just that the love part wasn't for him. He was missing the for-keeps gene, both the ability to love that way, and to be loved that way.

"You're not a spreadsheet," Jade said. "Or I would."

"If you gave it a shot, I'd let you at my accounting system, too."

"Don't tease me," she said, her eyes dilating with even more lust.

His own reaction was far more base, making him laugh, at himself. Time to call it a night before he did something really stupid. He leaned past her to open the door for her.

Jade's eyes dropped to his mouth, lingering a moment before returning to meet his gaze.

He had the brief thought that he hadn't called it a night fast enough because then one of them moved, he wasn't sure who, but they were kissing. She made a soft sound of approval that went right through him, as did the hand she set on his chest, landing right over his heart as she pressed in closer. God, yeah. Closer. His hand slid around the back of her neck, over satiny soft skin, his thumb brushing the exquisite hollow behind her ear.

Her hands slid to his shoulders, his biceps, and dug in as if to hold him here, right here. But he wasn't going anywhere. He liked her hands on him, liked her tongue in his mouth, and when she made that noise deep in her throat, the one that said she was as lost as him, he groaned, both in pleasure and with a good amount of what-the-fuckery, because he knew.

He was in trouble.

Down to the bone trouble, and he didn't give one single shit. Knowing this was crazy, that they had no place to go with this kiss, he still slanted his mouth over hers and took more, took everything she gave, and she gave her all, her soft sigh as they pulled apart turning him on almost more than the kiss had.

Still, she didn't move far, only a fraction of an inch, which meant that they sat there, still wrapped up in each other, noses touching, their exhales coming in fast pants on each other's skin. One of his hands was still in her hair, his fingers brushing the nape of her neck, the other just brushing the swell of her breast. The temperature of the night had dropped considerably but here inside his truck it was at least two hundred degrees.

Sanity was painfully slow to return. It helped to remember that she was leaving in a month. Theoretically, that took him off the hook. *She* was going to be the one to walk away.

Pressure off.

"Okay," she said shakily, finally pulling back.

Apparently the only one of them with a lick of sense.

"Not sure what that was," she said. "But for now, I'm going to ignore it."

He wasn't sure how to do that but he kept his doubts to himself and got out with her.

She narrowed her eyes.

"Just walking you to the door," he said.

"Fine." She pulled out her keys. "But I'm going to still be ignoring this tomorrow."

He'd be watching her try. "Night, Jade."

"Night." She didn't go in right away.

He didn't move, and not just because he hadn't been inside her place and was curious.

Though he was curious, very much so.

But mostly he wanted a repeat of that holy-shit kiss. He wanted that bad. Because she was leaving. Which mean that he wouldn't be the one to have to walk away, not this time.

The slight darkening of her eyes said she was considering the same line of thought. He looked at her mouth but the moment had passed and she was shifting back, away from him.

Already ignoring.

Thankfully Jade's workday was predictably crazy. Thankfully, because then she couldn't think too much about the night before.

The Kiss That Had Rocked Her World.

Dell had indeed mucked up the schedule. This demoted him from wildly sexy to downright irritating. It took her all morning and quite a bit of juggling to get it back to a manageable pace but she did it. And to be honest, nothing perked her up or kicked her brain into high gear faster than a problem that she could solve with a spreadsheet.

The phones stayed busy and the waiting room at a dull roar thanks to the patients and the owners that filled it. She knew the chaos would drive most people nuts but it was an organized chaos and she felt right at home, the noise settling over her like a security blanket.

In her not-too-distant past, her day had been filled with grumpy, sick, tired, distraught, rude people trying to get medical attention. She'd discovered that she preferred animals any day of the week. They didn't talk back, they didn't scream in your face if you were five minutes late getting them into their appointment.

Peanut the parrot sat in her opened cage, eyeballing the room with interest, occasionally squawking out a "mew" or "wuff wuff" because she liked to be a part of every conversation. Behind Jade's chair lay Gertie, Dell's ten-year-old "baby." The St. Bernard liked the chaos as much as Jade did and had decided she liked hanging out with Jade.

Gertie was currently snoring over the din.

The stray kitten was still with her and had gotten very attached to the carrier that Jade had been using to transport her to and from the loft. Jade kept it in a position of honor on her credenza, door open.

From the carrier, the kitten loftily surveyed her kingdom, looking down her nose at the waiting patients.

Jade had named her Beans because . . . well, she wasn't exactly sure but the kitten seemed to like it.

"She still here?" Dell asked, coming through the front room holding a chart.

"Just until she gets fattened up a little."

Dell just smiled, sure and confident and smelling amazing, damn him. "I am going to give her up," she said. Tomorrow.

Okay, so maybe next week. It had to be sooner than later because Jade *was* going back to Chicago.

At some point.

"Would it be so bad to want to keep something in your life?" he asked.

She laughed. "Okay, Mr. Pot. Meet Kettle."

"I have animals."

"Just not women. At least not permanent ones." She immediately clamped her mouth shut, with no idea where that had come from. With a shake of her head, she turned back to her computer.

Dell stepped to her side, but before he could say a word, Keith, their animal tech, squished in between them, reaching for the sign-in sheet with his usual cluelessness. He brought the patients to the exam rooms for Dell and took notes and stats. He divided a look between Dell and Jade. "What?"

"Nothing," Jade said and nudged Dell out of the way.

When he was gone, Keith looked at her. "We in trouble?"

"No." They weren't in trouble. *She* was in trouble, all by herself.

Keith sighed in relief. He was a twenty-four-year-old mountain biker and mountain bum. He was great with the animals but more forgetful than anyone she'd ever met, and he moved slower than molasses. "Dude," he said—just like he did every time Jade passed him in the hallway, assisting him in bringing the animals to the back. "You in a race?"

"No, but you could pretend to be."

Keith merely grinned. "You know what you need?"

Yes. Yes, she knew exactly what she needed.

"You need yoga. Or Xanax."

"What I need is you to move it."

"Move it," Peanut repeated.

Keith grinned. "I only move it on the mountain or in my bed."

Jade sighed but kept cracking the whip. By pushing the patients along, continuing to fill and empty the exam rooms as fast as Dell worked his way through them, she made up even more lost time. This she used to help Adam as needed, who was working from the center today as well. He gave a S&R training class in the morning, and then puppy obedience classes all afternoon, and Jade helped him stay as organized as she could.

Eventually, sometime after five o'clock, the place slowed down. The last of the patients were seen. Jade was straightening up the front room when Bessie arrived from the cleaning service.

Actually, Bessie *was* the cleaning service. She came at the end of the day and sometimes at the lunch break as needed. "That's my job," she snapped at Jade, who was straightening out the waiting room.

"Move it," Peanut said.

Bessie eyeballed the parrot. "I know how to make a mean parrot soup."

Peanut ducked her head beneath her wing.

"I'm just trying to help," Jade told Bessie. The benches were heavy and she knew Bessie's back bothered her by the end of the day.

But Bessie's eyes flared with temper as if she'd been insulted. "You think I can't do my job?"

Bessie was somewhere between fifty and one hundred. Hard to tell exactly. Time hadn't been kind, and neither had gravity, but Bessie had been cleaning offices in Sunshine for decades and wasn't ready to admit defeat. "I think you do your job better than anyone I know," Jade said.

"Then leave me to it," Bessie said.

This was a nightly conversation. Jade lifted her hands in surrender and went back to her desk to close up.

Keith left, as did Mike, Dell's animal nurse. Dell, done seeing patients, was holed up in his office, hopefully catching up on returning phone calls and making final notes to the animal charts and other various but necessary paperwork.

Adam came in from the outside pens, bringing a blast of autumn air in with him. He had a golden retriever puppy tucked beneath each arm. There was a woman with him. "Thanks so much for today," she was saying as he walked her to the door. "Timmy's already in the car, but I just wanted to confirm we're on for this weekend, for the special-needs kids."

"I'll be there," Adam said.

"It'll mean so much to the kids. Your dogs just have such a way of reaching them. Having you bring your puppies, letting the kids see how you train and treat them, is such a wonderful experience for them. We can't wait."

"Looking forward to it." Adam nudged the door open with his foot for her. He walked out with her and then surprised Jade by coming back inside, still holding two pups.

"Heading out for the night," he said. "I'll walk you to your car."

One of the puppies barked happily, earning him a low, authoritative look from Adam. The puppy seemed to smile at him but obeyed and fell quiet.

"I'm not ready yet," Jade said. "I'm backing up the files right now."

Adam nudged his chin in the direction of Dell's office. "Then call him when you're ready to go."

"Believe it or not, I think I know how to find my car."

Adam didn't return her teasing smile, just shook his head. "Another animal clinic was hit last night. No one walks to their car by themselves."

"You are," she pointed out.

That did make him smile. He was over six feet, solid muscle, and intimidating as hell. "Don't worry about me," he said, lifting the puppies higher. One licked his nose, the other licked his chin. "I've got guard dogs."

Jade came around her desk, kissed each puppy and opened the door for them. Then she went back to her desk. "Gertie," she said. "Go to Dell."

Well used to the night routine, Gertie trotted off to Dell's office, where she'd wait patiently for her master to take her home.

Jade covered up Peanut, then settled Beans in her carrier. She slung her purse over her arm, dimmed the lights, then stuck her head into Dell's office.

He'd had a long day and was still in his scrubs and white lab coat, sprawled in his big leather office chair talking on the phone. He had his feet up on his desk, his laptop in his lap, and he was hunting and pecking keys with an impressive speed for someone using only their pointer fingers. He had his cell phone open and on speaker, and at first she thought maybe he was consulting, as he often did for the other vets in the area.

That or going over the stack of paperwork she'd left for him. They had plenty of it, the most pressing tonight being the blood drawn from a jet-setting Boston terrier heading for England on a month-long vacay with his owner. The sample needed to be sent out to a lab authorized to give a rabies-titer clearance proving the dog had an adequate level of rabies antibodies to avoid Britain's quarantine. But . . . big surprise, a soft female voice was speaking.

"I've got a steak on the barbecue with your name on it, Big Guy," that female voice said.

Big guy?

Dell's dark eyes warmed at the sight of Jade. "Sorry, Kel. I have work." His hair was even more disheveled than usual. He'd shoved his fingers through it. He did that a lot when he was tired or frustrated, and today he'd been both. He'd lost a very ill cancer-ridden cat on the table, not entirely unexpected but never easy.

I'm going, Jade mouthed, and waved to indicate she was heading out.

"Wait," he said.

"I'll wait as long as you need," the woman said.

"Sorry," Dell said, putting his feet down and setting his laptop on the desk. "I meant Jade."

"Who's Jade?"

Jade rolled her eyes at Dell and left his office. The man was gorgeous as sin, and incredible at what he did for a living, but if he couldn't see that he went through women like other men went through socks because he insisted on choosing the *wrong* women, it was really none of her business.

Not that she was one to talk. She hadn't exactly been successful in the relationship area herself, especially lately. "People in glass houses shouldn't throw stones," she murmured to Beans as they stepped outside.

It was a relatively mild night, but she could hear the rustle of the dry leaves on the trees. They were getting ready to fall. The ground crunched beneath her heels as she walked across the parking lot. She was halfway to her car when it happened.

A figure darted between her car and Dell's truck. He was tall, lean, and had a face chalk white with hollow, sightless black eyes and a black mouth, gaping wide open in a soundless scream.

Four

Terror gripped Jade by the throat and between one heartbeat and the next, she was transported back to another time and another place.

To the night of her attack. And this time it was worse because she knew she was weak. She was supposed to be getting better and she wasn't. She was hiding behind the same routines, different place, and she was no better than she'd been before the first attack.

Run.

She told this to her feet. *Run.* But like the last time, her feet didn't obey. And also like last time, she froze.

That long ago night she'd been snagged up in hard, gripping hands, and dragged away by gunpoint. Knowing she couldn't survive that again, she opened her mouth to scream but only a whimper escaped.

The dark figure stopped short and tilted its head. The white face wavered in her vision, then floated disembodied as it was torn away. A mask. A zombie, she thought dimly. A cheap zombie Halloween mask.

And the figure? Just a teenager, and a young one at that. But it was too late for logic. Panic had stolen her breath, stopped her heart, and she couldn't breathe.

Couldn't move.

From a great distance she heard the second horrifyingly pathetic whimper that came from her throat. Her legs wobbled and gave, and she hit her knees, bracing herself with one hand on the rough asphalt.

The kid reached out to put a hand on her shoulder and she further embarrassed herself by cringing back.

A woman appeared, the woman who'd been talking to Adam only a few moments before, Jade realized. Michelle something. She crouched before Jade and tried to take the kitten carrier.

"No!" Jade gasped, tightening her grip on Beans.

"Your hand's bleeding, you must have scraped it when you fell," Michelle said. "I'm so sorry. Timmy didn't mean to scare you."

"He . . . he didn't say anything."

"He's deaf, he doesn't speak. I'm so sorry. I know I should take the mask from him, but he's so attached to his Halloween costume. He loves to wear it."

Only seconds ago it had been terror blocking the air in Jade's throat. Now it was humiliation. She got to her feet, still clutching Beans. "It's okay, I'm fine."

But she wasn't. With the memories she'd beaten back now pounding just behind her eyes, she was barely holding it together.

"Your hand's bleeding," Michelle said again. "Please. Let me—"

"No." Jade's jaw was clenched to keep her teeth from chattering. "I'm really fine." Whirling away, she practically ran to her car. Her hands were shaking badly, and it took three tries to find her keys in her own pocket. Glancing up, she caught sight of Dell's office window, lit from within. He was there, looking out, his phone to his ear.

It felt like five years had passed since she'd fallen, but it'd probably been less than a minute. Had he seen her mini freak-out?

Their gazes connected, and in the next beat he was gone from the window.

He was coming out.

She couldn't be here when he did, couldn't let him see her like this, shaken and trembling like a baby. Knowing she had only seconds—for a laid-back, easygoing guy Dell could really move when he wanted—she talked herself through it. *Don't lose it, not yet.*

Not.

Yet.

Shoving the key into the ignition, she mentally accessed her to-do list. One, pull the seat belt over the carrier. Two, shut the door. Three, open the driver's-side door and get in.

There. At least now she couldn't fall down again. She gripped the steering wheel with white knuckles and gulped in air. For a single heartbeat she gave into the emotions battering at her and dropped her head to the steering wheel. "Get it together," she whispered. "Get it together." Lifting her head, she turned the key. Her engine came to life just as she saw movement from the doors.

Dell was striding through them. She caught the glint of his dark hair beneath the bright outside light hanging above the entry way of the center.

Heart in her throat, she put the car in gear and hit the gas. *Don't look back, don't look back, don't . . .*

She looked.

Dell stood there in the center of the lot, hands on hips, a grim expression on his face.

Her tires squealed a little bit leaving the lot, but she didn't slow down. From in her pocket, her cell phone vibrated. Swallowing hard, she kept driving.

She was nearly a mile down the road when her phone vibrated again. Still shaking, heart still pounding, she pried her hand from the wheel and grasped the phone.

She didn't have to look at the screen to see who it was.

Dell.

With her vision already far too blurry for safe driving thanks to the tears she refused to acknowledge, she hit ignore and kept going.

Jade made it home and knew exactly how lucky she was to do it in one piece given her condition. Running on panic and adrenaline, she stumbled out of her car and got to her door before she remembered.

Beans.

"I'm sorry, I'm so sorry," she murmured after she'd run back to the car for the kitten. "God. I'm the worst kitten mom on the entire planet." Hugging the carrier close, she ran up the walk, up the stairs, unlocked the door and disabled her alarm.

Inside, she hit the switch that lit up the place like Christmas and then stood stock-still, her hand on the wall for balance.

Everything was in place and she was alone. Her purse hit the floor and she slid down the wall to sit on her butt next to it, gulping in air, still hugging Beans in her carrier.

"Mew."

Beans wanted dinner. Understandable. But Jade's mind was doing a rewind and repeat.

Dark parking lot.

Dark face mask.

Dark growling voice in her ear. "Do as I say, bitch, and I won't hurt you. Yet."

Dark fear as he emphasized the words with the cold muzzle of a gun thrust under her jaw.

Frozen with fear, she tried to turn her head to get a look at him, but he stopped her cold. He ran the tip of that gun from her jaw along her throat, over her collarbone and down, skimming her breast. "Let's go," came the low, rough voice. "Unless you want to spend some time out here with me first . . ."

The only sound in her loft was her harsh breathing until Beans gave another soft, questioning "mew."

Jade opened the cage and let the kitten out. Beans wound her way around Jade's legs, giving out a rumbling purr. She accepted a scratch behind the ears and then trotted off to the kitchen nook in the obvious hope that the bowl fairy had filled hers.

Jade let out a choked laugh and thunked her head back against the door. One little thing, a silly zombie mask, a frigging kid's Halloween mask, and she was back to a complete wreck, worse than ever.

Her first instinct was to run. Hell, that's how she'd ended up here. After the attack, she'd run to get her head on straight. She'd gotten in the car and driven west.

She'd ended up in Sunshine.

And she'd never left. She'd found this sweet place to hole up and had taken a job she was way overqualified for, just so she could do something well.

A safety net.

She'd needed the confidence booster, and at the time, she'd truly believed it a very temporary move. She just needed to find herself again, that was all.

She thought she had.

Clearly she'd been wrong. Clearly she'd been living in Denial City. She'd built herself a little fantasy here, a temporary geographical cure, that was all.

Now she had to decide what to do about that. She could pack and go. Again. Just get in the car and go. Maybe south this time. Arizona. California. Hell, she could hit Mexico and keep going if she wanted. She wrapped her arms around her knees and dropped her head.

But running meant once again leaving everyone and everything that mattered. And she'd already done that. She didn't want to do it again.

The knock at the door had her jerking upright as if shot. She stared at it, still as stone.

"Jade, it's me."

Dell, of course. Who else?

"Let me in, Jade." She covered her mouth and shook her head, like he could see her.

After a moment, the knock came again, less patient now, again accompanied by his low, unbearably familiar voice. *"Jade."*

"Mew."

Jade stared down at Beans, who was once again doing the head bump against her legs. "He's never been here," she whispered to the kitten. "Why's he here?"

Because he saw your freak-out in the parking lot, you idiot. Because he came down to check on you and you sped off into the night. Because you didn't answer your phone.

Pick one . . .

Leaning her head back on the door, Jade closed her eyes and fought with the conflicting urges to open the door and throw herself at him for the comfort she knew his very nice arms could provide or to continue to huddle in a pathetic little ball and pretend the world didn't exist.

"I can hear you breathing," he said.

Slowly she stood up. She could *feel* Dell on the other side, tall and strong, warm. Calm.

Waiting.

And he could outpatience Job, too. Once she'd seen him outwait a furious gelding who'd been out of its mind after being stung by a bee, so enraged that everyone had truly thought the poor thing would break its own leg, or worse.

Dell had stepped into the central pen while the horse ran in circles around him, and when the horse finally exhausted itself, Dell moved in, getting the thing to literally eat out of the palm of his hand.

Jade's cell phone rang, and shock, it was Dell.

Since he wasn't going to give up, she answered with, "Jade's unavailable at this time. Go away."

"Jade—"

"Leave a message at the beep," she whispered, trying for sarcastic wit, which is where she felt the most comfortable while completely coming undone.

"I want to talk to you."

"Sorry, you've been rerouted to the Office of Too Freaking Bad."

He hung up on her and she breathed a sigh of relief. Which turned out to be too soon because his voice came through the door. "Open up."

His voice was low. Calm, assertive. And she actually turned to face the door before she stopped herself. *Don't be the horse that needs taming!* "Stop woman-whispering me."

There was a pause, as if he was considering his options, weighing each against her mood. But unfortunately his silence was as compelling as his voice.

Dammit. "Go," she said, even though he hadn't spoken again. "Please, Dell. Just go away."

"I can't do that."

She began to mentally compile a new list: Dell's negative qualities. Stubborn. Single-minded. Nosy . . .

"I'm busy," she said.

"You're not."

"Yes, I am. Very, very busy."

But Dell had gone to the No Bullshitting School of Life and wasn't buying. "Jade, you're standing there right this minute, just staring at the door."

"I'm sitting." She let out a sigh, really hating it when he

was right. "I have a date." The only date she'd had all year had been with her secret stash of Ben & Jerry's.

And Netflix.

And maybe once or twice with her pulsing five-speed showerhead.

"Just tell me if you're okay," he said.

No, she was most definitely not okay. In fact, she was an inch from a second meltdown and she desperately needed to be alone to have it, thank you very much.

"Jade."

Her throat burned so badly she couldn't speak so she nodded like an idiot even knowing he couldn't see her. "Yes. I'm okay."

"Open the door and prove it."

Goddammit. She tossed back her hair, lifted her chin and forced an impassive expression before pulling open the door. "What?" she asked. "What is it?"

He said nothing, but his dark eyes swept over her, doing a quick and efficient visual exam.

"I could take a picture for you, if you'd like," she offered.

Those warm brown eyes lifted to hers, the briefest flash of humor momentarily dislodging his concern. "If I thought you meant that . . ." Belying the teasing in his voice, his eyes stayed serious, and he lifted her hand to eye the scrape that she'd cleaned and bandaged. He took a step forward to cross the threshold but she put her hand to his chest.

"We need to talk," he said.

"Yeah, now see, that's the *last* thing I want to do." She meant to shove him away but she'd been so shaken for the past hour, so on edge, she felt momentarily confused when she felt the warm heat of him, the easy strength radiating beneath his shirt.

And suddenly all she wanted to do was lose herself in that heat and strength. Almost against her own will, her head tilted back and she stared up into his face.

At his mouth. Because she knew now. Knew how it felt on hers. Knew the power of their connection.

As if he felt it, too, he went still as stone, then dropped his gaze to her mouth as well, and for the first time since the parking lot, she warmed—thanks to him. She didn't even realize she'd leaned in toward him until with a low groan and a curse, he put his hands on her arms. "Jade."

Galvanized into action by sheer mortification, she broke free and turned her back on him. She scooped up the kitten, pressing her red face into Beans's fur. "I told you, I'm busy."

"I'll see you tomorrow, then," he said quietly.

Tomorrow was far too many baby steps away to think about at the moment, but she nodded. When he said nothing else, she turned back to him.

A mistake. Just another one in a long line of mistakes today alone. Because Dell had a way. For as unflappable and affable as he was, he had instincts honed as sharp as any wild animal, and he saw right through her. "You'll call me if you need anything," he said. Not a request.

A demand.

If she called, he'd be back here in an instant. She knew that. They butted heads, they teased and pushed buttons, but there was no one better than Dell in a crisis. She could count on him, she knew that. She just didn't *want* to count on him. She wanted to be able to count on herself. God, how she wanted that.

"Jade."

"I'll call," she said. "Go." *God, please, go.* "I'll see you tomorrow." She'd have promised him the full moon if it would make him leave.

With one last long look, he nodded, and then was gone.

She stared down at Beans as she let all the air out of her lungs. "What now?"

"Mew," Beans said.

"Right." Baby steps. She headed straight to the kitchen,

specifically the freezer, grabbing a big wooden spoon on the way. She had a date, after all. A threesome with Ben & Jerry. Then she'd take a long shower, go to bed, and figure the rest out in the morning.

Baby steps.

Five

D ell rose before dawn. Not that he was a morning person by choice. Nope, if left to his own devices, he would stay up all night, but these days he had early morning responsibilities.

Of his own making, at least. He'd made this life for himself. He'd bled and sweated for it.

And he loved it.

But as he rolled out of bed at the asscrack of dawn and into a shower, he'd have given his left nut for a few more hours since he hadn't fallen asleep until an hour ago.

Couldn't, not when he kept reliving the look on Jade's face from the night before.

Mindless terror. That's what he'd seen when she'd torn out of his parking lot.

It'd been so different from anything he'd ever seen from the coolly poised woman who sat running his world every day that it'd taken a moment to compute.

It'd been all he'd thought about all night, the image of her beautiful face, pale and stricken. She'd collected herself somewhat by the time he'd gotten to her loft, but when she'd opened the door he could practically feel the vibrations from the trembling she was trying so desperately to control.

Her fake bravado had broken his heart. What the fuck had happened to her? He'd stepped inside, intending to get answers, but one look at her face had told him no answers were going to be forthcoming.

And then she'd looked at his mouth. He'd read her thoughts and body language as clearly as if she'd spoken out loud. She hadn't wanted to discuss what was wrong, but for that single beat at least, she'd been amiable to losing herself in his arms.

Not much shocked him these days, but that had. All this time and she'd never expressed an interest in him that way. In fact, she'd gone out of her way to make sure he understood that she *wasn't* attracted to him.

Until two nights ago after Crystal's. In the cab of his truck, giving each other mouth to mouth, everything had changed.

And then changed again when she'd vowed to ignore their connection.

Neither of them seemed to be capable of that, but not for lack of trying. "Come on, Gert," he told the still sleeping St. Bernard. "Let's hit it."

Gertie closed her eyes. Her version of possum. She wasn't a morning creature, either.

"If you don't get up, you won't get a cookie."

Gertie scrambled to her feet. Dell drove to Belle Haven and parked next to a freshly washed, shiny truck, its interior so squeaky clean he could have eaten off the dash.

Adam's.

It'd been the military to drum home that neatness in his brother, but Dell didn't have the same compulsion. His truck was covered in a fine layer of dust on the outside and Gertie hair on the inside.

The front door of the center was locked, lights off. Alarm

on. The security system was being upgraded this week, a
direct response to the vet clinic robberies.

It wasn't going to be his place they hit next. Or if it was,
he'd be prepared. Once upon a time he might have been an
easy mark but those days were long over.

It was an hour before any of his staff would show up,
and as he knew Adam had, he walked around back.

He kept their horses, Reno and Kiwi, here. Dell handled
most of the day to day care of them, but on this foggy morning
as he made his way to the pens, only one equine head appeared to pop through the fog as she neighed a soft greeting.

Kiwi.

Reno and Adam were gone. "Aw, you got left behind," he
said, laughing when she butted her face to his chest, knocking him back a step, letting him know what she thought of
being deserted.

Kiwi always played hard-ass. "Much like another
woman in my life," he said.

Kiwi snorted and searched his pockets. When she found
the apple, she softened her limpid eyes and batted her lashes.

Her version of the femme fatale.

He laughed again when she ate it nearly whole and then
burped in his face. "If only you were all so easy." Saddling
her up, he rode into the nearby hills, where as a boy he'd gone
to be invisible instead of the easy, skinny, scrawny target he'd
once been.

He rode hard, grateful to not be on foot as he mostly had
been in those years, trying to outrun his demons.

Halfway back, he ran into Adam and Reno.

At a wordless command, Adam halted Reno and studied
Dell's face. He said nothing, just arched a brow in query.

It was rare, extremely rare, that Adam beat Dell into
Belle Haven.

"Overslept," Dell said.

Or not slept at all.

Adam just looked at him and Dell sighed. "Everything's fine."

With a nod, Adam urged Reno onward.

"Good talk," Dell muttered, and followed.

They made it to the center a good half hour before any patients were due. Normally Dell cut it closer than that, but Jade always came at exactly seven thirty and he wanted to be there when she arrived.

Assuming she *would* arrive this morning.

But as he walked Kiwi onto the property, she pulled in, and he knew a moment of unrelenting relief. He hadn't realized until that very moment exactly how afraid he'd been that she might simply vanish as mysteriously as she'd arrived.

Going to happen sooner or later, he reminded himself. Because no matter what had set her off last night, she was temporary here. She'd been telling him that since the day she'd walked in with his help-wanted ad in hand.

She got out of her car and hesitated. Their gazes met for one long, charged moment.

"Well, that's new," Adam said.

Dell ignored this comment as he dismounted.

Adam slid off Reno at the same time and casually grabbed the reins from Dell's hand. He didn't say anything more, just led the horses away.

Jade reached into her backseat for Beans's carrier, then headed across the parking lot toward him. Hard to tell what she was thinking behind her big, dark Hollywood glasses.

All he'd managed to piece together about last night was that fourteen-year-old deaf and slightly mentally handicapped Timmy, had run by her, wearing a mask.

At the sight of it, Jade had completely lost it.

Clearly she'd found it again because she walked right past him now and into the office, her usual implacable self.

The phone was ringing as he followed on her heels and

she answered it while unbuttoning her jacket and slipping out of it.

She left her glasses on.

"Belle Haven," she said, the phone in the crook of her neck as she gathered her hair up and held it there with two tongue depressors, the kind he had in small jars in each exam room.

She wore a black wraparound top, tied with a neat bow over her hip, and black pinstriped trousers. The sophistication was broken by the kick-ass boots with the stiletto heels and the pin above her breast in the shape of a dog cookie that said: REAL DOCTORS TREAT MORE THAN ONE SPECIES.

She looked both prim and outrageously sexy as she let Beans out, and Dell's brain stuttered and twitched. His dick also twitched, but he ignored both responses.

"He just walked in," she assured the person on the phone, not looking his way as she uncovered Peanut and booted up the computer. "We'll work you in before he heads into surgery. No problem, see you then." She hung up and nearly plowed into Gertie, who wasn't at her usual spot but standing very close to Jade staring up at her.

"Gertie," Jade admonished. "Out of my way, please."

Gertie stayed at attention, still staring up at Jade, and then let out a low whine.

With a noise of annoyance, Jade walked around the dog, avoiding Dell by turning to her computer, even though he'd stopped and leaned against the counter, also right in her way.

Dell eyed Gertie, who was watching Jade with worried eyes, clearly noticing the tension in Jade's body language. "Jade."

"Jade," Peanut squawked. "Jade, Jade. Pretty Peanut. Peanut so pretty."

"You're going to have to hustle this morning," Jade told Dell, handing him a file comprising all of the faxes that had come in.

Yes, but hustle was the usual speed around here, especially

in the mornings where they always had to hit the ground running to keep up. Dell typically began his day checking on any of his patients who'd been hospitalized during the night, reading through the lab results that Jade pulled for him off the fax machine. That's what was in the file she'd just handed him.

The closest overnight animal hospital was in Coeur d'Alene, and sometimes he'd have to go there to see his patients in person and do rounds. Either he'd drive or Brady would fly him in their Bell 47 helicopter, but he flipped through the file and saw that wasn't required this morning.

Jade had turned to her printer, which was now spitting out his schedule for the day. "You've got your usual early morning rounds and four surgeries; a spay, two neuters, one dental cleaning, and then—"

"Jade."

She went still for one telling beat, then turned to face him.

Pushing away from the counter, he crossed her work space and pulled off her sunglasses. As always, her makeup was flawless. She wore lip gloss that smelled like vanilla mint and there was no sign of a sleepless night.

She'd made damn sure of it.

But as he stared at her, she drew a deep, bolstering breath and just like that, he knew. She wasn't cool, calm, or collected. Not even close. But she had a hell of a store of bravado, probably because she was braced for him to mention last night. In fact, her eyes, those mesmerizing green eyes, were daring him to.

He wouldn't. Not here, not now, when she so clearly needed to keep her shield. He handed her back her glasses.

There was a flash of surprised relief and then she slowly turned away. "I'm really swamped," she said. "So—"

"I need some help." He paused, waiting until she turned back.

"What kind of help?" she asked suspiciously.

And with good reason. He rarely, if ever, asked for help. "Work help." He'd made it a point to never let anyone fuck around with his files. It was a lifelong habit deeply ingrained from growing up having to watch every penny, and it had carried over. His receivables and payables were as personal to him as his patients, and he handed them directly over to his accountant quarterly.

In between those times, he muddled through, sometimes messing everything up without trying, more often than not simply neglecting them. He knew the piles on his desk drove her nuts. And he'd always enjoyed driving her nuts. She looked so pretty steamed.

But today felt different. She felt different. He felt her tension, her fear every bit as much as Gertie did. Whatever it came from, he wanted to assuage it. Not that she'd let him, but she needed something to distract her, then. Something more challenging then making appointments, and he could give her this. "I'm waving the white flag," he said.

She just looked at him. He nearly smiled at having his own trick of loaded silence played against him. "If you have time," he said, "my billing needs help."

Her mouth opened, then closed. The spark that had been missing in her eyes didn't come back, but much of her wariness vanished, and she at least finally spoke to him. "Did hell freeze over?"

"Not yet."

"Did you forget your password to get into the system again?"

"Okay, one time."

"Weekly." She continued to study him, eyes narrowed. "Is this a pity offering?"

"If I were going to make a pity offering, it wouldn't be in my office."

She stared at him, then let out a low laugh. "In your dreams."

"You keep saying that. Makes me think you're the one having the dreams about me."

She bent and scooped up Beans. "Are you getting a load

of this?" she murmured to the kitten, then kissed her on the nose. "He thinks I'd dream of him over Nathan Fillion."

"Mew."

Jade tapped a finger on the schedule in Dell's hands, pointing to one of his eight o'clocks. "Dixie's in heat. We're going to have to be careful that she doesn't excite every male in the place."

"What?"

"If we don't rush her through, we'll have a clinic full of boners. What's wrong with your hearing this morning?"

"Nothing," he said. "I just really like it when you say things like excite and boner."

"Boner," Peanut said.

"Oh, no," Jade said to the parrot. "No, no, no . . . you can't say—"

"Boner."

"Oh God." Jade panicked. "Peanut—"

"Pretty bird," Del broke in, smiling at the parrot and speaking low and soft. "Such a pretty girl, Peanut."

Peanut preened under his admiring tone. "Pretty Peanut."

Jade shook her head in disbelief.

"It's all about distractions." Dell eyeballed the schedule. Jade was right, it was manageable. She always made sure of that. "So are you in on the books?" he asked casually.

She stared at him for a long, interminable beat, clearly attempting to see how much of this was because of her.

All of it . . . But if she hadn't figured out that he'd do anything for her, he wasn't about to tell her. He gave her his most harmless smile.

"Dell," she said softly.

"Jade," he said just as quietly. "Or should I say Goddess Jade?"

She closed her eyes. "Is this because we . . . kissed?"

"Is that what that was? I thought it was the Fourth of July."

"Dell." She grimaced. "Tell me this isn't about last night. Because I'm not good with sympathy."

"Noted. How are you with just some good old-fashioned caring?"

"Not so good with that, either."

"Huh," he said, and crouched to rub Gertie's belly. "Maybe you should work on that."

"My family's been trying to drown me in it for a while now, but I just keep floating to the top."

He straightened. "Keeping your head above water is good, Jade. In or out?"

She blew out a breath. "You know I'm in."

"Good." He smiled. "Don't tell Adam—he'll whine like a little girl because he actually thinks he's good at the books. But he screwed up last month's billing so badly that we might have to start completely over."

Instead of looking nervous, she actually looked thrilled, and he shook his head. "You are one odd woman, you know that?"

She laughed, *laughed*, and he felt like he'd won the lotto. He turned to head into the back but she surprised him when she set her hand on his arm.

"Thanks," she said. "For not pushing."

He looked down at her fingers on his. "You're safe here, you know that, right?"

She nodded, and for a second, neither of them moved as that something new zinged between them. Smarter than him, and also faster, Jade pulled free and stared at him.

"Boner," Peanut said.

Six

As Dell walked away, Jade drew a deep breath and attempted to shrug off her tension. Only it didn't shrug off. Her shoulders were so tense they felt like pins and needles were stabbing into them, and now there was something odd going on low in her belly as well.

You could be halfway to somewhere new by now, said a little voice in her head. She told the cowardly weasel to zip it and held her chin high.

She wasn't going anywhere. So she'd had a minor setback yesterday, she could recover. She could go back to burying the past.

She could.

She would.

Her cell phone rang. Normally she'd ignore it at work, but she pounced on that sucker.

"Just looked at the calendar." It was Sam, her cousin. "And guess what, J? It's the first of October."

"Happens every month," Jade agreed, ignoring the significance. "What are you doing calling so early, is everything okay?"

"I was going to ask you the same thing."

She glanced at her watch and added an hour for Chicago time. "Wow, so you no longer sleep late?"

"Haven't slept more than five hours straight since med school. And then, to make it worse, a certain cousin of mine skipped out on her job and left us all in the lurch. I'm working my ass off."

"Poor baby. And that fat paycheck doesn't help at all?"

Sam blew out a breath and softened his voice. "Okay, truth, J. How are you doing really?"

"Fantastic." But they'd grown up together and were as close as family got. She couldn't bullshit him, she didn't even try. "I've been better."

"Goddammit," he said quietly. "Tell me you're still on track to be here by November first as promised. And if you say you need more time, I'm coming out there to drag you back here myself."

"I'm on track."

"Good," he said. "Because your town house misses you."

"My town house misses me?"

"Yeah. And the office misses you."

"Now that I believe," she said, thinking if all that missed her in Chicago was inanimate objects, why go back?

"Things are going downhill, Jade. Sandy's not on top of everything like you always were. We're suffering without you."

Guilt washed over her. "That can't be true."

"Believe it. I hate to ask anything of you, but . . ."

"But you're going to, anyway?" Jade asked dryly.

"Can you call in and talk to Sandy? She came from running just the Urgent Care, she's not used to this. She's got some computer problems and—"

"Sam, Sandy's good. She knows what to do." Jade had made sure of it.

"Yes but she's not you. The office management has gone to hell. We're losing patients, babe. People are tired of the long wait at the front desk. Phone calls are getting routed to our service in the middle of the day. We're losing out on business."

"You're not—"

Sam laughed mirthlessly. "It's a 'we,' Jade. We're a 'we,' in business and in family. In everything."

She pinched the bridge of her nose. "I'm working on it, Sam."

"I know."

The worry in his voice made her want to try to reassure him. She'd spent most of her life being the center of the family, the go-to girl. When she'd bailed from Chicago, she'd left a lot more than the city behind. "I keep thinking I'm working my way back to myself," she admitted. "But the truth is I'm not. I don't think I'm who I thought I was."

"You're still our Jade," he said firmly. "You are."

She wished she was as sure.

Sam blew out a breath. "Listen, don't worry about us right now. Tell me what's going on with you. I woke up with this need to talk to you and there's something in your voice."

"It's nothing. I just had a little setback, that's all."

"Flashbacks? Nightmares?"

"Some."

"Fuck, I hate this. I'm caught between that stupid promise I never should have made and—"

"Not a stupid promise," she interrupted. "I'm going to be okay, Sam. Really."

"You've been saying that for *eighteen* months." His voice softened. "Everyone got counseling but you."

"I wasn't hurt."

"Bullshit, you weren't. Now get your ass back here so we can take care of you. We have the best of the best, and you know it. Come home now."

There were built-in stakes to that plan, of course. Her parents. Sam. A business she'd been born to run. A town house she'd bought and loved . . . It was hard to say no.

It'd always been hard to say no. She hadn't been bred for the no. She'd been a pleaser. And that deep-seated instilled need she had to make people happy had nearly killed her. She glanced around her at the animal center that she'd made her life for now.

For now . . .

A temporary haven, that's all she'd expected it to be. But Sunshine had opened its arms for her, taken her in, given her refuge. She'd made connections here, deep ones. And through those connections she'd discovered a different side of herself. A side that believed *no* was a full sentence. A side that was beginning to have her own hopes and dreams, not the ones she'd been born into.

Her eyes locked onto a pair of warm, curious brown ones.

Dell's.

"I'll be there by the first, as promised."

"Jade—"

"Bye, Sam." She closed her phone.

"Problem?" Dell asked.

"Yes, but not yours." She paused, then felt compelled by the sheer force of his personality to say more. "My old job."

He arched a brow. "You didn't list any past jobs on your app."

No, she hadn't.

"You going back to that same job when you go home?"

"Yes."

He nodded and she paused, trying to decide how best to handle this. "I didn't list the job on my résumé because I didn't have any vet experience."

"But you have office experience," he said softly. "Big office experience. You were more than a receptionist."

"Yes."

"What were you, Jade?"

The gig was up a long time ago, she reminded herself. "Chief operating officer of a medical center. It's really just a fancy title for office manager and full-charge bookkeeper." She braced herself for the questions. Like why was she a thousand miles from home working a job she was obviously *way* overqualified for? And why had she given up that job in the first place, and did it have anything to do with whatever the hell had given her a near mental breakdown in the parking lot the night before?

But Dell didn't ask her any of those questions. He didn't ask her anything. He merely nodded and slid his hands into his pockets. Totally at ease.

"I should have told you," she said.

"You didn't have to." He walked back into her work space, Gertie so close on his heels that when Dell stopped, the dog bumped into him.

Gertie slid Dell a reproachful look.

Dell ruffled the top of her head, and Gertie's expression softened with unconditional love. "Down, Gert."

"Down, Gert," Peanut said, and Gertie plopped to the floor, the ground shaking under her graceless descent.

"I like hearing about you, Jade," Dell said. "I'd like to hear more."

"Trust me, you don't."

He gave her a small smile. "Not for you to decide, is it?" He leaned over her and reached for her keyboard, logging her in with his pass code.

That was new.

At her look of surprise, he said, "For the billing." He paused. "Unless you're leaving."

"Not yet."

He held her gaze until Keith walked through the reception area and unlocked the front door. Then he came up to the counter for the first patient file. "Dudes," he said. "We ready?"

Dell didn't break eye contact with Jade. "I am. You?" he asked Jade quietly.

They weren't talking about work and she knew it. Was she ready? Hell, no. Not for anything but she'd long ago learned that to fake it was to make it. So she nodded.

Dell smiled at her in approval before turning to head to the back, stopping to greet a Newfoundland who'd just come inside with his owner. Dell laughed at something the man said, and the sound scraped at something low in Jade's belly as she let out a careful breath. One more thing she wasn't equipped to deal with at the moment.

Completely unconcerned with that fact, Dell vanished into the back, his shoulders square, that long-legged stride confident and sure.

Jade had grown up with confident men. Highly educated men. Sophisticated and elegant. Polished.

Dell was highly educated. He had to be in order to become a vet. But he wasn't sophisticated and elegant, or polished. He'd as soon be on the floor helping a dog give birth than in a boardroom.

It was one of the most attractive things about him, how much he cared about his work. He had hundreds of patients and just about every single one of them was owned by a client completely and totally devoted to providing their animal the best care available. Dell was the best, and he was beloved in these parts.

Jade hadn't had pets while growing up. Her mother was allergic, and after Jade had been out on her own she'd just never thought of it. It'd been quite the learning curve when she'd first come to Belle Haven. Dell was fairly closed off emotionally with people, but he seemed to be able to access whatever an animal needed. An injured dog, a sick kitten, a horse in labor, it didn't matter . . . Dell gave his heart and soul, and in less time than it took humans to shake hands, an animal would become part of Dell's pack for life. But for as many animals in his pack, Dell's human pack was much smaller.

But he'd included Jade in that pack . . . which she'd resisted.

The room was filling up and Keith hadn't come back for the next patient to fill the other waiting room. With a sigh, Jade grabbed the file and stood. Typically, the morning brought in the clients and the animals that were the most sick or had become endangered overnight. These early appointments often began with Dell walking into the exam room to face worried and stressed-out people and animals.

He was good at assuaging fears.

He'd be good at assuaging yours . . .

"Sergio," she called, and managed a smile for Sergio's owner, Leanne Whitfield. Leanne could have been a Beverly Hills housewife, except she didn't have a husband and she lived here in Sunshine. What she did have was a short-term plan to rectify the lack of husband pronto. She wanted to marry the most eligible man in town, and she'd decided that man was Dell.

To that end, Leanne brought in her kitten every few weeks, manufacturing odd illnesses. Leanne had somehow concluded that Jade was the biggest threat to her marry-Dell goal, which could be construed as amusing given that Dell was a serial dater and Jade was a serial social hermit these days.

As for Dell's opinion on the situation, he and Jade had an understanding. Jade's job included making sure Leanne never trapped Dell alone in an exam room, where she'd "accidentally" grope him. "What's the problem with Sergio this morning?" Jade asked, pen poised over the chart.

"I'd rather go over this just once," Leanne said, and flashed a smile that said, *Bite me.* "I'll just tell the doctor myself directly."

Jade smiled a *Bite me* right back at Leanne. "Sure. I'll just go tell him so. He's running a few minutes behind."

"Oh?" Leanne didn't look happy. "He have a late night last night?"

"Here you go," Jade said, ignoring the question as she showed her into exam room two.

"When we get married," Leanne said, "your services won't be necessary."

"Married?"

"It's only a matter of time before he realizes how perfect we are together," Leanne said, eyeballing herself in the small mirror over the sink. She adjusted her boobs higher and her neckline lower. "We'll honeymoon in Cabo."

Okay, Jade wasn't in the mood for this. "Listen, it's not going to happen."

"Why?"

Yeah, Jade, why? She thought about being brutally honest and telling Leanne that she managed to do what no one else could do—she terrified the big, bad Dell Connelly, but sometimes honesty just wasn't the way to go. "Because we're engaged." The lie rolled right off her tongue so easily she couldn't even believe she'd said it.

Leanne's sharp gaze flashed immediately to Jade's ringless engagement finger.

"Getting it sized." Jade left the room, hung the chart for Dell, and practically ran down the hall, nearly plowing right into him.

He put his hands on her hips to steady her. "Oh no you don't, you're not deserting me with her. Let's go." He began to tug her back to the exam room.

"Um," she said. "She won't exactly be bothering you anymore."

"What did you do?"

She patted his chest. His hard, warm chest. "A thing."

"A thing? What thing?"

"Yeah, we don't have to talk about the thing," she said, relieved when the phone started to ring.

He caught her arm. "We'll talk about the thing later."

"Sure." *Or never.* And because just his hand on her was stirring up sensations best not stirred up, she backed away and returned to her work.

Seven

D ell was in the main surgery area cleaning up sometime later when Adam came through after a training session. "I've got the Moorelands in room two," Dell told him. "Want to come in with me?"

The Moorelands were clients of Adam's. They'd brought in their seven-week-old Labrador puppies.

"First exam?"

"And vaccinations. Eight puppies. You can help."

"Maybe you'd rather have someone else. Say, your fiancée."

"How many times do I have to tell you, crack kills brain cells."

Adam flashed a rare grin. "Didn't you wonder why Leanne didn't play grab-ass with you this morning? It was because your receptionist turned herself into your fiancée." Adam slapped him on the back. "Congrats, by the way. I didn't think you had it in you."

"Shut up. You're making this shit up."

"Are you kidding?" Adam asked. "No one could make

this up. It's too good. The question is, though . . . why would Jade come up with such a story? Unless something's happened between you . . ."

Dell didn't respond to that. Didn't know *how* to respond to that.

Adam gave a shocked Dell a push down the hall and into exam room one.

Eight puppies were crawling over everything, making soft, snuffling puppy noises. Their owners, Joey and Donna Mooreland, a couple in their midfifties were sitting, supervising the best that they could with four hands against thirty-two little paws.

Adam had sold the couple their first Labrador several years ago now and had helped them through their first breeding cycle. He scooped up a black pup attempting to eat his shoelace.

"I'm nervous," Donna admitted, hand to her chest. "This is our first batch of babies."

"No worries." Adam slid Dell a look. "There's a lot of firsts going around here today."

Dell ignored him and bent over the puppies. There were four brown, two black, and two white Labs, all in various stages of mewling and climbing over each other, tails wagging, tongues out.

"It's just that we've been so frazzled with our daughter's engagement," Donna said, stopping the biggest pup from climbing on top of his siblings like a circus performer.

"A lot of that going around," Adam said.

Dell gave Adam a look that said quite clearly *Shut up or die.* But Donna smiled at Adam. "Someone you know just get engaged?"

"As a matter of fact," Adam said. "Dr. Connelly here—"

Dell stepped on Adam's foot and ground into it a little bit.

Adam drew a careful breath and stopped talking.

But it was too late. Donna had caught the scent of a possible engagement. "Doctor?" she asked Dell. "Are you engaged?"

"He is," Joe said.

Everyone looked at him in shock. Joe shrugged. "One of your clients in the waiting room was talking about it as she left."

Adam started to laugh, but Dell put more weight on his foot, and Adam turned it into a cough.

"Oh, this is so lovely!" Donna said, clapping her hands, then leaning in conspiratorially. "You probably don't know this, Dr. Connelly, but just about all the single women in the country have their hearts set on you. You're going to break them all with this news."

Adam coughed again, and Dell took his weight off Adam's foot because he felt a little woozy. And he was sweating. Christ, this was ridiculous. "The puppies," he said. "Let's concentrate on the puppies."

Adam smirked. Dell ignored him and picked up the runt, a girl. The tiny brown Lab had eyes bigger than her nose and mouth and her head bobbed as she stared at him solemnly. He smiled at her and she licked his chin.

"So when's the big day?" Donna asked.

Try never, as it would be difficult to be married to a woman who lived seventeen hundred miles away. "The reports of my"—*Christ*—"*engagement* are overexaggerated."

Adam snorted.

Dell checked the puppy's teeth to make sure they were properly aligned, then inspected her eyes, examined her skin, and palpated her hips.

"Is she okay?"

Dell set her on the scale, having to keep a hand on her because her legs were scrambling for purchase. She had places to go, things to explore. "She's slightly underweight, but she's looking strong."

Both Donna and Joe looked relieved. "That's the one my daughter wants to keep," Joe said.

"We're going to wrap her up in a white silky bow on the day of the wedding," Donna said. Her voice went sly. "Maybe you'd like us to save you one for your wedding?"

Adam grinned and looked at him. "How sweet."

Dell resisted the urge to punch him and busied himself checking for defects the Mooreland's might not have recognized, like heart murmurs. He found nothing ominous, and after the longest ten minutes of his life he managed to escape. He strode toward his office, taking a quick glance out front.

Jade sat at the front desk, talking on the phone while simultaneously working on the computer, checking someone in, and checking two people out. She sat there, an oasis in the middle of a circus. As if she sensed him, she glanced up. And if he wasn't mistaken, she grimaced slightly.

He raised a brow.

She bit her lower lip but didn't look away.

Adam, hot on his heels, leaned in and whispered, "Think we should tell your fiancée that you're allergic to commitment? That you have abandonment issues? And, oh yeah, that you're never going to let your guard down enough to actually marry anyone?"

"You're an asshole."

"So are you."

Dell sighed. "Yeah," he said as Adam walked away. "But knowing it is half the battle."

By noon Jade had checked in and out a dizzying number of patients while managing to avoid being alone with Dell. He'd seen a bulldog with an ingrown tail, a duck with a mysterious throat infection that turned out to be a swallowed quarter, and a kitten with acne. He'd performed four surgeries.

Jade had grabbed the sandwich from her bagged lunch and walked outside, needing a moment of sunshine.

A soft nicker from the horse pen caught her attention.

Reno. He was close to the fencing and flirting with her. She reached out to touch him and he snapped at her fingers. It was so unexpected that she jumped back and fell to the dirt. She scrambled back to her feet as a big hand settled on the nape of her neck.

She screamed and whirled around and would have fallen again if Dell hadn't caught her. "Just me," he said calmly. "You okay?"

They both knew she wasn't but she nodded. "Reno tried to bite me."

Dell didn't say anything for a moment, just slid an arm around her, making her realize she was backing away from both the horses and the man. "What do you know about horses?" he asked quietly, his delicious warmth seeping into her.

"I know that the porcelain horse collection I had as a child wasn't made to be played with," she said, trying to lighten the tension. "But I did it, anyway, and kept breaking off their legs. My grandmother got fed up and stopped buying them."

"The grandmother you were named after?"

"Yes." She closed her eyes, concentrating on the feel of his hand on the small of her back. Comforting but something else, too. Her heart rate should have slowed by now from her fright, but it was still racing—for another reason entirely now. "They wanted me to be strong and tough like her."

"It worked. You're the strongest, toughest woman I know."

She managed to choke back her startled laugh at that.

"It's true." He paused. "Do you know anything about *real* horses?"

"I know Reno used to like me."

"He still likes you." He stroked his hand up her back, letting it settle at the nape of her neck again. "It's important with any animal, especially a spooked one, to be calm, assertive. Dominant."

"Okay."

"A horse's emotions depend on its surroundings and also on the emotions of its human counterparts."

She went still. "Are you saying that my emotions caused Reno to try to bite me?"

His silence said he was going to let her wrestle with that one. "Relax your arms," he said, making her realize she was hugging herself tight. She dropped them to her sides with effort.

"And breathe," he said.

He was right, she wasn't breathing. She sucked in some air.

"Better," he said, and leaned past her to rub Reno's neck the way he was rubbing hers.

Reno gave a snort of pleasure and shifted closer.

"It's calming," Dell said.

Yes. It was calming as hell. If he kept it up, she'd do as Reno just had and make sounds of pleasure and shift even closer, too. "You have a bond with him," she said, managing to sound like she still had bones in her legs.

"Yes, and so do you. You just have to find it, and use your touch and voice to assure the animal that you're not going to let anything harm him."

His hand was slowly moving up and down her back now. And she got the message.

He wasn't going to let anything harm her, either.

"Jade."

She closed her eyes. "I still don't want to talk about it," she said. "Ever."

The sun was warm on her face, telling her that even though it was fall, summer hadn't quite given up the fight yet. She could almost pretend that they weren't having a conversation she didn't want to have.

"Ever is a long time," Dell said.

"I mean it."

"I know." He nodded. "I felt the same."

She shook her head. This didn't compute. "What are you talking about?"

"I know what it's like to suffer a trauma. What it's like to struggle to get past it."

Deny, deny, deny. "I'm not struggling."

He just looked at her, and she blew out a breath. "Okay, so sometimes I struggle, but don't change the subject! You're six foot two and outweigh me by at least sixty pounds. How were you ever a . . ."

"Victim?" His smile was grim. "I wasn't always thirty-two and built like a linebacker, you know. Actually, I started off more like a pipe cleaner with eyes."

That surprised a laugh out of her and she sidled him a glance. No one in their right mind would confuse that well defined, tough, rugged body with a pipe cleaner. "Come on."

"Jade, trust me when I tell you that in my freshman year I was five foot three and weighed a buck twenty soaking wet. I got my ass kicked every which way, every single day."

An ache built in her chest for the boy he'd been. "Why?"

"Because I couldn't keep my mouth closed to save my life. I was a punk-ass kid whose mother had walked away and whose dad had died. I had a chip on top of the chip on my shoulder."

His mother had been Native American. According to Lilah, when the woman had been a teenager, she'd fallen for a white kid—a big offense in her family. She'd run off with him, but after having her second baby—Dell—she'd run off again, back to the reservation. When the boys' father had died several years later, she hadn't wanted her sons back.

Jade and her own mother had some issues, basically control issues, but Jade had never once doubted that she'd been wanted, cherished and fully, one hundred percent loved.

A luxury Dell nor Adam had been given. It made her hurt for him, for Adam, too. For the men that they'd become, not that they'd thank her for the sympathy. They were both far too proud for that. But in spite of what had happened to them, they'd become good men. For both of them, trust had to be earned, and Dell certainly didn't give it away easily. He shielded his emotions behind his intellect and his job, though he completely surrendered himself to every single patient.

"I'd been dumped into yet another foster home and was pissed off at the world," Dell said casually, letting her know it could no longer hurt him.

But she didn't believe that. He had Adam and Brady now, and Lilah. And that was about it, other than a bunch of four-legged creatures.

He wasn't all that much better than she at letting people in. The thought brought the crazy urge to . . .

Hug him.

The thought was ridiculous and almost made her laugh. Dell was the strongest, most self-reliant person she knew. Comfort wasn't anywhere on his list of needs. "What happened?"

"My first day at the new school, I picked a fight with the biggest kid there."

"Dell. *Why*?"

"Hell, I don't even remember. Because I was stupid."

"What did he do to you?"

"For starters, he had the entire football team drag me to the park after school for retaliation. They stripped me naked and told me if I begged real nice, they'd let me go. They lied."

Her heart was in her throat. "Oh, Dell."

"Yeah, it sucked."

"Who saved you?"

"Nobody."

"They just stood there?" she asked, pissed and horrified for him.

"No. They beat the shit out of me, swearing that if I ever

told anyone, it'd be worse next time." He shook his head. "Later, at the hospital, I tried to tell the nurses I'd walked into a door."

She gasped. "You didn't tell the truth?"

"I still had to go to that school," he said. "And I wanted to live." He rubbed his jaw ruefully, as if soothing an old ache.

"Who was in charge of you?" she asked.

"We went back into the system. Then we were taken in by a guy named Sol Anders." He said the name with fondness. "It was the last foster home I ever had. He kept us, Adam and me. Brady was already there when we arrived and he quickly became our older brother. After I healed up from the attack, Brady and Sol took turns teaching me self-defense. Luckily that summer I grew six inches, and then another five the year after. And I hit the weights."

It had done a body good . . .

"It wasn't about vanity," he said, reading her mind with his usual ease. It was about survival. I did what I had to in order to survive, and so have you. But you already know that . . ."

Reno bumped his big head to Dell's chest.

Dell made a soft clicking sound with his mouth and the huge horse bumped him again, knocking him back a step, making him laugh softly.

Reno snickered in response, almost as if he was trying to imitate Dell's laugh.

Dell ruffled the horse's ears and gave him a smacking kiss right between the eyes, then turned to Jade, eyes serious. "You're only as strong as your biggest weakness."

"Is that right? What's your biggest weakness?"

"Back then, it was trying to be something I wasn't."

"And now?" she asked.

His mouth quirked. "Apparently, it's my fiancée."

She froze. "So you did hear."

When he just looked at her, she sucked her lower lip between her teeth. "It was for you, you know. A favor."

"Yeah? How do you figure?"

"I saved you from having to worry about Leanne. Hell, I saved you from messy emotional problems with *any* woman. You're saved from having to deal with real love and genuine passion. You are welcome."

He went brows up. "So I should be thanking you, then."

"I . . ." She let out a breath. "Okay, not exactly."

"You know that news travels fast out here. People'll have us married with children in no time."

"Oh God."

Because she looked much as he imagined he'd looked earlier with Adam, he could laugh. "It wouldn't be that bad."

She shrugged but looked unconvinced. And he realized he really had no idea what her hopes and dreams were for herself. None. "You don't see yourself married? A mom?"

"I try not to look that far ahead."

"And they call *me* tight-lipped," he said. "Come on, Jade. Tell me about you."

"What do you want to know?"

"More than you get a hard-on for organizing things."

"Like?"

"Like . . . why you come all photo ready to a job you're obviously overqualified for, wearing designer clothes when you're going to get dog and kitten hair all over you."

She shrugged. "I know how to run a washing machine."

"Okay, so why don't you date? You're sexy, smart as hell, and know your way around a good conversation. Yet whenever a guy approaches you, you use cynicism and sarcasm to scare him off."

"Not my fault if a guy's scared off by a little attitude."

She was throwing off some good 'tude right now. "Tell me what scared you so bad you ran from Chicago," he said. "Don't you think it's time?"

She stiffened and turned away. "What it's time for is to get back to work."

Eight

The next morning, Jade arrived at Belle Haven before dawn's first light for their biweekly vaccine clinic. She sat in her car, eyeing the walk to the front door.

Another vet clinic had been hit in Coeur d'Alene the night before, and it was all over the news. Dell had upgraded the security system, adding cameras at the front and back doors and several panic buttons throughout the clinic with a direct line to emergency dispatch.

His cool, calm, almost ruthless efficiency told her that he was very serious about this. And if Dell was serious, it meant he had a good reason. Dell had a lot of really great qualities, but allowing others to see his weaknesses wasn't one of them. This place, and the people and animals in it, were his. No sharing. The protective, possessive side of his nature should have threatened her peace of mind but at the moment she was glad for it.

Still, she had to make the walk from her car to the door. "Going to need reinforcements for this," she told Beans and put in her iPod earphones. She hit shuffle and Eminem came on.

Eminem was an ass kicker.

Still, she kept the volume down so she could hear what was going on around her. Normally she liked to get in a half hour before anyone else to set up, but nerves jittered through her stomach as she headed across the lot.

Inside, past the alarm and behind the locked door, she started breathing again. She let Beans loose, uncovered Peanut, and began to get ready for the mob scene that always occurred on free clinic days.

Because she couldn't deny the slight nerves still jangling, she cranked the volume on Pink and was singing along, trying to enjoy the solitude and quiet. After a few minutes she felt herself begin to relax at the regular, familiar routine of turning on the equipment, checking the supplies, organizing the files for the day. She walked past the drug cabinet, as always automatically reaching out to make sure it was locked.

It was. It was always locked, but to make sure was a comfort. She went still when the hair at the nape of her neck rose, then tore out her earphones in time to catch a whisper of sound, the soft brush of a man's footstep. And then another, telling her that there were two of them behind her.

"Do as I say, bitch, and I won't hurt you. Yet."

Dark fear as he emphasized the words with the cold muzzle of the gun thrust under her jaw.

Frozen with fear, she tried to turn her head to look at him, but he ran the tip of the gun from her jaw down her throat and over her collarbone to skim her breast. "Let's go," came the low, rough voice. "Unless you want to spend some time out here with me first . . ."

She felt the hand on her arm and heard her own whimper.

"Jade. Jade, it's just me—"

"Man, she's too far gone to hear you."

"I know. Fuck—"

Jade felt herself being picked up. She struggled auto-matically, panic welling, blocking her throat so that all that escaped another pathetic whimper.

"You're okay. Jade, can you hear me?" A hand rough with calluses stroked gently down her hair. "You're safe."

Just a flashback. That's all. A flashback triggered by the Halloween mask from two nights before, not to mention hours of tossing and turning, culminating in having the bad timing of being nearly scared out of her own skin in front of the drug cabinet.

Which is where she'd faced her own nightmare once before.

"Here," Adam said to Dell, dragging a chair over. "Sit with her here, I'll get her some water."

Her brain didn't seem to want to connect with reality, and she couldn't draw air into her lungs. Embarrassed, she buried her face into the crook of Dell's neck and tried to breathe him in instead.

"Jade. Jade, listen to me." Dell, speaking in that quiet calm voice of his, the one that made her struggle to settle just so she could hear more of it. "You're safe. I've got you."

She nodded, hoping she looked like she was back in con-trol of herself. But she figured she must have failed because he ran his hands slowly up and down her back, soothing her, whispering softly to her, words she couldn't quite catch but it didn't matter. His voice was heaven. If he kept talk-ing, just like that, she thought maybe she could even start breathing again.

Adam came back with a glass of water. "She okay?"

"Yes." Dell cupped her face in his big hands, his own face so close to hers. "She's okay."

Jade nodded, even though she had a grip on his shirt, tight enough to hurt her own fingers. But she didn't let go as she drew in a desperate gulp of air and let it out.

"She's hyperventilating," Adam said quietly.

"No, she's got this. You've got this, Jade," Dell assured her and took the water from Adam to hand to her.

"Slow sips," Adam said, hunkering down at her side, his eyes on her face.

"I'm fine," Jade said, and gulped down the water, relieving her parched throat. Apparently freak-outs made one thirsty. Who knew?

Adam took the glass from her and that's when she realized . . . she was in Dell's lap.

"Careful," Adam said when she stood up. "You don't have your sea legs back yet."

"I'm fine," she said. A broken record. It didn't escape her notice that Dell made sure to be very close to her, close enough to grab her if she started to lose it again.

But she wouldn't. Hell no. She was overcoming.

Dammit.

"I'm sorry," she said.

Adam and Dell exchanged a long look and she grimaced. "Okay, so I'm working on it."

Dell's eyes never left hers. "What's setting you off?"

She shook her head. Not going down that road. Luckily for her the phones were starting to ring, and that was her cue. "Nothing. It's nothing. Got to get the phones."

"Jade—"

But she was already scrambling out of there for the sanctuary of her front desk.

Dell's last few appointments of the day were worming puppies—always fun—and examining a twelve-year-old German shepherd suffering from pneumonia. The owner was Gil Roberto, the local mechanic. He and Max had been together for all twelve years. Gil was sitting on the floor with Max's head in his lap, looking like he was about to face the firing squad. But Dell drained Max's lungs in a quick procedure, and Gil was able to take Max home.

It was a good end to a rough day. Dell had kept his eye on Jade, but she'd played things close to the vest. Still, there was no doubt she was working hard at keeping it together, but whatever the other night had dragged back up for her, it had shaken her to the core.

Tired and dirty, Dell showered in the bathroom attached to his office. When he came out, he found Adam in his office chair, feet up, leaning back, messing around on Dell's laptop. "You'd better not be looking at porn," Dell said. "You crashed the entire system last time."

Adam didn't bother to acknowledge his brother's presence.

"Don't you have your own office right down the hall?"

"It's your turn to buy dinner," Adam said, still staring at the laptop screen. "I'm thinking pizza."

"Yeah. Sure."

Adam looked up and eyeballed him. "You figure out what's up with our fearless girl?"

"No."

"She's still not sharing?"

"Would you?"

"Something bad happened to her," Adam said.

"I know."

"You going to ask?"

"No," Dell said.

"Why not?"

Dell slid his brother a long look. "Did pushing ever help you?"

A ghost of a smile crossed Adam's mouth. "No."

Dell shoved Adam's feet off his desk, and that's when he realized . . . the office was clutter-free. He had two filing cabinets—usually fully loaded with stacks of shit on top—and then a credenza, as well as a set of chairs used as crap collectors. But everything was completely cleaned off. "Holy shit."

Ever alert, Adam looked around. "What?"

"The entire room is clean."

"Yeah, I assumed you finally shoved the entire mess into the trash to start over."

Dell hauled Adam out of the chair, then sank into it himself, whipped around, and opened the drawers of the credenza.

Organized and neat as a pin.

"You get some sort of extreme makeover TV crew in here when I wasn't looking?" Adam asked.

"Jade," Dell said.

"Jade what?"

"She did this."

"Actually," Jade said from the doorway. "I brought in a hazmat team to handle it."

Adam flashed her a rare smile.

"Wow," Jade said, smiling back. "You ought to do that more often. Oh, and line one. It's Holly for you."

Adam's smile faded.

Holly was the daughter of Donald Reid, an extremely wealthy businessman who'd bought up a bunch of failing ranches and had somehow turned them around in a bad economy. His daughter Holly had recently joined him from New York. She was some big financial wizard and the bane of Adam's existence. Donald was rich, but also a big old softie, and often fostered young search-and-rescue puppies for Adam until they were old enough to be trained and adopted. The problem was, Donald had been spending a lot of time up north helping upgrade his sister's ranch.

This left Holly handling the entire Reid empire, puppies included. She and Adam were oil and water, which was hugely amusing because it was nice to see the infallible Adam messed with for a change.

"I'm busy," Adam said to Jade calmly, also amusing. The calmer Adam appeared, the more rattled he was.

"Already told her you were in," Jade said. "Sorry."

Adam's left eye twitched.

Jade nodded. "And yeah, you should be afraid. Very afraid. That woman is one pissed-off client."

Dell snorted, taking care to step out of the way before Adam could smack him upside the head.

"Why is she mad?" Adam asked Jade.

"Because you're breathing," Dell said. "She's always mad at you. Question is, why? What did you do to piss her off this time?"

Adam's expression was one hundred percent impassive. A battle-ready soldier. One who was staring at the phone like it was a spitting cobra. "I dropped off her father's new puppy yesterday," he said.

"Donald out of town again?"

"Yep."

"Well, pick up the phone," Jade said. "You can't just leave her on hold."

Dell leaned in and hit speaker on the phone.

Adam flipped him off, but with a resigned expression, he said, "Connelly."

"*You*," came Holly's voice, crystal clear, and so cold icicles nearly formed in the air. "You did this to me on purpose, didn't you? What was it, some kind of sick revenge?"

Jade looked at Dell but Dell shrugged. Hell, he had no idea. If Jade played things close to the vest, Adam was the master.

"Revenge?" Adam repeated as if discussing the weather. "For what?"

"You know damn well for what."

"I'm in the middle of a meeting, Holly," Adam said. "You'll have to get to the point."

"Okay, the point. The point is you're an ass—"

Adam scooped up the phone, taking her off the speaker. "Calling me names isn't going to encourage me to come rescue you. Again." Adam paused, the picture of polite listening. "Is that even anatomically possible?" He listened some more. "Only if you ask me real nice—" He winced and set the phone back into its cradle. "She had to go."

Jade shook her head. "It's really such a surprise that you're not married."

When she was gone, Adam looked at Dell. "Pizza."

"If you tell me what Holly said."

"She said that if she ever got ahold of me, she was going to do to me what the puppy did to her Prada pumps."

"Ouch."

"Yeah. And she was pretty specific about where she planned on shoving the shoe remains."

Dell winced. "So maybe we should go get the puppy and rescue Holly before we eat?"

"Hell, no. I'm going to bring her two more puppies later on tonight."

Dell stared at him. "You're insane."

Unconcerned, Adam shrugged.

"She's going to kill you."

"She can try."

Adam wasn't playful much these days; in fact, he hadn't been since he'd left the National Guard after a rescue had gone bad a few years back where half his team had been killed. In the time since, he'd been dancing around a boat-load of guilt and a dash of PTSD for good measure.

But he was definitely showing signs of playfulness now. Or so Dell hoped. "Or you could stop baiting her and try something else."

"Like?"

"Like sleeping with her."

Adam slid him a look.

Now it was Dell who shrugged. "Or hey, go on living like a monk, driving the rest of us out of our fucking minds. Your choice, man."

"Not all of us feel the need to sleep with anything in a skirt."

"You used to," Dell pointed out.

"Things change."

Dell shook his head and left his office. Jade was standing at her desk pulling on a long, fuzzy angora sweater that Dell happened to know would cling to her every curve.

"Adam and I are getting dinner," he said. "Come with us."

She slapped a couple of disks into his hand.

"What's this?" he asked.

"Your backups."

"I like my clean office," Dell said.

"You mean you like having furniture that's furniture instead of crap collectors?"

"It wasn't that bad."

"No, it was worse."

Adam was grinning as he joined them. "Aw. Your first fight as an engaged couple."

Jade ignored this. "I've laid out the payables that need attention and brought up all the outstanding receivables that I could find, though it'd be more accurate if you finished entering your accounting for this month."

They'd all been running like crazy for most of the day. How had she managed to do all this as well?

"And with another few hours I could probably get your checking account reconciled." She gave him a look of reproach. "You're three months behind."

"I'm getting to it."

"If you do it in the first week of the new month, you can close that month out and your accounting system takes you all the way to the financial statements. Assuming you finish entering your receivables."

Dell blinked. "For eighteen months you've been answering my phones and setting up my schedule and bringing my patients back to me like you were born to be a receptionist. You never once mentioned all these other talents."

She grabbed Beans's carrier and her purse and headed for the door. "My talents are on a need-to-know basis."

Adam raised a brow.

Yeah. She was definitely feeling better. But then he saw it, her slight hesitation at the door.

She didn't want to go to the parking lot.

"Adam," Dell said. "I'll meet you at Risolli's."

Adam never took his eyes off Jade, frozen in clear agonizing indecision. Nodding, he shifted around her, gently squeezing her arm before slipping out the door.

Jade mentally put on her big-girl panties and strode out the door the same way Adam had. Of course it was much easier to face her demons with one hundred and eighty pounds of solid muscle at her back, and Dell *was* at her back. He followed her to her car, waiting silently while she set Beans in the back and buckled her in. A breeze blew across the lot, and a branch cracked. She stiffened, but Dell's hand slid to her lower back, warm and sure. Steadying. She closed her eyes. "I'm just thinking about where I want to go for dinner," she whispered.

"Risolli's. Risolli's is where you want to go for dinner."

"Risolli's is a heart attack in the making," she said automatically.

"They have salads. Just think about it. And while you're thinking . . ." He wrapped his arms around her, all the way around her from behind. "Think about this," he said.

The hold was almost an exact replication of how she'd been grabbed that night and she froze.

"Where are your keys to the meds lockup, bitch?"

"I don't have keys," she said.

"Wrong answer."

She heard the pathetic little ragtag whimper drag up from her throat. "Dell."

"I know," Dell murmured very softly. "It's an aggressive move, and your heart's pounding and you're probably hardly able to hear me over the roar of the blood in your ears but listen to me, Jade. It's just me, and you have nothing to be afraid of with me. Break free."

"I can't."

"Goddess Jade doesn't know the meaning of the word. Fight, Jade. Do whatever you have to do to get loose. You don't have to be a victim."

A moment ago she'd been happy to have him at her back but now that he was using it on her it was a different story entirely. She could feel the strength in his arms, the heat of him behind her and could hardly breathe.

He didn't rush her, just gave her that same, steady patience he gave his animals. But she wasn't an animal, and she couldn't turn off her brain. This wasn't going to work. "Dell," she said hoarsely, the panic choking her. "Please—"

"First rule of self-defense. Stay calm and think as the situation develops."

Calm was out of the question. Not with flashbacks making her vision blurry. Or maybe that was the lack of air since she was holding her breath.

"Second rule, show no fear or hesitation."

Right. She'd get right on that.

"Breathe, Jade." He brushed his jaw to hers. "Come on, tough girl," he murmured softly, in direct opposition to the tight, unforgiving hold he had on her. "You can do this. There are many ways, but we'll take it one at a time. I'm a bad guy. How do you get away from me?"

"I don't know!" she cried, her hands coming up to grip his arm around her waist. But all that did was remind her of just how strong he was.

"The human skull is a powerful weapon all on its own," he said. "Don't waste your time trying to step on my toes or elbowing me in the ribs. None of those moves will do anything but piss someone off. Bash my face with the back of your head."

"What?"

"Connect once, maybe twice with your attacker's face or collarbone and you'll deliver some serious damage, trust me. Do it."

"Do it, give me your keys. Now."

She shook her head, and another guy in a mask moved into her line of sight, roughly pushing someone.

Karen, a floor nurse.

Jade gasped when the second masked guy casually set the muzzle of his gun to Karen's temple. "Bet you can find the keys now," he said.

He was right. Jade pulled the keys out and threw them at him. He snagged them out of midair and, with a smile that still haunted her dreams, dragged her along with him to the drug storage.

"Jade." Dell was saying her name, quietly but firmly, in a voice that demanded she pay attention. "Jade, you can do this. As soon as the adrenaline kicks in, everything will seem to happen in slow motion. If you stay calm, your mind will process thoughts so rapidly that it will even seem like you've got hours to make a decision on how to react."

She closed her eyes and tried to fall into her adrenaline instead of fighting it. She didn't manage until he tightened his grip. Then she drew in a breath and snapped her head back.

Dell dodged to the side, but she still managed to hit him on the cheekbone, and he immediately dropped his hold on her.

Spinning around, she stared at him, horrified.

But when he straightened, he was smiling. "Nice." He lifted his hand to touch his cheekbone, already reddened.

"Oh my God. I hurt you."

"That's the point," he reassured her, looking proud. "It

works, Jade. Every time. I was only able to dodge it because I knew you were going to do it. With the element of
surprise, you'll break anyone's hold on you."

"Anyone's?"

"You have to be confident. You have to picture it. You
have to believe it. But yeah. Anyone's. Now can we get
some pizza? Adam's a fucking diva when he's hungry."

She let out a breath, marveling over what she'd just
done, more than a little desperate to believe. It'd been a
long time since she hadn't worried about the shadows and
the boogeyman. She thought she was good at hiding it but
apparently not. She'd seen the look Adam and Dell had
exchanged. It wasn't a new look, she saw it every time they
dealt with a hurt or abused animal. It was their protect-the-
innocent-animal look.

She hated that she was the hurt animal. Hated.

At least they hadn't pressed her to talk about it, hadn't
called her out on her undeniably odd and peculiar behavior—
at least not really—and for that, she'd been eternally grateful.

But she was pretty sure her pass was over.

"There are more moves, Jade," Dell said. "I can show
you how to break the hold if you're grabbed from the front,
too, and lots of other self-defense tactics."

The power of that surged through her and overcame her
embarrassment and shame. "Really?"

"Sure. After a couple of months of practice, you'll be in
lean, mean fighting-machine shape."

A couple of months . . . "Dell. I've told you, I'm leaving
at the end of the month."

His expression didn't change. "You've said that before
and not gone back."

Oh God. Is that what he believed? That she wasn't leaving? "This time I am. I have to."

A muscle ticked in his jaw. "Fine. You still have a
month." His face was still calm. Controlled. "We'll make it
work."

Nine

Once again Dell rolled out of bed before dawn. He showered and headed out. Way out, passing through Sunshine, past Belle Haven and into the hills.

She was leaving. By the time the first snow hit, Jade would be gone. He felt more for her than he wanted, way more, so it was just as well that she was leaving.

Shaking his head at that ridiculous logic, he kept driving. Forty-five minutes later and light-years away from anything remotely resembling a town, he pulled to a stop. He got out of his truck, waving some of the dust away from his face. The road out here was always a dust storm, every single time. Grabbing his bag, he headed toward the double-wide.

The trailer had been here for as long as he could remember, sitting square on thirty acres of absolutely nothing.

He came every week. Nila didn't ask him to. She wouldn't.

But he came, anyway.

He couldn't explain why. Adam thought he was crazy, but he never said a word about it.

He didn't have to. Dell already knew it was stupid and pathetic.

But still he came. As he reached out to knock on the door, it opened and she stood there in ragged jeans, an old sweatshirt, and no shoes. Her long black hair was streaked with gray now and plaited in a single braid down her back. Her eyes were black and gave little away.

Dell got his eyes from her.

She didn't smile, she never did, but he could tell she was relieved to see him as she stepped aside to make room for him.

Waiting there, lined up on the narrow orange and brown trailer couch, were others: two women, an old man, a teenager, and two younger children—all with an animal at their feet or in their laps.

Dr. Doolittle time.

Nila handed Dell a cup of coffee, not meeting his eyes. She never did. He accepted the coffee and moved to the small Formica table, opening his bag, pulling out his laptop. This was an unofficial visit, it always was, but he still kept records as well as he could. "Who's first?"

The youngest, a girl who couldn't be more than five, stood up, a tiny kitten clutched in her hands as bedraggled as the little girl.

And Dell's day began.

Two nights later, Jade walked up to the front door of Dell's house, not quite sure if she was excited or nervous.

Both, she decided.

Definitely both.

The other evening, when he'd grabbed her from behind . . . she'd thought she'd expire on the spot from fear and panic. But then he'd shown her how to break free of the hold.

She went to the occasional yoga and Pilates classes, but

that was about it for her. She'd never done martial arts or self-defense, but Dell was a big guy and she'd broken free from him.

Crazy as it seemed, it had given her hope. And she'd followed the scent of that hope all the way here.

She'd been to Dell's house before. They all played poker every few weeks, usually in his dining room. But she'd never come alone, and she might not have now either but he'd been asking for two days and . . .

And she was curious. And afraid. And . . . and he opened the door wearing black workout shorts and a T-shirt that was wet and clinging to his torso.

And then she forgot to think at all.

His hair was damp, and he was rubbing a towel over his face, breathing hard, looking like he'd been enjoying whatever he'd been doing. "You came," he said.

He'd thought she wouldn't. She did her best to roll her tongue back into her mouth. "You look busy."

"Nope. Just kicking Adam's ass."

Dressed similarly, Adam came into view behind him and snorted. "Not even on a good day, man. Though I'll give it to you that you're better these days." He nodded to Jade. "You should have seen us when we were kids. He was so uncoordinated, he couldn't walk across a room without falling over his own scrawny legs. At least he outgrew his glasses. Christ, was he ugly. It took him years to grow into his current look."

"Hey," Dell said. "You do realize you look just like me."

"No, *you* look like *me*."

Jade followed them both into the kitchen, marveling at how they seemed to take perverse pleasure in making fun of each other's vulnerabilities at every turn. And yet the connection between them was unmistakable.

She shrugged it off to the mystery of the male psyche, watching as Dell grabbed two bottles of water, tossed one at Adam, then downed his in long, greedy gulps while Jade stood there looking at two of the finest male specimens she'd ever seen.

Adam tossed his empty bottle into a recycling bin and nodded to Dell. "Be sure to thank Jade for saving your hide. Five more minutes and I'd have been wiping the floor with you."

Dell grinned. "Whatever you have to tell yourself to sleep at night."

Adam shook his head, like he couldn't believe how lame his own brother was. Moving to the door, he slowed in front of Jade and lightly tugged on a strand of her hair. "I'm better than he is," he said with a head jerk in Dell's direction. "When you're done pounding him into the mat, I'll be happy to step in."

"Yeah, yeah." Dell shoved him out, then turned to Jade. "Want something to drink first?"

"Only if you think a tequila shot before learning how to kick ass is a good idea."

He smiled. "You're nervous."

That was putting it mildly. She'd been thinking about this for two days now, in between fielding calls from everyone in town about her supposed engagement to Dell. Knowing that if *she* was getting cornered, he had to be getting it way worse, she'd called Leanne and told her that the engagement was off.

Now the story running through town was that Dell had dumped Jade because he was a tragic alpha hero, wounded and terrified of love.

Dell had laughed it off, assuring her he couldn't give a shit what people made up about them. And she knew he was being honest—he definitely didn't worry about what others thought. He was classic alpha that way.

But she'd wondered . . . how much of the whispers were really made up? He'd been very careful in his life in regard to the chosen few whom he trusted. She hadn't worked for him for eighteen months and not understood that much of that easygoing and laid-back nature was only skin-deep, that no matter what he showed the general public he was actually intensely private and quite closed off.

She figured the mock engagement, and then the supposed cancellation of said engagement—leaving him "wounded" and needing some alone time—worked for him.

"Come on," he said, leading her down a set of stairs to a basement. "We'd better start before you change your mind and run out on me."

She was already beginning to sweat. "I don't run." *Liar, liar.* "But I could use that tequila shot now."

"Be good," he said, "and I'll get you something after. Sol used to serve us tea when he was kicking our butts."

"Tea's only good if it comes with cookies."

He laughed. "Tea's good never."

"Sounds like Sol was a sweet man."

"He was two hundred and fifty pounds, and six feet four inches of solid muscle. He was also ex-marine, and didn't know a smile from his own ass. He wasn't sweet, but he was . . . everything else. At least to us."

The basement was completely finished and had been turned into a gym. Equipment was lined on one wall, a treadmill, elliptical trainer, a selection of machines with a large maximum-load capacity, and free weights were in front of a bank of mirrors. Along one side, across from the riders, was a large padded mat area, as well as a huge flat-screen TV and entertainment center mounted on a wall. Music was blasting out of it. "The man cave," she said. Feeling a little intimidated, she pulled off her sweatshirt. She hadn't been sure what to wear but had settled on yoga pants and a tank top.

Dell aimed the remote at the entertainment system and the music cut. He tossed the remote aside and took her to the mats in front of the mirrors. "Anyone can learn this, I promise."

She nodded, hoping that was true. "Like you learned it."

"There's something about getting your ass handed to you daily that motivates you."

She looked around, curious. "How many women have you brought down here to . . . help train?"

She expected him to laugh, or at least give off a wicked smile, but he slowly shook his head, his warm brown eyes even on hers. "None."

"Come on. The way you date?"

"I've never brought a woman to my house."

"Ever?"

"Ever. And you're stalling. Step onto the mat."

She touched it with her toe. "Usually a guy buys me dinner first."

He held out his hand for hers, eyes steady. Calm. "Come on now, tough girl," he said in the same tone she'd heard him use on a wild stallion just before horse-whispering the thing into a puddle of goo.

She wasn't a puddle of goo *yet*, but she followed his soft command and reached for his hand. "Where do we start?" Her voice didn't sound as confident as she'd have liked. Being in Dell's very nice arms to be kissed was one thing. And a very nice thing. Being there to try to escape wasn't nearly so nice. It was claustrophobic and terrifying. He was big, bigger than either of the two men who'd held her that long ago night.

"Let's finish teaching you how to break out of a hold from behind," he said, going directly to the source of her anxiety without passing Go.

She nodded and he moved behind her, and this time when his arms came around her, she was prepared.

Or so she told herself.

But he was built like a wall of granite, and her breath hitched. "I know," he said. "But remember. Let the adrenaline work in your favor." His voice was low and steady, and she nodded.

But this hold was different. He had one forearm banded tight around her waist like before, but the other was at her throat and she didn't have the mobility to get him with a head butt.

Plus there was the added rush of it being Dell, not a bad guy. Dell, with his familiar scent and voice . . . and confusing emotions, battered her.

Fear.

Excitement.

Panic.

Arousal.

"Turn your chin toward my elbow," he said. "Force it down to relieve the pressure against the side of your neck so that you don't go unconscious if the pressure increases. Then you stomp the shit out of his insole with your heel. If you can, reach over your shoulder and poke out his eyes. Or, if your arms are pinned too low, like I've got you now, grab and twist his nuts."

"What?"

"Trust me, that's the most effective tool in your arsenal. He'll drop like a stone."

"Have you thought about any possible future children you're risking?"

"Well, maybe you could skip the twist part." He tightened his grip, signaling that he wasn't going to let her slip into brevity. "You want to make it so that they can't see, can't breathe, and hopefully can't run after you."

"Dell." She gripped his forearm, the one over her throat, her legs trembling.

"I've got you, Jade. I promise. Nothing bad is going to happen to you here. Ever."

"I'm sorry. I don't know why I'm shaking."

"Don't be sorry. You know I'll stop if that's what you want."

She closed her eyes and tried to collect herself.

"Jade?"

"No. Don't stop." She drew a deep breath. "Do you really want me to stomp on your foot and attempt to poke your eyes out?"

"Yes."

She closed her eyes again, drew in yet another bolstering breath, and stomped the shit out of his foot. When his arms fell away from her, she whirled and took a step back.

But he didn't drop like a stone. He came at her and grabbed her again, from the front this time. Suddenly she was up against him in a tight embrace, her chest, belly and thighs pressed to his. Completely overwhelmed, she gasped.

"Backing away was good," he said. "But you stopped. Never stop. Because once you do, you have to be prepared to fight, in which case you need to be either two arm lengths away from him—outside of his kicking range—or all the way in tight against him. Anything in between is leaving yourself too open. If you can, run. Fucking run for the hills and scream for help while you're at it. You okay?"

She nodded, all she could manage.

"Good," he said. "Couple of ways to get out of this. A knee to the groin works. Move fast and hard. Follow it up with a kick to the guy's knee or lower abs if you can reach them. Kick straight ahead using the bottom of your foot like you'd kick in a door. If he somehow manages to come at you again, use your elbow and smash him in the face, throat, or neck. Then back to your standby option—run like hell."

She was doing her best to stand there flat up against him and be casual, but she was so incredibly aware of every inch of him that she couldn't find an ounce of casual. "Dell," she whispered, and dropped her head to his chest.

"Okay, it's okay," he said, mistaking her distress. His warm exhale tickled her ear as his arms loosened. "Breathe, Jade. Then think. What's your first move?"

She breathed as ordered, then came up with her knee.

He deflected enough that she grazed his thigh, but he still went down to his knees.

It worked. Holy shit, it really worked. Shocked, she covered her mouth and stared down at him.

As he had earlier, he lifted his head and flashed her a grin. "Nice. Except you forgot to scream and run like hell."

Before she could move, he'd grabbed her and tugged her down to the mat, pinning her beneath him. Taking her hands in his, he yanked them over her head and peered into her eyes. "First," he said. "Remember. It's just me. Second . . ."

She came up with her knee.

"Yes!" he said, deftly rolling aside and coming up on an elbow with another dazzling smile, by which time she'd run across the room, away from him. "See? You're a natural."

He spent the next two hours putting her through the paces. And that night, she slept like the living dead, with only the weight of Beans on her chest instead of the usual ball of anxiety.

By the end of the next day, they'd seen forty patients, among them seven-week-old Rhodesian ridgeback puppies, a four-year-old shih tzu with colitis, a basset hound with OCD, and a bunny who had nothing wrong with him other than he was owned by Mrs. Wycoff, who was old and very lonely.

Dell healed them all with equal ease.

Oh, to wield that power, Jade thought. Good thing he had no idea exactly how much power he had. She began to close up. "Peanut want a cracker?" she asked the parrot.

She'd been trying to teach Peanut to say the sentence "Peanut want a cracker" to distract the parrot from saying "boner" at inopportune times. But Peanut was pretending to be mute today.

Jade was just about ready to switch to the phone service for the night when the phone rang, so she grabbed it.

"Hello, Jade. It's Melinda. Is Dell in?"

Melinda ran a thirty-thousand-acre ranch up north. It

was one of the ranching accounts Dell had added now that
Brady had fixed up their Bell 47 chopper to fly to farther
locations. Dell went to Melinda's ranch one Saturday a
month, where he tended to her animals' care.

And, according to the rumor mill, he attended to Melinda's care as well.

Dell was in his office with Brady, and his office phone
line was lit. "He's on the other line," Jade said.

"No problem, I'll call him on his cell later tonight. Let
him know I'm ready for him tomorrow."

"Sure." And if Melinda could say "ready" with more sex
in her voice, that would be just freaking fantastic. "Will
do." Jade forced herself to hang up calmly. "I'm ready for
him tomorrow," she mocked in a sex kitten voice.

"Ah. Melinda."

Jade nearly fell out of her chair and Bessie the cleaning
lady cackled good and hard over that. "She does seem to
have her hooks out for him, doesn't she?"

"I . . . I didn't notice."

Bessie cackled again. "And I hardly noticed that lovely
shade of green on you, dear."

"I'm not jealous."

"Of course not." Bessie looked pointedly at the message
Jade had written and crumpled. "Don't worry. Your secret
crush on the doc is safe with me."

"Crush on the doc," Peanut said.

Jade glared at the parrot. "What?"

"Boner."

Jade stood up and pointed at her. "You can't say 'Peanut
wants a cracker,' but you can say 'crush on the doc' and
'boner'? Are you kidding me?"

"Crush on the doc! Crush on the doc!"

Bessie laughed so hard that Jade thought she'd cough up
a lung right there, but she went back to sweeping. Jade narrowed her eyes at Peanut.

"Pretty Peanut," Peanut whispered.

Jade sighed and went to work, fantasizing about her next self-defense session and kicking Dell's very fine ass. She was halfway there, picturing taking him to the floor and . . . and what? She had lots of options, as he'd taught her.

Kicking.

Hitting.

Jabbing.

But there was something wrong with her brain. It wouldn't go there. Instead, she imagined dropping him to the mat and . . .

Stripping him. Stretching out over the top of him and . . .

Eating him up like a hot buttered biscuit.

Dammit. Now she was heated up herself and having a hot flash to boot. She fanned the air in front of her face, which didn't help.

"So . . ." Lilah said at her side, making Jade jump. "What's got you all hot and bothered?"

Bessie came through with her broom again. "Ask Peanut."

"Crush on the doc," Peanut said.

Jade closed her eyes.

"Fascinating," Lilah said. "*That* I have to learn from a parrot? You've been holding out on me."

"Don't be ridiculous. Peanut has no idea what she's saying."

"Boner," Peanut said.

Lilah grinned. "Okay," she said to Jade. "Start at the beginning and leave nothing out. Tell me what's up."

"The temperature, dammit. Too many bodies in here."

Lilah's gaze slid across the room to where Dell and Brady had come out from the back. Dell's gaze tracked directly to Jade.

"Uh-huh," Lilah said.

"I know what you're thinking," Jade whispered. "But stop it. So there's a little sexual tension in the room between Dell and me, it's nothing. *Nothing*. In fact, picturing him as old and flabby right now. Flatulent. And see? I'm cooler already."

"I was going to suggest turning down the thermostat."

"Or that," Jade muttered to Lilah's laugh.

The next day, Jade got an e-mail attachment from Dell—a spreadsheet to-do list with only one thing on it.

Training session #2 tonight. My house, seven o'clock.

There was a code, too. The key code to his front door, she realized. She wouldn't have to knock, she could go right in.

Which is why he'd given it to her, of course, so she wouldn't get there and while standing on his porch waiting to be let in, change her mind.

But she couldn't just let herself in. Could she? Besides, he'd been gone all day, up north at Melinda's.

He wasn't spending the night up there?

She showed up at his house exactly on time and after some hesitation, entered the code and let herself in.

Dell was in his kitchen, staring into his refrigerator, which had not magically filled itself. It'd been a hell of a long day at Melinda's ranch, and he was dead on his feet.

Normally he spent the night up north. Usually with Melinda. She was smart, funny, and beautiful, and with two ex-husbands, she wasn't looking for anything more than a good time. No harm, no foul.

But last month he'd had Brady fly him home the same day as well.

He'd repeated the pattern today, marking two full months of dateless Saturday nights for him.

A first.

He heard his front door open and Jade's footsteps coming through the living room. He knew without looking that she was wearing her Nikes, which she wore only for him. For the rest of the world she wore designer heels or boots.

He liked her stripped down to casual. To what he thought was the real Jade beneath the glamorous veneer. He liked that he alone saw her this way. Not that he could explain to himself why.

"Thought you had a date tonight," she said, appearing in his doorway.

"My date's you." He shut the refrigerator. "I can make you dinner after you finish wiping the mat with me."

He added her quick smile to the list of things that he liked, though he had no idea if her grin was because he hadn't stayed at Melinda's or the idea of wiping the mat with him. He suspected the latter.

The list of things he liked about Jade was very long and growing, he thought as they went downstairs and she pulled off her sweatshirt. He liked how she threw herself into any task with everything she had, including this one—which she wasn't altogether comfortable with yet. He liked the way her skin glowed. He liked the way she shoved her hair back from her face to stall before getting on the mat, and he *really* liked the way her nipples hardened and pressed against her T-shirt.

Yeah, that was his favorite. "Ready?" he asked.

"I was born ready."

Not for me, though he suddenly wished otherwise. They worked for a half hour before she asked for a water break. As she tipped her head back and drank from a bottle he handed her, his gaze drifted up the length of her body where she was draped over a weight machine trying to catch her breath. Her T-shirt was sticking to her, and it made her look tough, like maybe she could kick some serious butt. It also emphasized her curves, making his mouth water.

Her hair had dared to disobey and was coming out of her

fancy twist but he could still see the nape of her neck. The creamy pale skin there was driving him insane. It was the vulnerability of that one little spot, the way a few strands of red silk curled damply to it.

He wanted his mouth there. Of course he was shit out of luck on that particular fantasy, which could get in line behind all the other fantasies he had filed in his brain under Goddess Jade.

"Dell?"

She'd finished her water and was facing him, expression determined.

He was so going down.

And not ten minutes later she went for the slam dunk and he was on his knees on the mat, hands holding his junk, gasping for breath and trying not to throw up.

Yeah, she was not nearly as soft and vulnerable as he'd thought.

"Oh God. Oh God, Dell, I'm sorry! You said jam my knee up and—"

"It's okay," he croaked, and slowly fell over. "I'm okay." Or as okay as he could be with his nuts in his throat. Hell, he wasn't ready to have children, anyway. He felt her crawl close and put her hand on his lower abs. "Back up, I don't want to throw up on your pretty Nikes."

She didn't back up, she leaned over him, her fingers drifting lower to cover the hand he was using to cup himself. He knew why *he* was doing it, he was holding on to the goods to make sure they were still there. But she . . . "Jade—"

"Did I hurt it?"

"It" twitched. "No," Dell said, both to her and to his dick's unspoken and hopeful question of getting lucky.

"Are you sure? Maybe I should . . . look."

He opened his eyes and met her worried ones.

"I worked at a medical center for eight years, remember?"

Because he wasn't ready to move—or let her look, *Jesus*—he said, "Tell me about the job."

"I was in charge of . . . everything."

He choked out a laugh. "So what's so different from now?"

That earned him a small smile and she wrapped her fingers around his wrist and tried to lift his hand off his groin. Her fingers brushed against him and in spite of the fact that he was still hurting, he got hard. Perfect. "Jade—"

"If you're bruising up, we need to ice—"

"I'm not bruising."

She pulled his hand away and stared down at the crotch of his basketball shorts.

He lifted his head and looked, too, the both of them taking in the very obvious bulge between his legs. "I think I'm going to live," he said wryly.

She swallowed hard and wet her lips.

Groaning, he thunked his head back on the floor. "Not helping."

Her gaze met his, and that's when they heard it. The front door slamming shut. And then Adam's boots on the cellar steps.

Jade leapt to her feet and practically ran for her sweatshirt, which she was just pulling over her head when Adam appeared. Jade sent his brother a weak smile. "He might not be in fighting condition at the moment."

And then she was gone.

Adam looked at Dell prone on the mat. "She flatten you?"

"Yeah."

Adam just shook his head. "Food?" Then he went back upstairs, apparently in search of said food.

Dell rolled to his knees, disgusted with himself. *Great way to make her feel comfortable and safe.* He scrubbed a hand over his face feeling . . . discombobulated. It took him a minute to realize that was because she'd walked. Usually he did the walking. That's how it always worked. "I guess not this time," he said to Gertie, who'd lumbered down the stairs to investigate. Gertie snuffled and plopped down at his feet. She might not have a graceful bone in her body, but she wouldn't walk away. At least not unless someone bribed her with food . . .

Ten

Dell spent Sunday deep in the Bitterroot Mountains with Brady and Adam, working volunteer S&R. Late that night they'd located the lost hiker and flown back to Sunshine.

Brady went home to Lilah. Adam had a class to give.

So Dell was on his own, and he crashed early in his own bed. Not that being exhausted helped him sleep. He woke up several times, the latest at dawn when Gertie leapt on his bed and slobbered on his face.

Her version of the good-morning kiss.

He shoved her off him and got into the shower. At Belle Haven he rode Kiwi, then let himself into the office just as Jade arrived. He'd called her several times since Saturday night, all of which she'd ignored.

Which made sense. He'd invited her over for self-defense training, promising to teach her moves to make her feel safe. And then he'd turned into a fifteen-year-old boy and gotten hard in class. "Jade."

She had the phone headset on. She raised a finger to indicate she needed a minute. He could see now that she was accessing the center's messages from their service, typing them into the spreadsheet that she had up on her screen. She was crazy about her spreadsheets. She'd uncovered Peanut, and the parrot was preening and humming to herself. Beans was watching Peanut with avid, narrow-eyed interest.

Gertie had found the sole sunny spot in the room and was already snoring.

Jade's fingers were a whirl on her keyboard. She worked hard here, and she was his responsibility, as much as any of the animals were. He took that very seriously.

He wanted her to be able to count on him.

Always.

Which meant he needed to work on the self-control. The only thing that kept him coming back to the straight-and-narrow was that clearly she'd been hurt. Some fucker had put his hands on her and terrorized her, and seeing her suffer the aftereffects killed him.

That was not to say that having her sweet, curvy body so intimate with his wasn't having a toll.

It was.

And that toll had kept him up at night. Hell, last night he'd had to get up at two in the morning to abuse himself in the shower.

He probably should have abused himself again this morning just to cover his bases.

Jade's fingers were a blur on her keyboard, but then suddenly she stopped and pulled off her headset. "Twenty-five messages today. Must be Monday."

"Jade, about Saturday night—"

"I never thanked you."

This derailed him. "What?"

She lifted her head and met his gaze. "For spending so much time with me."

"Sure, but I wanted to apologize for—"

"Nothing," she said, shaking her head. "You have nothing to apologize for. It was my fault. I, um, put my hand . . . there, and then it—"

She broke off suddenly, eyes locked on something over his shoulder.

Dell turned around to find Adam standing there, brows up.

"Don't stop on my account," Adam said. "It's just getting good."

Dell blew out a breath and considered killing him but he had patients arriving. "Go away." He turned back to Jade, but she was gone, heels churning up the big reception area as she went to the wall of files and began pulling down the day's scheduled patients.

"So," Adam said, "she put her hand where?"

Two days later, Jade was sitting in Lilah's kennels. They were in Lilah's office, surrounded by Abigail the duck, Lulu the lamb, and several dogs, all snoozing.

It was naptime in Lilah's world.

Lilah and Jade were munching on deli sandwiches, which Jade had brought over to spend her lunch hour with some female company.

"He's going to be back any minute," Lilah was saying as she decimated a pickle, talking about her favorite subject.

Brady, of course.

Dell had been gone all morning with Brady, out on a ranch about a hundred miles east where Brady had flown him, taking care of a difficult high-end breeding mare's birth.

"It didn't go well," Lilah said, patting one of the dogs who lifted its head and sniffed. Twinkles belonged to Brady, but Lilah considered him hers. She handed him a piece of turkey from her sandwich. "In fact, it went awful."

"What do you mean?" Jade asked.

"They lost the mare. She'd stroked out and Dell had to put her down."

"Oh no," Jade breathed.

"The owners were so distraught they couldn't sit with the horse during the euthanization."

"They let her die alone?"

"No." Lilah shook her head and Jade knew. Dell. Dell had stayed with the horse. Jade's throat ached for him because she knew him. He'd have sat on the straw-covered barn floor with the horse's head in his lap, stroking her face and talking to her until she closed her eyes for the last time.

It was who he was. "Damn."

Lilah nodded. "Been a long week. How are you doing?"

Jade sipped her iced tea. "Good."

"Good as in 'I don't want to talk about it' or good as in 'good.'"

Jade looked at her.

Lilah looked right back, innocent-faced.

Jade had no idea how Lilah could have heard about her kissing Dell. But she planned to play it cool just in case. "Maybe we should save some time and you should just skip to the part where you tell me exactly what you want to know."

"Okay, well something scared you last week in the parking lot and you've been jumpy ever since."

Not where Jade expected this conversation to go. "Who told you that?"

"Hell, honey, this is Sunshine."

Right.

"And Dell's been teaching you self-defense, and now you're talking about going back to Chicago—which you left to come here because, as you told us, you wanted better skiing in the winter. Now I'm thinking that's not true." She paused, brows up. "How am I doing so far?"

Jade stared down at her turkey on multigrain. "It's . . . complicated."

"Are you okay?"

"I'm working on it."

"Is there anything I can do?"

Again, Jade's throat tightened. She'd lied, omitted, kept a good part of herself closed off, and Lilah didn't care about any of that, all she wanted to know was if Jade was okay. "You're already doing it."

Lilah smiled and offered her some chips. "He's a good man, you know."

"Who?"

"You know who."

Yeah. She did.

"A *really* good man."

Jade nodded. "I know."

"Do you?"

Jade looked at Lilah.

Lilah smiled sweetly. Expectantly.

And Jade had to laugh. "You're fishing."

"Yes," Lilah admitted without shame. "I'm totally fishing."

"Why?

"Why?" Lilah just shook her head. "You know how insatiably nosy we all are. Something's going on. We just don't know what, and it's killing us."

"There's nothing—"

"Oh, please. If there's nothing going on with you two, I'll eat Abigail."

Abigail the duck lifted her head and looked reproachfully at Lilah.

"Seriously," Lilah said to Jade while patting Abigail on the head. "There's no way it's nothing."

"Based on what?" Jade asked.

"Based on the fact that whenever you and Dell are in the same room, all these little flames flicker between you."

"Flames."

"It's a metaphor," Lilah said.

"For?"

"Sexual tension."

Jade stared at her, then laughed.

"And Adam told Brady he interrupted the two of you in Dell's gym."

"What, is this high school?"

Lilah grinned. "Well, we've all been together that long, so yeah, in emotional years, we're still in high school. You two doing it or what?"

"Okay, wow." Jade shook her head. "We are so *not* going there."

"Please! Oh, please, let's go there!"

"I didn't ask you about your . . . *flames* when you first started circling Brady," Jade said.

"Aha!" Lilah jabbed a finger into Jade's direction, triumphant. "You are! You're circling Dell."

Jade sighed. "Okay, maybe I'll cop to the circling. But that's no secret. We've always circled each other."

"But something's different," Lilah insisted. "I can feel it."

Was it? All her life Jade had been the master at compartmentalizing the people in her life. She'd put Dell in the slot for boss and left him there for eighteen months. She'd been okay with adding him to the friend slot as well, but that had taken him a good long time to earn.

And he *had* earned it.

He was a friend, a good one. She knew he'd give her the shirt off his back without a moment's hesitation. That had made it easier to feel safe in Sunshine, she'd be the first to admit. And she loved Lilah. She loved Adam and the others, too, but Dell . . . From the start he'd been different. Somehow he'd burrowed deeper, gotten past her walls though she couldn't have said how.

Or why.

But Lilah was right—something *was* happening between them. She didn't know what exactly but whenever he was close, her senses went on high alert and she strained to get even closer. When he touched her, her entire body tingled.

She wanted him.

She, who hadn't had sex in over a year and a half, wanted the guy who'd probably had sex last weekend.

It made no sense but in her mind he was changing, becoming something other than just her boss and her friend, something that was both safer and far less safe at the same time.

"Maybe you two can fall in love and get married, like me and Brady."

"Lilah. You know I'm going back to Chicago."

"So? We have the chopper. You'll commute."

Jade stood. "Would you look at the time? I've got to get back to work now."

"Oh, come on, just give me a hint."

"You want a hint?"

"Yes!"

"Abigail just pooped on your shoe."

Lilah was still swearing when Jade made her escape.

The next night, Jade let herself into Dell's house again. He'd left her an e-mail about another training session and she'd dropped everything to be here.

Everything being season one of *My So-Called Life* on DVD . . .

She found him in the gym, already stripped down to black basketball shorts and a black T-shirt, and she stared at him because he didn't look like her boss. Or her friend.

He looked . . . hot.

He turned and their eyes met. Yearning flowed through her, yearning for a man. This man. She felt silly for staring, but he was staring, too.

"I'm wearing a cup," he said, and she laughed. Tension broken, as she knew he'd intended.

But she still wanted him.

For two hours he reviewed joint manipulation and using an attacker's own weight and momentum to bring him down. It was fascinating but involved close hand-to-hand contact.

Body-to-body contact.

In short, he was all over her, his hands on her body, maneuvering her into place and positions as he worked her hard, harder than she'd thought he would.

Finally she flopped to the mat flat on her back, gasping for air and sweating. "I can't feel my legs."

He crouched at her side, not breathing hard at all, the bastard.

"The least you can do," she said, between gasps, "is pretend to be winded."

"There's no pretending between us, tough girl. If you want to be as good as me, you have to work for it."

She laughed. "Conceited much?"

"No. Just good. Thanks to Brady."

"Did he beat you up until you cried, too?"

"More than once. But you're not crying. Get up. One more time."

She wanted to whimper and curl into a ball. Instead she rolled to her feet.

"I'm going to come after you, right at you," he said, warning her but not babying her. "You know what to do."

She inhaled, accessed all the knowledge he'd given her, and let her brain select one of the judo moves he'd taught her. It was a lot like taking on a charging bull, but she managed to catch him when his weight shifted off his leading foot.

His momentum should have taken him down hard, but he was still better than her, and at the last second he brought her with him.

She landed on her back, with him on top. He lay along the entire length of her, his hands holding her wrists to the mat. Lifting his head, he looked down at her. The raw intensity of his dark gaze spoke to the woman inside of her. The sound of his deep voice was like a caress of warmth against her chilled skin. "Your move," he said.

Thanks to his careful tutoring, she did have moves. She could pick one and be efficient because she wasn't panicked.

Nope. She was something else entirely.

But he was braced, ready for her, and aroused as hell or not, she intended to win today. Hell, every time. So she picked an option that she knew he didn't expect. Using her newfound confidence, she looked into his dark eyes and let all the yearning and heat that had been gathering for months now show in her eyes.

He immediately relaxed, his own eyes softening. "Jade."

It was inevitable, really. They'd been in close quarters, touching and grappling and grabbing. Sweating. It didn't get more personal than that, and another man might have taken advantage of it.

But he'd been careful not to. And he didn't now, either. She waited until he rose lithely to his feet and reached down to pull her to hers. She gripped his hand hard with hers . . . and fell back, into a roll.

Surprised, Dell followed her completely over, and while he was still in motion, she dropped on him and set her elbow to his windpipe.

There was a long beat of silence and then Dell laughed. Jade was still enjoying the sound of that laugh when he abruptly switched their positions, rolling on top of her, once again pinned her down, his face hovering an inch from hers. "Who taught you to fight dirty?"

"You."

He laughed again, kissed her on the tip of her nose and sprang up gracefully in one smooth motion, pulling her with him. "Just remember that all fights are dirty." He tossed her a bottle of water and grabbed one for himself. "You did great tonight."

"Yeah?" His praise washed through her, warming her from the inside out.

"Oh, yeah." His eyes met and held hers. "I think you're amazing, Jade."

She started to look away but found she couldn't.

"Amazing," he repeated softly, simply, as he moved closer. "Strong as hell. Smart. Brave. Resilient."

She opened her mouth to thank him, but her throat was too tight to speak. Once upon a time her family's approval had meant everything to her, but though they'd always meant well, she'd arrived in Sunshine with no sense of self.

Over the last year and a half she'd started to find herself. The real Jade, and that real Jade wanted to be those very things that Dell had just said: strong, smart, brave, resilient. He didn't use empty platitudes or pretty words, ever. He didn't have to. So when he said something, he meant them.

And damned if she didn't like looking at herself the way he saw her. Damned if she didn't want to be *that* woman. No, he hadn't taken advantage of their closeness. So she would. "Dell?"

"Yeah?"

She tossed her water aside and put her hands on his chest, running them northbound, winding her arms around his neck.

He went stock-still. Well, except for closing his eyes and a sexy muscle in his jaw that bunched tight. "Jade—"

"Shh," she said, watching his lips quirk as she animal-whispered *him* for a change. "Just stay calm, Dell. And keep breathing. This won't hurt, I promise."

He let out a rough exhale that turned into a groan when she brushed her lips against his, once.

Twice.

His eyes opened, dark and intense.

Hot.

One big hand ran down her spine to rest at the small of

her back; the other gripped her hip. They were inches apart from each other, sharing air.

One inch one way, Jade thought. One more inch would change everything.

Everything.

She gave a brief thought to stepping back, but it was too late.

Far too late.

So she closed the gap, absorbing the heat of him and the fact that he was so big. And hard.

Everywhere.

She let out a little hum of pleasure at that as she slid her fingers into his hair and drew his mouth back to hers.

Eleven

Dell was lost in the kiss before Jade tightened her grip on him and made a soft, sexy whimper, but when her tongue touched his, desire exploded as the kiss deepened into a hot, intense connection that blew the circuits in his brain.

She moaned and melted into his body, her fingers tightening painfully in his hair. Hell, she could make him bald if she wanted, he didn't care, just as long as she kept on kissing him just . . . like . . . that . . . *God*.

"Dell—"

"I know." He dipped his head and dragged his mouth down her throat, one hand fitting low on her back, the other sliding down her leg, lifting it to his hip so he could grind against her. The insanity continued when she clutched at him and arched closer, as if she couldn't get enough. Her hands where everywhere, running her fingers through his hair, stroking them down his neck, giving him a shiver all the way to his toes. Then she worked her way beneath his damp T-shirt and dug into the muscles there. He was already granite hard when she rocked herself against him. This was because he had no blood left in his head. He sucked in a breath and once again took her mouth with his.

Like a match on dry timber.

Her arms wound around his neck as she went up on tip-toe, molding her body to his. Yeah, God yeah. Her lips immediately parted and her tongue slid to his, hot and wet, and he groaned into her mouth as he stroked up her ribs, his thumbs lightly brushing the underside of her breasts.

Making a low purring noise, she tried to climb up his body. "Dell—"

His answer was to press her up against the wall, dragging his mouth down her throat to taste the pulse racing at the base of her neck.

She moaned and held his mouth to her skin with a hand on the back of his head, again rocking the apex of her thighs into him. He wanted to take her right there against the wall, he wanted that more than he'd ever wanted anything in his life. He sucked in a breath and reached for the hem of her T-shirt to rip it off when he heard someone clear their throat behind them.

Jade went stock-still, and Dell pulled his mouth away and rested his forehead against hers.

"Huh," Adam said behind them. "The hand thing makes a lot more sense now."

Jade tore free of Dell. Putting her hand to her lips, she stared up at Adam, her chest rising and falling like she'd just run a mile. "We—we were training."

The corners of Adam's mouth quirked as he rubbed his jaw, doing his best to hide his amusement. He failed. "Yeah? You could make a million bucks off a DVD of that kind of training."

Dell gave him a shut-the-fuck-up look. Jade moved past them both and grabbed her purse.

"Jade—"

"Sorry, it's late. I didn't realize how late. I've gotta go, I have a thing . . ."

"Jade."

But she was gone and two seconds later the front door shut somewhere above them.

"You are such an asshole," Dell said to Adam, and shoved past him, heading for the stairs.

"Really? Because I'm not the one kissing my receptionist, the receptionist who's clearly battling some demons."

Dell turned around on the stairs and nearly plowed Adam over. Adam arched a brow, silent.

Dell blew out a breath. "You're an asshole."

"Repeating yourself. It's the first sign of guilt, man."

"She's not just a receptionist. She's . . ." More. She was much more to Belle Haven, and it was to his own shame that he'd only begun to realize it as she'd effortlessly taken over the dreaded bookkeeping with seamless ease, freeing up hours a day for him. "And I told you we were training tonight."

"Yeah. You were training real hard." He shook his head. "Do you have any idea what you're doing?"

Dell shoved his hands in his hair. "Does it look like it?"

"You could hurt her." Adam paused. "Don't."

"I—"

"Don't."

"You really think I'd hurt her?"

Adam just looked at him.

Okay, so he didn't have a good track record. Who did?

"Just slow down," Adam suggested.

Slow down? He and Jade had been co-workers and friends for a year and a half already. She was leaving in a matter of weeks. How much slower could they go? He pushed free and took a shower and a drive, and look at that, he ended up at Jade's place. As he got out, he knew that for once Adam's radar was off. It wasn't Jade in danger of getting hurt.

It was him.

* * *

An hour later Jade was on her couch. She'd checked her locks, engaged her alarm, fed Beans, and had her *Oceans 11* DVD in and playing. Some people knitted when stressed out over things like kissing their boss. Some people ate potato chips.

Jade watched movies with Matt Damon in them. With the movie playing in the background, she was working her way through her things-to-do-in-her-spare-time spreadsheet. This meant she was painting her toenails, reading the stack of *People* magazines she hadn't yet gotten to, and catching up online with her financial obligations.

All while trying to not think about the fact that she'd thrown herself at Dell.

Because she had.

Thrown herself.

With a remembered groan and a hot blush, she covered her cheeks and closed her eyes. "This is bad," she whispered to Beans.

"Mew."

"I was hoping you'd disagree. Although . . ." She blew out a breath and leaned back. It'd felt good to have his hands on her. Really good. And his mouth.

God, his mouth.

It'd been too long for her, way too long. Her own doing, of course. For a long time after the attack, she hadn't wanted to be touched. Even though she hadn't been raped, she'd felt a disconnect from others and hadn't wanted physical contact.

Seemed that was changing.

On the coffee table, her cell vibrated an incoming call.

"Darling," her mother said. "You missed your weekly check-in, I was worried."

When Jade had left Chicago, her family had threatened

to come after her and drag her back. Lovingly, of course. They had only her best interests at heart, and she'd scared them.

She'd scared herself.

But she'd needed the space and the time, and they'd finally come to an agreement. She would call and check in once a week, and in return, they'd let her be. She called them every Wednesday evening. "*American Idol* isn't over yet. I didn't want to interrupt."

"I don't like the new judges," her mother said. "You need anything?"

This was always the first question asked. Followed quickly by the second: "And are you okay?"

Jade shook her head and pinched the bridge of her nose. "I'm fine, Mom. Really."

"You don't sound it. You sound nasally. Are you sick? If you catch a late-night flight, we could have you taken care of by morning—"

"Not necessary. How's Dad?"

Her mother sighed. "Okay, the same as always, I expect. Stubborn and working himself into the ground, of course. Which means he's overworking himself running the show. And we all know that only speeds up the symptoms of his Parkinson's."

"He's not listening to his doctors?"

"Your father? Hello, have you met him? He knows it all, remember? And we both know there was ever only one thing that kept him home, happy in the knowledge that he didn't have to work every day, and that was you being in the office instead of him. Baby, you know I don't want to rush you . . ."

Jade kept her unladylike snort to herself.

"But you're really coming home?"

Jade closed her eyes. "Yes."

"Have you given notice there then? At your little dog place?"

Jade rubbed her forehead and stared down at her toes.

She'd done a damn good job with them if she said so herself, though they needed another coat. "It's an animal center, Mom. We see all animals, not just dogs."

"And you . . . enjoy it. Checking in dogs."

"I know you don't get it, but I've been very happy here."

"In Idaho."

In Jade's mother's opinion, the entire country consisted of three cities. Los Angeles, New York, and Chicago. Anything in between belonged in some alternate universe, Idaho included.

"Idaho is very nice," Jade said.

"So you've said. Why don't I come visit?"

"No!" Jade lowered her voice with effort. "Like I said, I'm coming home."

"Before November first."

"Yes."

"I could help you pack."

Aka call a moving company. "I don't have much to pack."

And she didn't want any visitors here. So far she'd managed to avoid a family invasion by going home to Chicago on the occasional holiday. The last thing she wanted was for them to show up en masse and see her life here. Not that she was ashamed of it. She wasn't at all. But neither was she ready to share this world she'd found for herself.

Still, her mother meant well and missed her, so Jade made nice for a few more minutes, then hung up, feeling the usual guilt wash over her. She put a second coat of nail polish on her toenails and didn't think of Dell or how she'd nearly inhaled him whole.

Much.

And in any case, it was hardly her fault. He'd more than met her halfway, and good Lord Almighty, he was no slouch in the kissing department. She'd nearly gone up in flames for him right there on the mats. One more minute of his amazing mouth on hers and she'd have stripped off her own clothes to get his hands on her.

Except that Adam had shown up.

Again.

She was suspecting a conspiracy but really he'd done her a favor because she had no business starting anything with Dell.

None.

They'd had all this time and hadn't acted on their attraction. And now she was leaving. Getting involved with Dell was out of the question.

Not going to happen. And anyway, it'd been nothing but sheer hormones. That's all. And pheromones. And good God, sheer testosterone, the stuff came off him in waves when she wrestled around with him on those damn mats.

"This is why normal people have regular sex," she told Beans. "Keeps them sane. Sane by orgasms."

Beans didn't seem impressed by this kernel of knowledge.

"Okay, so I'm low on self-control," she admitted. "Sue me. But it's his fault—you should have seen him in those shorts, all hot and sweaty and . . ." *Gorgeous.* "Look, all I need to do is . . . not look at him." Ever.

She'd have sworn that Beans rolled her eyes on that one before she leapt to the back of the couch and began to wash her face. "Oh, please. If you'd been standing in front of him, all hot and intent and protective and . . . *hot*, you'd have jumped him, too."

Beans finished her face and went to work behind her ears.

Jade shook her head and set down the bottle of nail polish. She'd had a glass of wine, but she was still unnerved, quivering with tension and unused adrenaline. If Adam hadn't interrupted them, what would she be doing right this very minute? She was picturing it when the knock came at the door; she jumped and knocked over the nail polish. She righted the bottle, attempted to keep her heart in her chest by pressing hard between her breasts, and did the duck walk to the door so that she didn't smear her toes. She looked through the peephole, then went still.

Dell. He'd showered, put on jeans and a long-sleeved graphic henley that emphasized the chest and arms she'd had her hands all over earlier.

He looked . . . perfect.

She looked down at herself. She wore the oversized Harvard sweatshirt she'd pilfered from Sam years ago, *Toy Story*–themed pajama bottoms. At least she didn't have on her donkey slippers; they were by the couch waiting for her toenails to dry.

Yeah, she was a catch.

When she opened the door, Dell wore a solemn expression—until he took in her pj's.

At that, a small smile crossed his mouth.

She tried to remember if she'd put mascara back on after her shower. She hadn't.

When it became clear she wasn't going to invite him in, Dell simply stepped into her. And dammit if she didn't back up, and then she was watching his very fine ass as it moved into her place.

He stood in the center of her living room and turned to face her. "We have unfinished business."

Twelve

They had unfinished business?

Assuming he meant their near physical miss, Jade hesitated.

With another small smile, Dell shook his head. "I meant your training. You left early."

"Figured we were done."

"Yeah. That got a little out of hand." He paused, but she shook her head.

"If you're going to try to apologize again, don't."

He just looked at her with those dark eyes, and she let out a breath. "Look," she said. "We both know the truth is that I kissed you, so if anyone should be apologizing—"

"I'm not apologizing for the kiss."

"Oh." She blinked. "Then . . . ?"

Instead of answering, he sat on her couch in the same place she'd just vacated and took in the movie playing on the TV, the spread of fingernail polish, the half-eaten bowl of popcorn, the opened laptop.

Too late she realized what she had up on the screen.

He smiled, then laughed out loud, his amusement eradicating the lines of tension in his beautiful face. He leaned forward to read more.

"Hey," she complained. "That's private." She moved toward him to shut the laptop, but he held her off, easily grabbing both her hands in one of his wrists and tugging her down beside him.

"Watch the freshly done toenails!"

He grinned and did just that, taking in the pale blue polish. "Pretty." Then he went back to her screen, reading her things-to-do-in-her-spare-time spreadsheet:

1. Organize junk drawer.
2. Clean hairbrushes.
3. Relax.
4. Don't think about Dell.

Dell slid her a look but didn't point out the obvious, that she wasn't doing anything on her list.

"Cute pictures," he said of the piglet and calf pictures on the other half of her screen. Both were close-ups of two adorably earnest but wary faces. "Friends of yours?"

She sighed. "Yes." When he only looked at her, brows up, she shrugged. "I've adopted them from Adopt a Farm Animal." She tugged her hands free of his and refilled her wineglass.

"You adopted a pig and a calf?"

"It's the late-night commercials. They play sad music and show pictures of abused, neglected animals."

His smile widened.

"They look *right* at you! Oliver, the calf—" She pointed at the picture. "He'd been abandoned and had nearly *starved to death* before he was rescued. And Miss Piggy was heading to the bacon factory. Now I write a check for fifteen bucks a month and they live happily ever after. What's the big deal?"

"Christ, you're cute."

"I—" She narrowed her eyes at him. Cute? "You take that back."

"Okay, you're not cute. You're . . . sexy as hell."

They both looked at her attire and he laughed when she winced. "You are," he maintained.

"You're a very nice man to lie like that." She grabbed the laptop from him, shutting the screen. "And now you'll forget about the fact that I'm so pathetic that I watch DVDs on Friday and Saturday nights instead of going out."

He looked at her for a long moment and she groaned and covered her face. "Don't tell me that's why you're here, that you thought I was feeling . . . vulnerable." She dropped her hands and glared at him. "Because if you say that, I'm going to kick your ass, Dell, I mean it."

Reaching for her wine, he helped himself.

"Say something," she demanded.

"Are you kidding? I don't want to get my ass kicked. And you could do it now, too." He flashed a grin but she just stared at him, deadpan.

He sighed. "I'm not here because I thought you were vulnerable. I'm here because you ran off rather than face the fact that we—"

"Hey. I didn't run off."

"Jade, you left smoke in your wake."

Okay, so she'd run off. Bad habit. "It was just a kiss."

He slid her a look.

"Okay, it was an unexpectedly great kiss."

He nodded. "Yeah." His voice was low and a little rough, and she felt her nipples harden at the sound of it. "Each time gets even greater."

Oh so true. "But we'd be stupid to keep doing it."

"Right." He looked at her. "Why's that?"

"Because . . ." God, his eyes. And that gorgeous mocha skin, sun-burnished and so smooth, except for a five o'clock shadow across his jaw after a long day. She already knew how it felt beneath her fingers, which were itching for another touch. "Because we work together. Because you date like other men change socks. Because I'm leaving soon. Pick one."

"Right," he said, nodding agreeably. "I almost forgot about all that."

She nodded.

He reached out and ran a finger along her temple, making her . . . yearn. She leaned into him and closed her eyes.

"And we're more than co-workers," he said quietly.

"We're friends."

He didn't say anything and she opened her eyes.

"Yeah," he said. "We're friends."

"Friends don't kiss like we did without becoming . . . naked friends."

"And?"

"And you have a no-relationship decree in place. You've told me so yourself. And even if you hadn't, your actions speak louder than words."

"What does a relationship have to do with becoming naked friends?"

Okay, he had her there. There was a silence, and she waited for him to push the issue, but he just started eating her popcorn. Then he took another drink of her wine. "I thought maybe you were upset about something else," he finally said.

"Like what?"

"I thought maybe me touching you brought up some bad memories." His eyes never wavered from hers so when she grimaced, she knew he saw it.

"I . . . No. Not like you're thinking." She looked down at her hands, which twisted together until her knuckles turned white. She hadn't talked about this. She didn't want to talk about this. But she could admit he deserved a few answers. "I wasn't raped."

He covered her hands with one of his as he let out a low

breath that had a lot of relief in the sound. "I'm glad. But something happened to you."

"Yes." His skin was warm on her suddenly chilly fingers and she found herself turning her hand palm up so she could hold on. "A long time ago."

"Eighteen months."

She stared down at their entwined fingers. "Eighteen months." She shook her head. "But I'm fine now and getting more fine all the time. I don't need a babysitter, Dell. Or a shoulder to cry on."

"Well, that's a relief. I never know what to do with tears."

Not true. Just this morning she'd seen him holding forty-eight-year-old Missy Robinson, who'd fallen apart in the exam room when he'd had to tell her that her Alaskan husky had cancer. He'd held her for as long as she'd needed, looking devastated for her but perfectly at ease in the role of comforter. "With all those women you date, I'd think you'd have a lot of practice at tears."

She had no idea why she said that. His dating, or not dating, wasn't her concern.

Dell grabbed the bowl of popcorn and the remote and leaned back. "Maybe I'm not quite the hotshot you think I am."

She stared at him. He was good at letting people come to their own conclusions, and he'd certainly never tried to be anything he wasn't. His eyes met hers, clear and warm and open. "What are we doing, Dell?"

"Well, I'm hoping to watch a movie and eat the rest of your popcorn."

"Because . . . ?"

"Because I like this movie and I love popcorn. And because Adam's at my house barbecuing chicken and vegetables. *Vegetables.*" He shuddered again.

After *Oceans 11*, they switched to *SNL*. "I bet this isn't how most of your dates end," she said.

He was quiet a moment. "Was this a date?"

She met his gaze. "If it was, it'd be my first since—" She paused. "A really long time."

"How long?"

"Eighteen months."

"How does it feel?"

She thought about it. "Good," she said honestly. "But what about you—"

He put his finger on her mouth. "I'm good, too, Jade. More than good. Don't worry about me." He ran his hand up and down her back until she relaxed again. At some point she realized her eyes were closed and she lifted her head in shock.

She was curled up against Dell's side. He was asleep on his back, one arm around her, his torso rising and falling with his slow, steady breaths, even with Beans sitting on his chest.

"Hey," she said, sitting up and poking Dell in the side.

He mumbled something beneath his breath and didn't budge.

Jade scooped the kitten off of him, set her on the floor and poked Dell again. "Wake up."

Both arms came around her, snuggling her in close as he pressed his face into her hair. "Mmm. You smell good."

"Dell, wake up!"

His mouth was on her neck now. "I'm awake," he said, and licked the spot he'd just kissed. "You taste as good as you smell, did you know that?"

Then he cupped the back of her head in one big hand and kissed her again, her mouth this time, and she gave herself up to it, to the heat of him, his taste. Their bodies were plastered together and he was rock solid against her, his arms flexed tight around her. "Are you really awake?"

In answer, he tugged her even closer and deepened their kiss, taking his time about it, too, moving slow and almost unbearably erotic against her, his hands sliding under her shirt, his fingertips resting just beneath her breasts. She wasn't wearing a bra, and when he discovered that he lifted his head and looked at her, his gaze sleepy and heavy-lidded, pulling her in, making her want to fall into him and drown.

"Dell." She sucked in an uneven breath, shockingly turned on. "Are you up?"

"Yeah," he said, and pulled her over the top of him so that she could feel exactly how "up" he was. His chest was hard, his abs were hard, his thighs were hard.

Everything was hard.

Her eyes must have gone wide because a low chuckle accompanied the slow rock of his hips to hers. A tug of her hair brought her line of vision up to meet his once more. She quivered and he urged her down to him, and then somehow she was kissing him again. God, she could kiss him forever.

Beneath her shirt, his fingers stroked her skin and she thought, *Up an inch!*, and then in the next beat he'd done exactly that and the desire exploded.

When they she came up for air, Dell had one hand palming her breast, his thumb gliding back and forth over her nipple, making her squirm with pleasure. Or maybe that was his other hand, inside the back of her pajama bottoms, gripping a butt cheek, his fingers gliding over the silk of her bikini panties.

She was no better. She had both hands under his shirt, low on his abs, her fingers playing with the loose waistband of his jeans. She lifted her head and looked at him. "There's this thing about sleeping with someone. It creates a false sense of intimacy and leads to . . . things."

"Things?"

"Sleepy sex. It leads to sleepy sex. You know, the kind of sex you wouldn't have if you were all the way awake."

He laughed softly, his eyes black with desire. His hands

gripped her hips with a familiar possessiveness that maybe should have turned her off but instead turned her on. From his intense expression she knew that even though he hadn't come here for this, it was certainly what he was going to do. "I don't know about you," he said. "But I don't do a lot of sleepovers period. So this . . . sleepy sex is new for me." His eyes lit. "Be gentle."

His hands went to her hips as he slowly arched into her, making her realize he was still incredibly aroused. "Dell—"

He put a finger over her lips. "We're done denying, Jade." A statement not a question. He let his words hang between them for a long beat, then gently nudged her off of him. He rose and headed to the door.

She stared at him. "Wait—" What? That was it? Dammit! He couldn't leave now, not when she was all hot and bothered! To cover that, she sat up and pulled on her donkey slippers. She needed the armor. "No good-bye?"

Dell was looking hot and bothered, too. And . . . yum. He checked the lock on her door and came back, standing over her. "There's not going to be a good-bye," he said. He pulled off his shirt and dropped it to the floor. Then he covered her body with his, pressing a muscled thigh between hers to spread them, making room for himself. "Not until dawn. Hell, maybe not even then because my first appointment tomorrow isn't until nine."

Oh. *Oh.* She was surrounded by him, a bicep on either side of her face. She could turn her head and press her lips to his flesh and at just the thought she experienced a wave of desire that swamped her. "I have to be at work at seven thirty," she said. "My boss is a real hard-ass."

He smiled. "I could make you forget him."

She nearly climaxed at just the sound of his voice rumbling in her ear. He could make her forget everything, including how he never kept the women he slept with. "Kiss me."

He gave her one last long look before lust completely consumed him and his mouth came down on hers. He de-

voured her. There was no other word for it. He stripped her
out of her sweatshirt and pulled off her donkey slippers one
at a time, and she would have sworn he was laughing as he
tossed them over her shoulder. But then she slid her hands
down his chest, over hard abs and then lower, cupping him.

He stopped laughing.

She outlined him with her fingers, impressed and also a
little worried. It'd been a long time, a really long time, and
he seemed . . .

Big.

She must have let some of her worry show because he
cupped her face and kissed her deep, angling his head to get
more of her until she was clutching at him in desperation.
Shifting lower, he kissed her jaw, her throat, her shoulder,
moving to the swell of her breast.

A slow, warm heat began to fill her, building as he sucked
her nipple into his mouth, rolling it between his tongue and
the roof of his mouth. Gasping, she arched her back, lifting
herself to him.

He smiled as if he'd won a prize and then went back to
his diabolical torture, leaving trails of fire on her skin everywhere he touched or kissed.

Which was everywhere.

Her breath was catching with each new caress as she lay
writhing beneath him. She needed . . . God, she wasn't even
sure, she couldn't think, she couldn't form words, she certainly couldn't stop herself from making sounds she'd never
heard herself make before.

But Dell didn't appear to need words or direction. After
all, the man made his living reading the body language of
animals, and he was reading hers with shocking ease. His
hands were on the move southward, caressing her stomach,
her thighs, until her pj bottoms got in his way and he tugged
them off. Now she was beneath him in just her panties,
which he seemed to like because with a hand on each inner
thigh, he took a good long look and growled deep in his

throat. His fingers played with her through the silk and
came away wet, making him groan. The sexiest sound she'd
ever heard. The desire she was feeling was bordering on
untenable, stronger than anything she'd ever experienced.
"Dell—"

"I know." His hands slid down her hips, catching the tiger
silk along the way and pulling them down her legs. "Christ,
Jade. You're beautiful." He stroked a finger over her, then
inside her, and it was all she could do not to levitate off the
couch. At that moment she was so far gone he could have
done anything, asked anything of her.

But he didn't.

He wasn't taking, he was giving, shifting down her body
to do so, pressing his mouth to her hot center, teasing, reduc-
ing her to nothing more than a quivering, panting, begging
boneless mass. Yes, begging. He had her begging, adrift in
the sensations of the rough demands of his tongue, teeth,
and hands, which were sending shock waves down her body
until she felt her toes curl, until she burst.

Shattered, actually. Breathing like a lunatic, hot, sweaty,
desperate, she surged up and undid his jeans and shoved
them down to his thighs and found him as impressive as
she'd imagined.

They put on the condom together. Or rather, he worked at
rolling on the condom while she attempted to help but really
was just using the opportunity to stroke and caress him.

He didn't seem to mind, but she wasn't nearly done teasing him the way he'd teased her so mercilessly when he
apparently decided the hell with playing and slid into her in
one smooth, hard thrust.

The air left her body as she rose to meet him, pulling
him closer, digging her fingers into his flesh as he began to
move. Mindless, she rocked up into him, the pleasure was
so intense, she cried out with it.

How had she not missed this?

But she knew. It was him making her feel like this. No

one else but Dell could do it, the way he moved inside her, his muscles hot and tense beneath her fingers, his eyes dark and fiercely intense on hers.

Just looking at him, something in her chest cracked and opened.

Her heart.

It shattered right along with her body as she pulsed and throbbed, tightening around him. He was filling more than just her body and she knew it. God, she knew.

He sped up his pace and she met every thrust with her own startling level of passion. She could hear his ragged breathing in her ear, feel his heart pounding against her chest.

Or was that her breathing, her heart . . . she didn't know. "Dell."

His hands tangled in her hair, pulling her head to meet his mouth. This kiss was rough, demanding everything of her and she willing gave it. Her hands traveled everywhere on his body that she could reach and it still wasn't enough. She planted her feet on the couch and lifted her hips, pushing into him, doing some demanding of her own.

His control snapped and he thrust into her one last time, taking her right off the edge with him.

When she came back to herself, her heart felt as full and achy as her body. She didn't know what she expected to happen next. She never knew with him. But he stayed deep inside her, holding her tight, his breath warm against her temple. Snuggling in, she let her eyes drift shut as her heart pounded against his.

After a few minutes, he stirred. "You okay?"

"Mmm." It was all she had.

But it was apparently all he needed, because he grabbed the throw blanket from the back of the couch and covered them, then settled them more comfortably and kissed her. "I've wanted to do that for a long time."

"How long?"

"Long."

All the yearning and wanting in the world wasn't going to change anything between them but in that moment, with him holding her close, obviously content to stay here, right here, it was enough.

It had to be enough.

She woke up the next morning from a really great dream and stared into Bean's green eyes.

"Mew," she said. The cat was sharing Jade's pillow.

It was the same story every morning. But unlike every other morning, Jade was wrapped up in another body. A big, warm, mocha-colored hunk of tough muscle that was still deeply asleep.

He'd expelled a lot of energy last night. All night . . .

There was stubble on his square jaw, and his lashes were jet black and sinfully thick.

Definitely not a dream, she thought, and though she had to get up, she took a long moment to just look at him, knowing if she didn't move fast, get out of his arms instead of remaining snuggled in all perfect like she was made for him, it was going to be hard to ignore what had happened here last night.

Real hard.

Thirteen

One minute Dell was deep in the land of the living dead, the kind of sleep that comes after great sex, and then in the next, he was blinking at the sudden light.

"It's time to get up."

He squinted blearily at the woman wrapped in a sheet at the side of the bed.

Jade. Mmm, Jade. She looked good in nothing but a sheet but he knew how she looked even better.

Reaching out, he took a hold of a corner of the sheet and tugged.

There was a female squeak, then the flash of bare ass as she ran for the bathroom.

Grinning he rolled out of bed and followed, but she'd locked him out. "Hey."

"Just because we slept together does *not* mean we're going to share a bathroom," she said through the door. "Go away."

"Jade, I've seen every inch of you. Hell, I've had my mouth on every inch of you. Let me in, I have to—"

She opened the door and came out wrapped in a robe. She looked him over and her gaze softened.

Yeah, now that was more like it. With a smile, he stepped into her, the part of him happiest to see her arriving first, bumping into her belly.

"Oh, no," she said, slapping a hand on his chest. Her other went to his mouth. "No. Don't say or do anything more until I've inhaled some caffeine. I need caffeine." She closed her eyes when he slid a hand down her back to grip her sweet ass. "Dell, help me here. I can't be strong and make the right decision without caffeine."

He sucked on the tip of her pointer finger. "Decision?"

Her fingers began making their way slowly down his chest. "Yeah. The age-old question—round two or the walk of shame?"

He had both hands on her arms now, one working southward to get beneath the robe. "I vote for round two."

"We have work."

"I can hurry." Hell, if her fingers kept on their current southern trajectory, this whole conversation was going to be a moot point.

"I don't know," she said. "You weren't very good at hurrying last night. You took your sweet time, kissing and licking and touching . . . everything." She was a little breathless now.

He liked her breathless, a lot, and with a flick of his fingers, he tugged open the loose knot on the front of her robe. God, there was nothing as perfect as a woman all soft and warm in the morning. Pushing her robe off her shoulders to the floor, he kissed her hard.

"Dell—"

"Your way," he said against her mouth. "Whatever you want, Jade. Take it."

She took the suggestion with a seriousness that made him want to smile. "My way," she repeated, and nipped his earlobe between her teeth before pushing him up against the wall.

"I think I'm going to like your way," he managed as she dropped to her knees.

"That's a safe bet," she murmured.

After Dell left, Jade got into the shower and told herself that what had happened last night—and this morning, good Lord, this morning!—was nothing more than an expression of pent-up lust.

And now that they'd given in to it, it was over and done.

Pent-up lust quenched.

She had no idea what Dell was telling himself, he tended to keep his own council. Although holy sweet Moses, he'd looked knee-knockingly fine in her small shower, bumping those long legs and arms on the tile every time he'd moved. He'd used her soap and shampoo, and now he was going to smell like her all day.

The big Dell Connelly, smelling like peaches and cream.

She dressed and moved through her living room, stopping to stare at the couch. None of the cushions were in the right place. One of the three was on the floor, another upright on the arm, and the third lying haphazardly in the center of the room. The memory of what they'd done there made her flush, and not with embarrassment. She righted the cushions, found a condom wrapper on the floor and then caught sight of herself in the bathroom mirror when she went to throw it away.

Her eyes were bright, her cheeks flushed. Her nipples visibly hard. There were invisible reactions going on, too, and she rubbed her thighs together, feeling that she was damp from just thinking about Dell. *You need to get a grip,* she told herself sternly, and left for work.

Dell's first appointment of the day was with Lilah, who'd brought in a new rescue, a two-week-old kitten. Dell gave the little thing the once-over and pronounced her in decent health for being undernourished and abandoned.

Lilah nodded with relief and hugged the kitten close. "She's so little and yet so tough. It makes me want to keep her."

Dell's eyes drifted out the open exam room door to the front desk, where Jade sat running his world. She stopped typing to gently admonish Beans, who'd just taken a swipe at Gertie's face, then went back to her computer. He wondered if she was making one of her spreadsheets.

And if he was on it. She'd certainly had some Things To Do to him earlier, and though they'd "hurried," he'd still nearly been late.

But not too late for her to stop him as he was leaving and look solemnly into his face. "What just happened between us doesn't change anything."

Actually, it changed everything. "Like?"

"Like no preferential treatment at work from you. And in return, I won't be looking for a ring and a white picket fence."

"Well, that's a relief. I don't like white fences."

"Dell."

She'd been serious, and he could admit a huge relief that she felt so strongly about not getting attached. Getting attached to him was never a good idea. He hurt people that way because he didn't get attached back.

Ever.

He was pretty sure he was missing the attachment gene. Then he realized Lilah had said something to him several times and he'd missed it all. She was now staring at him with open amusement.

"I said," she repeated patiently, "like someone else we know."

"Huh?"

She patted him on the shoulder. "I said Beans is coming along nicely, too. Like someone else we both know." She paused. "She looks good today. Happy."

"Beans?"

"Don't be stupid, Dell."

Right. He busied himself with the chart, knowing *exactly* why Jade was happy. It was called multiple orgasms.

"Probably you never even looked in a mirror this morning," Lilah said, running her fingers through his hair fondly, then giving up when she couldn't get it in any sort of order that pleased her. "But you're wearing a matching expression."

"I'm always happy."

"Not always," she said. "Let's talk about it."

"Let's not."

"Oh, come on! Obviously something's up."

"Your hormone levels. You should have them checked."

She rolled her eyes, then her smile faded. "Seriously, Dell."

"Oh Christ, Lilah. You have a fiancé now. Bug him with this emotional shit."

"You know Jade's leaving." Lilah's eyes held worry, for the both of them. "What's going to happen then?"

"Nothing."

She stared at him. "Nothing? What do you mean, nothing?"

She was the closest thing he had to a sister. Which probably explained the urge to wrap his fingers around her neck. "Does Brady realize how annoying you are?"

"Yes, and he loves me, anyway. Dell, we have to do something."

"We?"

"Yes. Clearly you need my help."

"No, I don't."

"Oh, for chrissake." She clapped a hand to either side of his face and made him look at her. "You get that this isn't just about Jade's issues, right? That your abandonment issues are coming into play here, too?"

He stepped back from her. "What? I don't have—"

"Hello! You were abandoned by your mother, your father, then a handful of idiotic foster care providers, Sol, and every single bonehead bimbo you've ever dated, and now Jade if she really leaves as planned. So yeah. You do, Dell. You have abandonment issues."

Dell looked out the door. No one was paying them any attention but he shut it anyway. "Okay, first of all, my dad *died*. Sol *died*. They didn't leave me on purpose."

"It's still abandonment."

"Lilah," he said, shaking his head. "You're wrong. And I have people. I have Adam and Brady."

"Because they're the same as you, you're just all so frigging stubborn, you stick together like glue."

Okay, *that* might be true. "The women," he said, continuing his defense. "I've always been the one to walk away from any woman in my life."

"Yes. You've made sure of it. Walking the walk, talking the talk, but keeping it all deceptively shallow and casual so that you're alone. You've made sure of it. Because then you aren't going to get hurt."

He stared at her. "If I'm so busy being alone, why are you still in my life?"

"Because I'm a bully." She smiled and hugged him. "Oh, Dell. You've always been there for me, you've helped me so much. I love you, you know."

He sighed. "I love you, too."

"Then, for once, let me help you."

It'd be easier to just bash his head in.

She pulled back and looked into his eyes. "Let her in."

He'd deny that as a possibility but there was a problem with that. Because he was pretty sure Jade was already in. All the way in.

In general, Dell was excellent at compartmentaliz-ing, and he could reason and logic away most problems with little trouble. So it was frustrating that he found himself unable to do that with Jade, especially after Lilah's visit earlier. His day ran long. He lost track of how many dogs, kittens, and various other creatures he saw.

Let her in . . .

Dell trusted Lilah, but he wasn't altogether sure she knew what she was talking about this time. Both Keith and Mike had left when Jade appeared in his office doorway. "I need you a sec."

He followed her down the hall to . . . the supply cabinets?

She touched the drug lockup. "I just checked to make sure it was locked up for the night," she said quietly, turning her back to him to stare at the cabinet. "And it made me wonder if I'm better." She put her hands on the locked door and bowed her head slightly. "Do it," she whispered. "Attack me again."

Again? "Jade." Her name felt like it was torn from his throat. "I—"

"Do it!"

There was a terrible pause where he'd have sworn he heard her heart pounding from where he stood. With a sick feeling deep in his gut, he came up behind her just as Adam came into the room.

Jade froze. Dell felt the change in her instantly and glanced at Adam, who stopped where he was.

Jade's breath hitched.

"It's just me," Dell said quietly to her. "You can do this. Remember how I showed you in my gym." He stepped closer, into her space now. A strand of her hair stuck to the stubble on his jaw and then she trembled, killing him. "Jade—"

"Shh." Dropping her head to the cabinet, she spoke to herself. "It's easier in the gym. It's less real."

"We don't have to do this—"

"Yes, we do. Someone's still hitting vet clinics."

At the realization that she didn't feel safe here in his place, a helpless fury rushed him. "Jade—"

"Please, Dell? I want to do this here, in the real world, until I don't want to throw up at the thought."

No one understood that better than him. He wasn't sure exactly what had happened to her, but he was good at guessing. She hadn't fought back and that haunted her. She wanted to be strong. He understood that, too, the need, the passion driving her to make sure she was strong no matter what. So he tightened his arms on her and pressed her up against the cabinet.

She stomped on his foot, plowed her elbow into his belly, and when he bent with an "oomph," she whirled, a pen in her hand, ready to poke him in the eye.

Which, thankfully, she didn't. She dropped it to the floor and stopped short, breathing hard. "Oh God."

"Nice," Adam said, nodding. "Follow up?"

"A knee to the family jewels." She swiped her forehead with her arm. "Drop him like a stone."

"Sounds good," his brother said. "I wouldn't have minded seeing that."

Dell slid his brother a long look and received a rare but genuine laugh. Adam humor.

"I could use a pizza now," Jade said.

Still smiling, Adam raised his hand. "My treat," he said. "Promise to do that again tomorrow and I'll spring for the beer, too."

Two days later Dell was sitting in his office staring at the files on his desk. He needed to work, but he hadn't written a word in ten minutes. For the millionth time, his gaze landed on Jade out in the front room.

He'd thought that her request and his promise to treat her the same at work was just the usual womanspeak for we are now sleeping together so I own you.

But she'd meant it. She hadn't tried to discuss their night or, to his chagrin, repeat it.

She was closing up for the night; straightening the chairs along the wall, talking to Gertie who was padding along after her, then laughing at something the silly parrot repeated as she wiped down the front reception counter with her special antiseptic wipes.

He loved to watch her.

It wasn't just the clothes, he decided, taking in her black pencil skirt and kick-ass heels, the ones that had little bows at her ankles. It was the way Gertie loved her. The way she'd taken on Beans. The way both of them, dog and kitten, followed her around like she was the Pied Piper.

It was . . . well, fucking adorable, for one thing. And for another, he found it hot. Her loving his animals was hot.

She moved back to the computer and sat, staring at the screen, fingers whirling on the keyboard. Her hair was carefully contained and controlled in some complicated twist up on her head, and her white blouse . . . Christ, had it been unbuttoned that far when she'd first come in this morning? Because damned if she didn't look like every man's secretary fantasy. In fact, just like that, it started to play in his mind.

Slowly she rose to her feet. Licked her lips as she reached up and undid her hair, shaking her head, causing the soft, silky waves to tumble to her shoulders.

Oh yeah.

Nice.

Her fingers began working the buttons on her snug white blouse, revealing a black lace bra beneath which barely covered her nipples and—

"Jesus, where the hell are you, Disneyland?"

Dell blinked at Adam, who'd come and perched a hip on the desk. He stared at Dell with a straight face, but he knew his brother better than anyone on earth.

Adam was laughing his ass off on the inside, the fucker. "Not Disneyland."

More like *Penthouse Forum* . . .

Adam gave a purposeful, knowing look in the direction where Dell's gaze had been fixated.

Jade. Not giving him a naughty secretary striptease . . .

Dell kicked his office door shut.

Adam's mouth twitched and he leaned forward, opening the door again.

Jade glanced over, saw them, and gave a quizzical look.

Adam waved at her.

Jade paused, narrowed her eyes, then went back to her work.

Adam turned to Dell. "This is new, you doing all the mooning. Usually it's the women showing up or calling incessantly. But now it's you. You're the one mooning now." He shook his head. "Poor dumb bastard."

Dell shoved Adam off his desk. "Don't you have something to do to earn your keep?"

Adam smiled. He knew damn well that his business, the classes, the training, the breeding . . . all brought good money into their pockets. "You're pissy. You know what that means? That I'm right."

"Really? You want to go there? Maybe I should get Holly on the line for you. Then we'll talk pissy."

"Hey, at least I'm not changing my MO midgame," Adam pointed out.

"Huh?"

"You let Jade come to your house," Adam explained.

"Yeah. To train her. You'd have done the same thing."

"No, I'd have brought her to the gym in town. But you. You took her home."

"So?"

So they both knew that Jade was the first woman Dell had ever had out there.

"Next thing," Adam said, "you'll start thinking about giving her the key code."

The guilt must have shown on Dell's face because Adam

tipped his head back and laughed. He was still laughing when Dell, not liking where this was going, turned back to his work. "Why are you here, anyway?"

"Training."

"I mean why are you *here*, in my office, bugging the shit out of me?"

"Other than it's fun to fuck with you?" Adam shrugged. "Thought we'd get something to eat." He took another peek at Jade. "You figure you know what you're doing? Because both Brady and I have our doubts."

He had no clue. "You and Brady should fuck off."

Adam took one look at his face and shook his head, still amused. "Good to see this on the other foot for a change."

"Shut up."

"I'd be worried about Jade, but you know what? Even with whatever's clearly bothering her, she's still going to eat you up and spit you out."

Dell could get on board with the eating him up part. "What the hell does that mean?"

"Hey, if you don't know, I can't help you." He tapped Dell on the head with his knuckles. "Yeah, still hard as wood. You always did have to learn the hard way." He headed to the door. "My money's on you, though."

Fourteen

Late the next afternoon, Jade signed in the last patient of the day—Lulu the lamb was by turns sweet, curious, and holy hell on wheels.

Keith had brought Mrs. Robertson and Lulu to an exam room. Jade was at her desk doing the whole wind down for the day when she heard Mrs. Robertson and Dell laughing.

Two minutes later, Mrs. Robertson and Lulu checked out with Jade and left.

Jade turned to her last chore, Dell's laptop. The other day on the helicopter back from a S&R training, he'd made a bunch of notes for her to add to patient files. She'd been asking him to e-mail them to her, but he hadn't, so she'd confiscated the laptop to do it herself.

That's when she found the patient files she'd never seen before, a whole set of them that had never been entered on the books. Frowning, she scrolled through them. Well-puppy and -kitten checks, simple surgeries like neuters and spays, dentistry, vaccinations . . . Confused, Jade searched, but though she found names, dates, and detailed services provided, there was no billing information.

Because he hadn't billed, she realized. Not for any of it.

She went deeper and found that these services occurred approximately once a month and went back years. Thoroughly baffled, Jade went into the back and found Dell in front of the x-ray machine, laughing with Mike, who was cleaning up the equipment.

"What's wrong with Lulu?" Jade asked.

"She ate Mrs. Robertson's birth control pills," Mike said.

"That's not dangerous for her?"

"Not the pills," Dell told her. "But the case is . . . problematic."

Jade stared at Dell. "She ate the case, too?"

Dell smiled. "Yeah but no worries. The x-ray shows she broke up the case pretty good, though. It's going to all come out okay in the end."

Both men cracked up at this. When they'd composed themselves, Mike said good-bye for the night.

Dell surprised Jade by snagging her hips and drawing her in close, gripping her with a protective, possessive familiarity that should have pissed her off.

Instead, her heart stuttered to a stop. She looked down at his hands on her, at his fingers, the ones she'd had on her body all night long three nights ago now, tender. Rough. Demanding . . .

Tilting her head up, she looked into his face. "What are you doing?"

"Breaking my promise. I'm gonna kiss you, Jade." He flashed her a wicked smile that blew a few brain cells. "Want a breakdown of what happens next?"

"I—" It shouldn't be so sexy when he spoke in that low alpha voice. She lost her train of thought when his hands ran up and down her sides, dangerously close to the swells of her breasts.

"God, I love this top," he murmured, dipping his head to kiss her neck. "And you smell good enough to eat."

"Dell, we're at work."

"When we're not at work, you ignore me."

"That's . . . that's not true." Was it? "You didn't come by or call, either."

He went still and stared at her, looking genuinely flummoxed, as if he was so used to women coming to him that he'd not even thought of it. "You are so spoiled," she said. "And—" Her phone was vibrating in her pocket. She pulled it out, saw that it was her mother, and put it back into her front pants pocket.

Dell's brows went up.

"It's nothing." But the phone kept vibrating insistently.

Dell slid his hand into her pocket, taking his sweet-ass time pulling out the phone, making sure his fingers brushed against her hip bone, letting his thumb slip beneath the waistband of her skirt to touch bare skin as he looked at the ID screen. "It says *Mom*," he said. "Jade, you can't ignore your mom." Before she could say a word to that, he hit Answer and said "Jade Bennett's phone, how can I help you?"

Jade tried to snatch the phone back, but Dell used his superior height against her. "Yes," he said very sweetly into the phone. As if he were ever *sweet*. "As a matter of fact, Jade is right here. Hold on a moment."

She snatched the phone. "Mom, is everything all right?"

"Of course, darling."

"Okay . . . but I'm at work, you know that, right?"

"I know." Her mother's voice was clear enough for Dell to hear. "So who was that lovely young man?"

Dell preened.

"Was that your secretary?" her mother asked.

Jade smirked at Dell. "Not quite. Mom, you know that I'm the secretary here."

"Actually," Dell said. "You're more than—"

Jade slapped her hand over his mouth. "Can I call you back after work?"

"Oh, there's no need. Just wanted you to know that I went by your town house today and aired it out for you. I was thinking a fresh paint job."

It was difficult to concentrate with one hundred eighty pounds of solid muscle and testosterone pressing into her. "I just painted it."

"Eighteen months ago. And how about some new furniture? Just yesterday I found this adorable King James end table—"

"Mom—"

Dell made the most of their close proximity and sank his teeth lightly into the lobe of her ear. Desire rolled through her and she barely managed to swallow her moan. Shoving at him, she said, "I don't need new paint or new furniture, but thank you."

"Plants, then. How about a few plants, something to make it homey for your arrival."

"No plants," Jade said firmly, giving up trying to push Dell away as he kissed his way down her throat, his hands gliding up to cover her breasts. Damn. He was good . . .

Her mother gave a long-suffering sigh. "Okay, but new bedding and towels. I'm going to insist, Jade. It'll be a welcome-home present."

"I know you're trying to help," Jade murmured, her head thunking back on the wall when Dell's thumbs rasped back and forth over her nipples. "But . . ."

But she'd lost track of the conversation since only half of her was half paying attention; the other half was now quivering with anticipation of where Dell's mouth and hands would go next. "I don't need a welcome-home present." She felt Dell's reaction to that in the slight tensing of his muscles. "I've got to go, Mom," she said, and slid the phone back into her pocket. "And *that's* why I don't answer my cell when I'm on the job," she said, trying for glib.

He didn't play. In fact, his face was carefully cleared of all emotion. "You wanted to go over something with me," he said.

It took her a moment to change gears—he was much better at it than she was. "I got the files off your laptop." She handed over the computer. "And while I was there, some other files popped out at me. Services you've provided but not charged for."

His gaze flickered, but he said nothing as he took the laptop.

"Do you need help with the accounting?" she asked as Adam came into the back.

"There is no bookkeeping for these accounts," Dell said.

"Pro bono work?" Jade asked.

Dell flicked a glance at his brother, then back to Jade. "Yes. I go out to the Tall Rocks area once a month and give a clinic for the people out there who can't afford vet care for their pets."

"On the Indian reservation there?"

He looked surprised that she knew. "No, just off the reservation."

"If you put it on your books, it's a write-off."

"I don't want the write-off," he said.

"But—"

"No," he said, and walked away.

"Confused?" Adam asked her.

"Yes."

Adam nodded. "It's because you asked him the wrong question."

"What's the right question?"

"Why does he do it?"

Jade looked into the dark eyes so like Dell's. "Okay, why does he do it?"

"Because no matter what he wants us all to believe, he cares for people as much as he cares about animals. It's a pack leader thing. He won't let himself turn his back on anyone in his pack, like it or not."

"But why can't he take the write-off?"

"Not can't. Won't."

"Why?"

"Now that's a far more complicated question," Adam said.

After what had happened against the x-ray machine, and what hadn't happened, Dell made himself scarce the next day. Not hard to do with the schedule they had all morning, which had been double booked because he spent the afternoon out west making ranch rounds. From there he was called to an emergency at Melinda's, which Brady flew him to. When Jade had locked up for the day, it was Adam to walk her out to her car, standing there big and protective, making sure she got off okay. "You have a training session tonight," Adam reminded her.

"Still?" Jade asked. "But isn't Dell—"

"Still."

She went home first and changed. "Men are stupid," she said to Beans.

"Mew."

She sighed. What had she expected? That Dell would stop being Dell?

That they were in a relationship?

Of course they weren't in a relationship. She'd made it perfectly clear that she was leaving, and he didn't do relationships, anyway.

Which disturbed her more than it should. But regardless, she drove to his house for her scheduled self-defense session. She walked up to his door and stared at the keypad in indecision. She ran a hand over her clothes. Tucked a strand of hair in place.

Chewed on her lower lip.

She was nervous, which she hadn't been since their first session. But things were different now. They'd slept together for one thing. Before, using the key code to let herself into his house had been . . . a friend move, not a lover move. God, no. He'd never even had a lover here to his house.

And now . . . now she wasn't sure what they were.

The door opened unexpectedly, and she hurriedly pasted a smile on her face.

It was Adam. He stood back and let her in.

"Oh," she said in surprise. "Where's Dell?"

"I'm your stand-in tonight."

She ignored the ping of loss. "You should have told me. You don't have to—"

"Want to," he said. "And don't worry. I'm better than he is."

She smiled, thinking this would be far easier with Adam than Dell, but her nerves only increased as they moved down to the gym.

After her attack, she hadn't wanted to be touched. Dell had broken through that barrier, but that was Dell.

Adam was . . . not Dell.

Okay, so it didn't make any sense, but all she knew was that her feet didn't want to take her to the mats.

Adam stood stretching while she made a big production out of setting down her purse and removing her sweatshirt.

And then another long production of making sure her shoes were both tied tight.

And then double-tied.

One could never be too careful . . .

"Jade." Adam's voice was always low and measured. He never wasted a single word. If Dell was the laid-back, easygoing one of the family, Adam was his virtual opposite. Quiet. Guarded. Stoic. His version of the Connelly Self-Protection Plan.

She sighed. "Yeah?"

Looking at her with steady patience, he gestured to the mat.

She walked onto it.

"You look like you're going to the guillotine," he said, sounding a little amused.

"No, really. I'm fine. Really."

"That was one too many *really*s."

She grimaced and he shook his head. "How about we work on something not physical?"

She let out the breath she hadn't realized she was holding. "Like?"

"Weapons."

She laughed, the tension loosening a little. "Weapons aren't physical?"

"Not like hand to hand is, no. If you have a weapon, you're far less likely to ever be a victim."

"I'm not comfortable carrying a weapon," she told him.

"You don't have to. You can have something that can be *used* as a weapon, something easily and quickly accessible. Get your purse."

She grabbed it and hugged it to her chest.

He gave a little smile. "Don't worry, I have no desire to ever comb the mysterious depths of a woman's purse. Pull something out from there quick, just the first thing your fingers grab."

She pulled out a compact-sized can of hair spray.

"Perfect. If someone surprises you in a parking lot—"

She winced, and he continued on, more gently now. "If someone does, you'll spray him directly in the face. Best if you can get it right in his eyes."

She'd actually done that to herself once by accident and it had hurt like a bitch. But . . . that long ago night, she'd had her purse and the spray wouldn't have helped her. "If he's got a gun," she said softly with a remembered shiver.

"Then you bide your time to make your move. It's actually hard for an attacker to keep track of everything; the job, the gun, the hostage. When he takes his eyes off you for even one second, you smash the heel of the can into his nose, throat, or against his temple. Whatever's exposed. If you're already down on the ground, go for his foot or kneecap. Groin, if you can reach. Hit hard and don't hesitate. Women hesitate."

She nodded. "No hesitating. Got it."

"Now grab something else out of your purse."

"You don't want to test me with the can?" she asked, surprised. "Dell always makes me try everything on him."

He shook his head and muttered something beneath his breath about his brother being both a softie *and* a sucker. "Hell no, I don't want to test your smashing me in the face with that can. I've seen you beating up the copier. I know what you can do. Pull something else out of your purse."

She stuck her hand back in and this time latched onto a pen. She shrugged in apology.

"No, that's good," he said. "It's pointy."

She stared at the pen. "Yeah. So?"

"So all you have to do is remember that pointy things are more effective on something *soft*. Like the throat, the eyes, abs, groin."

She felt a little sick at the thought of using the pen on a man. "You guys sure are obsessed with your . . . groin area."

"No doubt," he said, sounding amused again. "But you have to be careful. If you use something like a pen to strike at a hard point—a kneecap, for example—chances are that your weapon of choice will just bounce off without doing any real damage, and then you'll have just pissed him off. That won't be good."

When the moment had come for her, she hadn't done anything to protect herself. She'd been too scared, and that was her secret shame—she'd *let* herself be a victim.

Adam's expression softened. "Just remember, something hard like the can goes to bone, pointy goes to soft tissue. It's really as simple as that, Jade. The next time you're walking from point A to point B, just make sure you're holding your keys or a pen or a can of hair spray. Hell, it can be a fucking can of vegetables, it doesn't matter. As long as you're thinking ahead, staying calm, keeping your head up and being vigilant, you'll never be a helpless victim again."

At the *again* her head came up, but he was moving away, toward the refrigerator to get them each a bottle of water. Grateful he wasn't going to push or ask, she let him talk her into giving the mats a try. They went over some of the other techniques that Dell had been working on with her, but they cut it short because her shoelaces were bothering her.

Aka she wasn't ready to wrestle with anyone other than Dell. Rather than face that, she made an excuse about being tired, and Adam walked her out to her car.

"So," she said, casually as she could, "where's Dell tonight? Still at Melinda's ranch?" Because everyone knew what Melinda and Dell did after a long day on the ranch, and it didn't involve work.

Hypocrite, she told herself. *He and I have the same relationship.* Or they had, for one night . . .

Adam shook his head.

"Is that no, you don't want to tell me?" she asked. "Or no, you don't know?"

He actually gave her a rare smile. "You're too smart for him, you know that?"

"He's on a date," she said flatly, not willing to be distracted, even if he had a pretty great smile.

"Listen, I'm not sure what happened between you two, but—"

"I reminded him that I'm leaving soon," she said.

"Ah," Adam said, nodding. "Well, that'll do it."

"Do what?"

"You're leaving," he said, as if it was the most obvious thing in the world. "Dell doesn't 'do' leaving. At least not anymore. He leaves first. Always."

Fifteen

Dell was already back in Sunshine, a hundred miles away from Melinda's ranch. At the bakery, to be exact, eating a half-dozen donuts, because for the third time in a row he hadn't stayed for a date with Melinda.

Although he should make a date—with a shrink.

He wondered what Adam was teaching Jade right this very minute. And if she was wearing that look of intense concentration she got when he was showing her a new move, the one that said she was earnest and serious and focused on kicking ass.

God, he loved that expression.

Adam appeared at his side and plopped into the other chair at Dell's little table. "You're an idiot."

"Aw, thanks."

Adam reached out and snatched an old-fashioned glazed donut.

"Hey."

Taking a huge bite out of it, Adam leaned back. "Don't you want to know *what* makes you a fucking idiot?"

"No."

"It didn't go so well with Jade tonight."

Dell straightened. "What do you mean? What happened?"

"She was nervous about tangling with me on the mat."

"She tell you that?"

"No, she told me that she was exhausted, so we had to stop."

Dell blew out a breath. "I don't get it, she's been doing so well."

"Yes, and this is where the fucking idiot part comes in. She's good with *you* touching her. She feels safe with *you*. What the hell is going on with you two?"

"Nothing. She's leaving."

"Yeah," Adam said. "I got that. But she's not gone yet. You're just backing out of her life?"

"What part of *leaving* don't you understand?" Dell asked.

"If it were me, I'd take every last second I had."

"Yes, well, I always was smarter than you."

"Come on," Adam said, shaking head. "If this were any other woman, you wouldn't give a shit that she was leaving. It wouldn't matter."

"We work together."

Adam waved this away as inconsequential. "You know what my point is."

"Not really." But Dell did. Christ, he did.

"You going to tell her how you feel about her before she goes, or are you going to be a total pussy about it?"

"Telling Jade that his feelings for her had changed, deepened, felt like the dumbest of all the dumbass moves he'd ever made. He didn't want Jade to consider him as her . . .

What?

Christ. "I have to go."

"Shock."

"What does that mean?"

"You're so smart," Adam said, stealing the very last donut as he rose. "You figure it out."

Jade went to the animal center instead of home. She'd been running some accounting reports and wanted to check on them.

Or . . . she wanted to keep herself busy.

She decoded the alarm, flipped on the lights, and sat at her desk, immediately losing herself in the comfort and stability of accounting. Accounting didn't require much. The numbers either added up or they didn't, and the predictability of the work was soothing all in itself.

After an hour, she got thirsty and headed into the staff room for a bottle of water. She stepped into the room and as her hand reached out to flip the light switch on the wall, she heard it.

A loud exhale.

Male.

Panic. Her hand flailed and instead of getting the light switch, she hit the counter. Her fingers wrapped around something and without thinking, she held it out in front of her as a weapon just as a large shadow surged upright at the table in front of her.

"Holy shit," she gasped.

"Holy shit," someone else gasped, and then there was a beam of light that blinded her.

Jade stepped backward, out of the room, then whirled and ran down the hall to the front desk, where she groped for the panic button, which she hit five hundred times in a row.

"Jade?"

She was still hitting the button as she looked up. Keith stood in the doorway wearing nothing but his long hair standing straight up on one side and a pair of Big Dog flannel boxers that said BLOW THIS down the fly. She was so shocked, she just stood there, her finger still on the button.

"Dude," Keith said, scrubbing his hands over his face. "You scared the shit out of me."

Knees wobbling, Jade sank to her chair. "What are you doing here?"

"My roommate got lucky tonight and he made me leave so he could have the place to himself."

"So you were sleeping here?"

He gave her a reproachful look. "*Was* sleeping. Jesus, you are one noisy chick. What were you going to do with that?"

Jade looked down and realized that she was gripping a plastic fork. It'd been what she'd grabbed off the counter. "I . . . I think I was going to stab you with it."

"Dude." He scratched his chest. "Gotta piss." He vanished in the back.

The front door crashed open and Dell burst in. Jade stared at him. He stared right back, concern and anger and fear all over his face as he came to her. "Jade." He sounded horrified as he reached her, hauling her up out of her chair and wrapping his arms around her tight. "You hit the alarm? What happened, are you hurt?"

"No, I—"

There was a scuffle of feet in the doorway to the back rooms, and in the same instant Dell whipped Jade behind him. There was a gun in his hand.

A gun.

Keith was in the doorway again, still in his BLOW THIS boxers, holding an opened soda. His eyes went wide at the sight of Dell standing there, gun drawn. "Holy shit," he said in a repeat of what he'd said to Jade, jerking, spilling his soda down his bare chest. "Am I dreaming?"

"I came into work because I knew I wouldn't be able to sleep," Jade started.

"Unlike some of us," Keith muttered.

"And I came in on Keith sleeping in the back room, but before I realized it was him, I'd hit the alarm. I'm sorry, Dell."

He swore and tucked the gun into his jeans waistband at the small of his back. Then turned and hugged Jade in close. "Don't be sorry. You did the right thing."

"It's my fault," she whispered, pressing her face into his chest. His *bare* chest because he was in jeans and an unzipped sweatshirt with nothing beneath it. His athletic shoes were unlaced and he didn't appear to be wearing socks.

He'd been in bed.

Beneath her cheek she could feel his heart pounding hard and fast. She'd wondered what it would take to ruffle the unflappable Dr. Dell Connelly.

She'd found it.

Her.

Her safety. "You have a gun?"

"I get notified at the same time as the police when the alarm goes off. I saw your car in the lot. I thought—"

He'd thought she was in danger.

Still holding her against him, Dell reached into his pocket. "Need to call this in and tell them it's a false alarm—"

Before he could finish that sentence, several squad cars came flying into the lot, lights flashing.

"Dude," Keith said on a sigh.

The next morning, Jade was at her desk staring down at the newspaper. There were two stories of interest. The first one was front page. The guys robbing the vet clinics in the state had been caught in Boise when they'd tried to hit a twenty-four-hour emergency pet hospital. No one had been injured.

The other story was on page three.

Dr. Dell Connelly's ex-fiancée and receptionist at Belle Haven catches their animal tech Keith Roberts In the Act. Of Sleeping.

Sighing, Jade tossed the paper aside. The police had been quite understanding of the mishap. Keith got over himself. Dell swore he wasn't upset with her, but something had happened.

He'd pulled back. She didn't know why.

After morning rounds, he'd gone into surgery and Jade spent the time reorganizing files and updating inventory. Dell was gone for a few hours, seeing pets at a vet hospital about an hour away. When he called her from there about some records he needed, he sounded perfectly pleasant.

And perfectly not himself.

"Dell," she said after she'd told him where to find the records. "Are you okay?"

"Of course," he said, then paused. "And you?"

An odd longing filled her. A longing for him, which was unsettling. She wanted . . . well, she didn't exactly know.

And wasn't that the problem.

"I'm peachy," she said, and when he'd hung up she smacked herself in the forehead with her phone, castigating herself aloud. "Peachy? You're *peachy*?"

"I think pineapple works better," Adam said, walking through the reception area. "It's prickly." He flashed her a quick grin, making her laugh and shake her head.

"You on for tonight?" he asked.

Tonight was poker night. Dell, Brady, Adam, and Lilah were religious about the twice-monthly get-togethers. Dell hosted them at his place and these guys took their poker very seriously. "Yes," she said. "I'll be there."

"Bring your cash and valuables," he said.

Two weeks ago Jade had cleaned Adam out. He wanted his revenge. "There's going to be an ass-whooping tonight."

"Hmm," she said. "I'll bring my can of hair spray, too, in case it gets ugly."

He reached into the candy jar on the counter that Jade used to bribe little children into behaving. "You can't scare me like you do Dell."

She went still. "Is that what I do, scare him?"

Adam flashed her a look of sympathy that she didn't want. "Jade—"

"No, never mind." Standing, she nudged him clear of her area. "Okay, out you. I have to close up."

He managed to grab a handful of candy before she pushed him away. When she was alone, she looked at Gertie. "Men are annoying."

Gertie cocked her head in agreement, but Jade let out a low laugh. "Oh, who are you trying to kid? The minute he shows his face, you'll drop everything for him. Face it, Gert. You're a Dell 'ho."

Gertie grinned and drooled.

Jade sighed. She was a Dell 'ho, too. She finished closing up and got Beans into the carrier, surprised when she straightened to find Adam back in her space. "You didn't have to wait for me. The bad guys have been caught."

He shrugged. "Humor me." He paused. "And about Dell. He—"

"You don't have to explain him to me." She pointed to a stack of phone messages from the day, which she'd already entered onto a spreadsheet and sent to Dell's e-mail.

Adam picked up the messages and flipped through them. "Okay, Tina's his housekeeper. Shelly's a good friend of mine. She called me, too, wanting to know what to get the man of mystery for his birthday next month. I told her a kick in the ass. Amanda . . ." He lifted a shoulder and stared at that message. "Okay, that's a new one," he admitted, rubbing his jaw. "And probably not worth remembering."

Jade sighed. "She's a drug rep."

"And you think Dell's into her?"

"No," she admitted. "He took her to lunch last week when she drove in from Boise, and since then she's called twenty times, but he hasn't gotten back to her."

"And how many times has Melinda called?"

"Four, and there's two hang-ups, which thanks to the magic of caller ID, are also hers."

Adam just shook his head. "Christ, you two are a pair."

Dell was slumped in his dining room chair as he gathered his cards in. He'd lost.

To Jade.

Fitting, he thought. Since he'd already lost her—a fact that had been slammed home to him last night. Only a few weeks ago, what had happened in the clinic last night would have paralyzed her with fear and insecurity. But the self-defense he'd taught her had bolstered her confidence and given her some belief in herself.

And now she was going to use that newfound strength to leave here.

Great job, Connelly. Well done.

Jade was smiling as she gathered all his nickels and dimes in close, making careful, perfect stacks.

"So you have what," Lilah said to Jade. "A few weeks left?"

Jade didn't look up from her winnings. "About."

"Wish you wouldn't go," Lilah said. "We're going to miss you."

"You're the only one who can keep the knucklehead in line," Adam said in agreement.

The "knucklehead" didn't speak because if he did, it would be to utter the two words that had been stuck in his throat for so long he was choking on them.

Don't go.

"This was always a temporary situation," Jade reminded them softly. "But I'll miss you guys."

"Me too," Lilah said, and pulled Jade in for a tight hug, the full-body kind that only women could pull off. "You're leaving me here with all this testosterone, it's not fair."

"I'll visit," Jade said.

"Promise?"

"Promise."

Lilah sniffed and nodded and then composed herself. Jade did the same. And just like that, it was over and the two of them were smiling again.

Not Dell. He couldn't have smiled to save his life. His throat burned. Fucking burned.

Lilah filled the silence, talking about flying to Chicago to visit Jade and shop, flirting with her husband-to-be, making fun of Adam for losing when he wanted to win so bad.

Brady was just sitting there, clearly enjoying Lilah's antics. Adam was quiet, probably calculating his revenge hand.

"Love how you always kick their asses," Lilah said to Jade. "Promise me you'll fly in for our poker nights once you go home. Brady can get you in the chopper."

Brady nodded his agreement of that and Adam said something about how he'd have to start saving up for that since she kept killing him, but Dell couldn't joke about it. Hell, he couldn't hardly fucking breathe.

And how the hell *she* could, he had no idea.

Two weeks . . .

"My deal." Jade took the cards, shuffling like a pro. "Five-card stud. Deuces wild." She dealt, then surveyed her cards with that same little smile she always gave her hand.

She had a helluva poker face.

And if she'd looked like a naughty secretary yesterday, tonight she looked like a gambler's wet dream. Snug, silky, long-sleeved T-shirt with an equally snug vest that tied up the center into a bow between her breasts.

He wanted to tug on that tie with his teeth.

Her jeans were cut low, and when she leaned forward to collect her winnings or to toss her cards, her shirt rose a little, revealing a mind-melting strip of smooth, creamy skin.

And just the very tiniest hint of twin dimples above the best ass he'd ever seen.

Christ, she was killing him.

He drew two cards and came up with three tens and a deuce. He went all in.

Brady shook his head and folded. "Sucker."

Adam looked pained and also folded.

Lilah grinned but joined Adam and Brady in folding.

Jade pushed her money to the center of the table. She was in.

Dell looked into her eyes, and it might have been just the two of them—except for their audience, of course. The Three Stooges, watching them like a prime-time sitcom.

"You packing any heat?" Jade asked, studying his face.

"A little late to ask," he said. "You're all in."

"In more ways than one," she murmured. "Going to show me what you've got?"

In more ways than one? What did that mean? He revealed his cards. "Three of a kind."

Jade's brows went up. "Nice," she said, but stopped him when he leaned forward to collect the pile.

"Not so fast." She laid her hand out.

Full house.

Brady and Adam grimaced in tandem. Lilah chortled with glee.

Jade smiled and gathered the booty toward her. "You lost, Dr. Connelly. All of it."

Yeah. A feeling he was getting far too used to.

*   *   *

Much later, Dell was alone on his couch. He had his remote in hand, and Gertie doing her best imitation of a lap dog, leaving a good amount of slobber on his thigh.

A knock sounded at his door.

Not Adam or Brady. They'd left an hour ago, and besides, they both had keys and absolutely no care for Dell's privacy whatsoever. They'd just barge in.

Dell glanced at his watch. Two in the morning. Frowning, he shoved Gertie off him and headed to the door, glancing out his living room window as he did.

Jade's car was in the driveway.

What the hell? Gertie peeked, too, and gave a bark of wild enthusiasm.

Speeding up his pace Dell pulled open the door, reaching down to grab Gertie's collar just before she could launch herself at Jade.

"Gak," Gertie said, back paws on the ground, front paws in the air as Dell held her back.

"Were you sleeping?" Jade asked, her hands tightly clasped together. She sent a quick look over her shoulder as if the dark night was unnerving her. "You were totally sleeping, right? Never mind." She started to turn away, but Dell used his free hand to snare his second female of the night, catching Jade in the back of her jacket and reeling her to him. Because it was cold, he pulled both woman and dog into his house and shut the door.

Gertie shoved her face into Jade's palm, blithely demanding a rubdown, which Jade granted. Everyone seemed happy with the momentary distraction, especially Gert. After a moment, the dog shuffled back off to her spot on the couch.

"I—" Jade let out a breath. "I'm sorry if I woke you."

"I wasn't sleeping. I was just sitting here thinking of how broke I am."

She smiled, and he felt the usual reaction in his chest. And south. "Not that I'm complaining," he said. "But what are you doing back here?"

She hesitated. "Remember how when you were a kid and you knew something was a really bad idea, but you wanted to do it anyway, even when everyone from your nanny to your best friend told you it was stupid?"

He'd been moved around too much for best friends. Adam had fit the bill, but if Dell had gone to do something stupid, Adam had most likely been the ringleader. "Never had a nanny."

She nodded with a little grimace. "I knew that. I didn't mean . . . I just . . . The stupid thing. I'm trying to tell you about the stupid thing I want to do."

"The thing your nanny and best friend would try to talk you out of."

"Yes. But they're not here. And you . . ." She shook her head and walked into his living room and looked around.

"Forget something?"

"No, I was just sort of hoping to find your Adopt-a-Farm-Animal type of secret thing you do when you're alone."

"Guys have . . . different alone-time activities than women. Very different."

She laughed and dropped her coat to his couch. Okay, that meant she was staying, for at least a few minutes.

Or maybe not.

He'd long ago given up trying to read her mind. She'd changed out of her gambler's wet dream outfit and was now in a snug black sweat suit. The bottoms were contoured to her body. The hoodie was unzipped to just beneath her breasts and beneath was a lacy white number that fucked with his head. She entwined her fingers and looked at him.

He looked back.

With a sigh, she sank to his couch and patted the spot next to her.

He joined her, trying not to notice that she smelled like heaven on earth or that he managed to sit as close as he could without actually sitting on her. Which made him no better than his own damn dog.

"You haven't been yourself," she said softly. "You know, since we . . ."

Actually, to be technical, it had nothing to do with their night and everything to do with the fact that she was leaving Sunshine. But he had just enough pride to keep his mouth shut.

Barely.

Because if he opened it he'd do it. He'd say it.

Don't go.

So instead he did something even more dumb. He dragged her up against him and kissed her, because he remembered how good she tasted, remembered that soft, sexy as hell little sound she made when he touched his tongue to hers. Remembered what it had been like to be inside her, how she'd felt all silky soft and naked in his arms.

She kissed him back until he was hard with hunger and need, but even he knew it wasn't all physical. There was a deep and overwhelming longing within him, one he'd successfully buried for a long time but he was having trouble putting it away again.

"Dell?"

No. No talking, because he knew damn well the wrong thing would come out.

The begging.

Because God, really? What the fuck did he know about keeping a woman in his life? Not nearly enough to keep Jade with him, that was for damn sure.

Which didn't stop him from pushing her down to the cushions and covering her body with his to kiss her again.

"Aren't you going to ask me what stupid thing I wanted to do?" she whispered.

"Please, God," he breathed against her neck. "Say me."

She bit her lower lip but burst out laughing, anyway.

"Dell." She dropped her head to his chest. "This is all your fault. I just keep thinking about our night. I know it was a one time thing, it *has* to be a one time thing. I'm leaving, and you don't do more than one night things, and . . ." She lifted her head and looked at him beseechingly. "Can you help me out here? Be the voice of reason?"

"What do you expect me to say, *don't* want me? Are you kidding?"

"Tell me it was bad," she said. "Like . . . *bad* bad. So bad that we don't need to repeat it because it was so *bad*."

Letting out a breath, he opened his mouth.

She nodded, eager to hear what he might say.

"Jade."

"Say it."

"It was bad. So bad we should repeat it to learn from it."

She went still, then snorted. "Way to be strong."

He knew every bit as much as she that this shouldn't happen. It was risking too much. Someone was going to get hurt.

Too late for that . . .

And in any case, he couldn't let her go. In fact, his arms came around her and held on. "Jade, what the hell am I going to do with you?"

"Are you as scared as I am?"

"Terrified," he said. "Hold me."

She laughed but did just that. "You know," she said, mouth against his ear. "Someone once told me that when I'm in an unsure situation, calm assertive dominance is best."

He stroked a finger over her jaw, tucking a strand of hair behind her ear. "You want me to assert some calm dominance now? Over you?"

She shivered and her eyes darkened. "Maybe just this once . . ."

As he went from zero to sixty in less than a second, rising with her in his arms to head for his bed, he had to wonder just who was the one in control.

Sixteen

The next morning Jade slumped at her desk and eyed the clock as she yawned widely. It was only eight o'clock.

She'd gotten maybe three minutes of sleep the night before, and so had Dell. He had to be dragging every bit as much as her.

Bringing up the day's to-do list, she added, *Get a nap*.

Dell came in wearing work boots, low-slung jeans, a hoodie, and an opened down jacket, looking far more like a Hollywood version of the mountain vet than the real thing.

Except the dirt on his boots and the straw on his shoulder and back were real, and so were the shadows beneath his eyes.

Yep, he was dragging as much as she. Only he looked much better while doing it.

He pushed his sunglasses to the top of his head and looked at her, his cheeks ruddy from the cold air, a day's growth on his square jaw.

He'd been riding. She'd seen him out the window tearing across the meadow on Kiwi's back, the man and the

horse beautiful in the weak sun that was trying to burn
through the fog.

She looked around her for a distraction, but everything
was in place. Her pencils perfectly lined up. The files were
pulled. Peanut was on top of Jade's printer. Beans was curled
up on Jade's lap. Gertie lay at her feet, staring up at her with
love and adoration.

None of them needing a damn thing from her, for once.

"You were gone when I got up," he said.

"Had things to do," she said. "The boss is real demanding. I left you a note."

"Yes, thanking me for last night." His gaze held hers.
"You sneaked out."

"Don't be ridiculous," she said.

"You *sneaked*."

Okay, she had. She'd held her breath and slipped out
of his warm, strong arms, grabbing her clothes off his floor
and dressing on her way to the front door. "Fine!" She
stood up and tossed her hands high. "I sneaked out. Are you
telling me no woman's ever sneaked out on you before?"

The look on his face answered her question, and with a
sigh of disgust, she started to turn away, but he took her by
the arms and lifted her up so they were nose to nose.

She wasn't sure where he was going with this, but by the
sparks in his eyes she was going to guess maybe some more
calm, assertive dominance . . .

Suddenly the door opened and in came Keith, with Mike
right behind him. And then Adam. All three stopped short
and stared at the two of them.

Dell set Jade back down and she backed away from him,
attempting a smile. "Morning," she said, and turned to her
workstation. She felt Dell looking down at her but she didn't
meet his gaze.

"Is everything okay?" Mike asked.

"Yes," Jade said, and felt Dell move off. She let out a

low breath and watched him go, then turned and nearly ran smack into Adam.

He picked up the schedule she'd printed out for him, and studied it. "Going to be a long day," he said.

He wasn't kidding.

At lunch Jade locked the front door after Dell and Adam left for their usual cholesterol overload. She looked around at the empty place and tried to rub the matching ache between her breasts.

She couldn't.

She and Dell had spoken several times since their . . . what had it been, a fight? Not exactly. There'd been no raised voices, no slammed doors, no pouting or brooding.

But things were off. He hadn't laughed when Peanut had announced to a room full of waiting patients that she had a "crush on doc."

He hadn't teased her when she'd brought him the lab reports to go over. He hadn't let his eyes warm when he looked at her. Actually, he hadn't looked at her.

With a sigh, she put in her earphones, cranked her iPod and turned to the accounting.

Her version of relaxing.

Now that she finally had all the accounts entered, it was sheer joy to balance the numbers out every day, and she watched with great satisfaction as reports ran down her screen.

Pink came on, her voice a gorgeous low, husky rock-and-roll rasp. Jade loved Pink. Pink was strong. Invincible. "You're fucking perfect," Jade sang along with the song, standing up to put more paper in her printer. Fucking perfect . . .

Dell. Dell was fucking perfect.

She couldn't help it, then, the song demanded it. She was already standing so her body moved with the music. It was her line dancing teacher's fault, she used this song sometimes, the PG-rated version, of course. With a little shimmy, Jade whirled and—dammit!—came face-to-face with Dell and Adam.

With a surprised yelp, she yanked out her earplugs and searched for her dignity.

There was none to be found.

"Do you think she was singing to you or me?" Dell asked Adam.

"Me," Adam said. "You're nowhere close to fucking perfect."

Oh God. Jade put her hands to her very hot cheeks.

"You might want to try a dance class," Bessie said, coming through with her push broom. "You're stiff as my broom."

"I'm in a dance class," Jade said.

"Maybe you should get a refund."

"I thought she moved pretty good," Dell said.

Jade would have shot him a shut-up-and-die look, but she was too embarrassed to meet anyone's gaze directly.

"I could teach you some moves," Bessie said, planting her broom right in the middle of the room and giving a little hip shaking boogey that had some parts of her jiggling more than others. Since Bessie was five foot two, both vertically *and* horizontally, she nearly gave herself a black eye, but she looked pleased with herself. "Yeah," she said. "I still got it. I'd show you my never-fail-to-get-me-some move, but the last time I tried it out for Mr. Southwick, I pulled something in my hindquarters. Had to go to the doctor and everything."

Dell grinned.

Even Adam was smiling.

Jade sank to her chair and stared at the phone. Why did it never ring when she needed it to? She did her best to look busy. Busy while sweaty and out of breath. She heard footsteps move away from her and she sighed in relief.

They'd left her alone.

"I like your moves," came Dell's low voice near her ear, making her jump. He put his hands on the armrests of her chair and whipped her around to face him.

"Everyone should dance on their lunch break."

She tried to glare at him but he wasn't laughing at her. His eyes were dark. And warm. "Don't be mad. Seeing you so comfortable here is the sexiest thing I've ever seen."

She gave him a push but she might as well have tried to move a brick wall. "You think everything's sexy."

He shook his head. "I'm pretty sure it's just you."

She hesitated. "Dell, are we okay?"

"You mean because of this morning?"

"Yeah."

"I don't know. Why did you leave like that, like I was your dirty little secret?"

There was something in his voice now. Same tone, but there was definitely something new. Temper, she realized. He was always so careful to show the world nothing but easygoing and laid-back no matter what the circumstances. For some crazy reason, seeing the extra depth went a long way toward defusing her.

Maybe because she knew that if he was showing her his feelings, she meant something to him. "I had to get to work," she said. "That's all."

"Or . . ."

"There's no 'or,'" she said, not sounding nearly as calm as him. She was good at hiding in a very different way than he was.

"There's definitely an 'or,'" he said. "You didn't trust yourself with me."

Okay, now that was annoying. Mostly because it was true. "I stayed all night. I trusted you right through what, a half box of condoms?"

He nodded agreeably, but she had his number now. He was feeling anything but agreeable. "So this is just sex," he said.

She stared at him, unable to believe that this had gotten so off track. "Is it ever anything else for you?"

For a moment there was a sort of horrible beat of weighted, awkward silence, and she'd have given just about anything to take back the words, but Dell let out a mirthless laugh. "Okay, let me get this straight," he said. "You tiptoeing off in the middle of the night is my fault?"

"It was dawn, Dell."

"Fuck, Jade." He pressed the heels of his hands to his eyes. "Uncle. I give up. I can't guess anymore. You're going to have to come right out and tell me."

"Tell you what?" She knew what, she knew exactly what, but she needed to buy herself a second. Or a bunch of seconds.

He dropped his hands to his sides. "What the hell I have to do so that you'll feel safe with me."

"I do!"

"With your body, maybe." He gave a slow shake of his head. "When I'm buried deep inside you and you're panting out my name, wrapped tight around me . . . yeah, you know you're safe with me, then, that I'll take you where you want to go. But any other time it's like pulling teeth to get you to tell me things about you."

Panic licked at her. "You know me."

"Some things, like you snub your nose at almost all crap food—except ice cream. Ice cream you hoard like it's your crack. You like your clothes and yet you don't mind getting animal hair on them. You have to have things in careful order because it makes you feel in control, and yet there's one area you like to be just a little bit messy and unorganized."

"Uh—"

"In bed," he said bluntly. "In bed you don't mind giving up control."

She blushed. "See that? You do know me."

He was already shaking his head. "It's not enough."

"What could you possibly want to know that you think you don't?" she asked.

"Why you're really here. What your life was like in Chicago. What happened to you to make you leave. Why you slowly came to life here, and yet you're still going back."

The little ball of anxiety in her chest, the one that had been there since she'd slept with him and then done something even worse, started to fall for him, grew and spread so that she couldn't breathe. "You say that like you're an open book," she managed.

His eyes never left hers. "I am an open book, Jade. For you. I may be a little slow on the uptake in the emotion department, but you can ask me anything and I'll answer."

Would he? His expression was intent. Focused.

And wrenchingly, bluntly open.

He meant it. She could ask him anything. Like . . . was he falling, too?

Except . . .

Except she wasn't ready for the answer.

"Only you won't ask me anything, will you, Jade? Because you're good with this, just as it is. And hell, why not? It's all I ever do, right?"

"Dell," she said softly in regret. She'd hurt him. She'd never even known she could.

"Give me a few minutes before you let Keith bring any patients back," he said, and vanished into his office.

There was little that got to Dell. Abuse or neglect of any kind. Someone fucking with someone he cared about.

But a woman? A woman hadn't gotten to him in a long time, if ever.

Which was what made the way he felt about Jade so difficult. He'd been waiting for her to make the next move. He'd been waiting for a week now, and he wasn't good with waiting. In fact, he sucked at it, mostly because he'd never done it before.

Adam thought he was an idiot. Dell was leaning toward agreeing with him.

Brady thought he should cut his losses and forget it. After all, she was leaving.

But Dell couldn't fold, not yet. He wanted . . . Christ. He wanted so much it hurt.

And yet it had to be *her* move . . .

It was the end of a very long day. Still in scrubs, he stood at the window watching a storm move in—not nearly as nice a view as the one from his desk if he leaned forward just so to catch a glimpse of Jade—but definitely safer.

Besides, he'd watched her enough today. Just a few minutes ago she'd been checking out Ashes, an Australian blue heeler, who'd managed to stab herself on a low-lying branch in the woods. The branch had caused considerable damage to Ashes, requiring surgery, a drain, and multiple visits. Nick, Ashes's owner, was an out-of-work construction worker who faithfully paid cash for each visit. He'd been standing there meticulously counting out money from his wallet and must have fallen short because Jade covered his hand and shook her head, sending him on his way.

Once Nick had left, she'd gotten up and added three twenties to the cash box.

From her own purse.

Behind Dell, he heard the click click clicking of heels coming down the hall toward him. Jade, of course. And given the attitude in every step she made, she'd discovered what he'd done and they were heading for their second fight in three, two, one . . .

She stalked into his office and stopped, hands on hips, giving him that teacher to errant pupil look that always made him so hot.

She didn't speak.

He could appreciate the tactic but he wasn't in the mood.

Besides, there was little he could do to get on her good side now. And it wasn't as if she cared about getting on *his* good side. "Problem?" he asked calmly.

"You know there is."

Her legs looked ten miles long in the skirt she was wearing today, and her cute little boots had given him dirty thoughts all day long. He really liked watching what he'd come to think of as the Jade show. Today, for instance, after getting caught dancing—Christ, he'd loved that—she'd sat at her desk, doing that little OCD thing she did with her pencils, lining them up perfectly, making her lists.

And she was leaving . . .

She ran his office, she managed his life, she made things . . . easy for him. Easy and good.

And in return he'd thought he was giving her something. Stability. Comfort. Safety.

When he pictured his world without her in it, something funny happened inside him.

He went cold.

She held up her paycheck. "This, Dell. This is the problem. My paycheck. It isn't right."

"No?"

"You know it isn't." She set it on his desk, then stabbed at it with her finger, pushing it across the wood surface toward him. "You seem to have given me a raise."

"Are you objecting?"

"Hell no. I've earned it. But double? You nearly doubled my salary?"

She was wearing peach gloss today, and he gave brief thought to yanking her onto his lap and settling this pent-up anger between them in the age-old way of the Neanderthal caveman dwellers.

He wasn't sure why he was giving her this big push now. It felt an awful lot like desperation, a last-ditch effort to see if she'd stay.

"Dell."

"You're doing the work of office manager and full-charge bookkeeper," he said. "I'm just giving you the money that goes with it. You're getting what's fair."

"This is hardly fair."

"No? Okay, how much more do you think—"

"Oh my God, you are the most stubborn-ass, confusing, arrogant man on the planet!"

"So I take it that you're not going to thank me for the raise by having your way with me then?"

She smacked him upside the back of the head with the envelope. Figuring that fighting back was fair, he went with the caveman urge and yanked her into his lap. He slid one hand to the nape of her neck, the other to her waist and leaned in, pressing his forehead to hers. "To first blood or the death?"

"I feel like we've already drawn blood." But she melted into him a little, his favorite ice princess, and for a long beat they just breathed each other's air.

"I know what you're doing," she finally whispered.

"Do you?"

"Yes." She cupped his face. "You're woman-whispering me with the alpha-dog move, touching my neck, pretending to be trying to get lucky to throw me off, but you're really doing the whole calm, assertive domination thing."

"No, the domination thing would be stripping you naked and sprawling you out on my desk so I could—"

"Dell." She shook her head but gave herself away by biting her lower lip and glancing at his desktop. "I can't take the raise or the job."

"You already have the job, Jade."

"But—"

"You're leaving," he said. "Yeah. Believe me, I know."

"Do you? Do you really? Then why haven't you put out an ad for my replacement? I could train them."

Fuck, how he hated that idea.

She sighed and dropped her head to his shoulder. With

a sigh of his own, Dell slid his hand down her back for the sheer pleasure of touching her. "Just tell me this. *Why* are you going back? Is it for duty or because you miss your life there?"

"What's the difference?"

"Missing your life is one thing. And a good reason to go. You tell me it's because you miss your life and I'll step back and be happy for you."

"And if it's duty?"

He gave a slow shake of his head. "I don't see how that can be a good enough reason to give up your life."

"And I don't see how that's your call," said a male voice from the doorway.

The guy was thirtyish, leanly muscled, and dressed like he was heading to an A-list event. And he was apparently familiar to Jade because she leapt out of Dell's arms with a surprised gasp.

"The front door was unlocked," the guy said. "But the front desk was deserted, so . . ."

"You're . . . here," Jade said, and walked into his arms.

Dell couldn't see Jade's face, but he could see the guy's as he squeezed Jade, his expression a grimace of relief and love, his hands fisting on her sweater as if he couldn't get enough. Jade appeared to be doing the same and Dell stood, fighting an entirely different Neanderthal caveman dweller urge now.

Jade finally pulled back from the warm hug and smacked the man hard in the chest. "I told you not to come here," she said.

"And I listened. For a year and a half." He tugged on a strand of Jade's hair. "Now introduce me to the man who just had his hands on you and is looking like maybe he wants to kill me."

Jade looked back at Dell, not giving much away. "Dell, this is my cousin Dr. Sam Bennett. Sam, this is Dr. Dell Connelly, my . . . boss."

At the slight hesitation, Sam's mouth twisted into a wry smile. "Interesting inner-office policies," he said directly to Dell, eyes cool in a way they hadn't been with Jade.

"Sam," Jade admonished, and pushed him toward the door, adding a little push. "Wait for me by the front desk." She added a second shove, then when Sam was gone, turned back to Dell. "Sorry about that. He's a little protective."

Dell just looked at her, willing her to talk to him without him having to give her the inquisition, but this was Jade. The Queen of Emotional Fortress.

"I'll see you tomorrow," she said. "Okay? We'll discuss this"—she pointed to her paycheck—"further."

"That's not first on my list," he said.

Her eyes met his and something happened. The air condensed and a fierce hunger gutted him.

Her expression mirrored what he felt and it was staggering. "I won't be here tomorrow," he reminded her. "I'm flying up north for the next few days to cover the ranches I'm under contract with."

"That's right." She nodded. "Monday, then." She started to leave the room, but paused and moved toward him instead. "Dell, I—"

He had no idea what she meant to say. He didn't care. His circuits had crossed and rather than go back to his desk, he reached for her.

She met him halfway and slid her hands into his hair as he hauled her up against him. Their mouths collided in a hard, deep kiss. No tenderness, not an ounce. In its place was a boatload of frustration and aggression, which was working for him until she abruptly pulled away and, with one last look, left him. Dell told himself to get used to it.

But he was starting to think that wasn't going to happen.

Seventeen

Jade cooked Sam dinner that night. She waited until her second glass of wine kicked in to ask. "Why are you really here?"

He smiled at her, as always utterly at ease in his skin. Which, given how handsome he was, couldn't have been too difficult. "Thought maybe you missed me," he said.

"Hard to, when you call me every day."

"Every two days, tops."

She shook her head, having to admit it was good to see him. "You know I'm coming back. You didn't have to show up."

"Sandy crashed the computer system."

"You flew here to tell me that? Aren't you busy? Don't you have any patients to see? Who's in charge?"

"See? We need you." He smiled. "Had frequent-flier mileage and a day off."

"We both know that Sandy's actually more qualified than me," Jade said. "She's a CPA." Sandy had been promoted from accounts manager, where she'd worked only part-time because she liked being home with her kids.

Everyone was happy with her work performance, though Jade's family complained that she had the personality of a pencil. "There's no way she crashed the computer system."

"Okay, she didn't," Sam admitted. "But she did leave coffee rings on your desk. Your pencils are homeless. And she doesn't use spreadsheets. She scribbles her notes on sticky pads and slaps them everywhere. It's raining yellow sticky notes."

Jade opened her mouth, then shut it again. "Some people don't find spreadsheets all that effective."

There was a beat of disbelieving silence from Sam on this. "Okay, who are you and what have you done with my favorite cousin?"

"Your only cousin."

"Jade."

"Sam."

"I mean you didn't even comment about the pencils. The pencils, Jade, are all over your desk every night. There's no organization. And she's not filing daily either, she's—"

Jade tried to ignore the pencils, but it took an embarrassing amount of effort. "I *am* coming back, Sam. By the first, as I promised you."

He was quiet a minute, his gaze reflective as he looked around at her loft. "But you're happy here."

She paused. "I am."

"You look it. You look good, Jade. Not like your old-self good but different good. Maybe even better good."

She didn't know what to do with that so she picked up the wine bottle and refilled both their glasses.

"You going to ever tell me about him?" Sam asked quietly.

"Who?"

Sam gave her an impressive eye roll. "The guy who had his hands all over you who."

"He . . . I . . ." She blew out a breath and shook her head.

"No." Dell was hers, and maybe she'd blown it with him in more ways than one, but if nothing else she'd forever have the memory of how he'd given her life back to her.

"He means something to you," Sam said.

He meant everything to her. "How do you know he's not just a wild fling?"

"You don't do wild flings. You don't do anything without your entire heart and soul."

"Yeah, well," she said, "do me a favor and don't let that secret out of the bag."

Sympathy and worry filled his eyes now, and he opened his mouth, but she jabbed a finger in his direction. "Don't do that. Don't suddenly start feeling bad for badgering me to come back."

"If I badgered—"

"*If?*"

"Okay, *when* I badgered, it was because I thought you were alone. I didn't want you to be alone."

She sighed. "It's a done deal. I've given notice to my landlord."

"And your boss?"

"And my boss," she said as evenly as she could, ignoring the little pang to her heart at the thought of leaving Dell. "But this was always a temp position. A service will fill it for him with no problem."

"But—"

"No. No buts. And no second-guessing or regrets. If there's one thing I've learned, it's that neither of those things does anyone any good."

On Sunday, Jade took Sam to the airport and went into work. She did that sometimes, went into the office to catch up on paperwork or clean up. She couldn't help herself. She went straight to her desk, pulled up her to-do-at-work list and got to it.

One of the things she wanted to do before she left Sunshine was upgrade Dell's computer system, so that things would run smoothly when she was gone. It was a perfect day for it, so she called Dell's cell just to make sure he wasn't going to be trying to access the system remotely.

When he answered, he sounded breathless and in a hurry, and then she remembered: he was still up north.

Melinda's ranch was up north.

"Connelly," he said again.

Clearly he hadn't looked at the caller ID. Jade paused, thinking about all the reasons why he'd be breathless and too harried to look at the screen. The number-one item was because he was in Melinda's bed.

In Melinda.

God. A root canal without drugs would be preferable to this, and her thumb hovered over the End button.

"Hello?" There was some rustling noise, then, "Jade?"

Great. *Now* he looks at the ID screen.

"Jade, you there?"

"Yes." She winced. "Listen, sorry to interrupt. Forget I called." She disconnected and tossed her phone into her purse. From the depths, it began to vibrate so she grabbed her entire purse and shoved it into a drawer where she couldn't hear it anymore.

That night, Dell and Adam were sparring in Dell's basement gym. They were going at each other street style, no rules, fighting dirty.

It suited Dell's mood. He'd been gone for three days, attending to his ranch accounts, working around the clock. He'd been getting in the chopper with Brady when Jade had called and then hung up on him. There'd been something in her voice that he hadn't liked, but she'd ignored his subsequent calls. By the time he'd gotten back to Sunshine, she was nowhere to be found. He'd tried the office, her place, Lilah's . . .

Finally, he'd left her a "Jade, call me now" message, born out of sheer frustration.

She hadn't called.

He and Adam were pretty evenly matched until the sound of soft footsteps coming down the stairs caught Dell's attention. He turned his head to see Jade in a fuzzy sweater, gauzy short skirt, and those boots of hers that always corroded all common sense. He opened his mouth to greet her and found himself eating the mat. When he could gasp some air into his lungs, he rolled to his back.

Adam was gone.

Jade was on her knees at his side. Actually, there were two Jades.

No, three. Dell closed his eyes. "Where did he go?"

"Home. Said he didn't want to embarrass you when you tried to retaliate and got your ass kicked for the second time."

Jesus. "I'll kill him later." With care, he got to his knees and then stood up, pulling her with him. No way in hell was she getting away. "Want to tell me what that was about earlier?"

"No. I want you to show me that move. The one Adam just flattened you with."

"Well, I wouldn't say flatten exactly. I—"

"Show me."

"It's a rough one—"

"Show me."

He showed her. He had to do it several times, it was a complicated move. Each time she hit the mat and was slower to get up. "Jade—"

"Again."

Determination and grit blared from her every pore. No fear, no hesitation, just as he'd taught her himself. So

damn if he'd tell her she'd had enough. They went over it
again.

And again she landed on her back. But this time she
stayed down, eyes closed, face pale and damp.

Goddammit. Dell swore and dropped to his knees at her
side, planting a hand on either side of her hips. "Jade. Jade,
talk to me, are you—"

With both hands she pushed hard, right into the crook of
his elbows.

With a surprised "oomph" his arms collapsed and he fell
over the top of her. "Christ, Jade. I'm sorry, I—"

She brought her knee up. Not hard or fast enough to hurt
him but only because she held back. Purposely. Protecting
the goods, he pressed her flat, holding her there with his
body and regarded her warily. "You're mad at me."

"Well, give the doctor an A plus."

Yeah, she was right. It'd taken him long enough. Slowly,
aware that she could absolutely unman him if she wanted,
he pulled back and sat up. "What did I do?"

"You're breathing, aren't you?"

He paused. "Is this about the other day at the center?
Because you're the one who said that this was just sex," he
reminded her grimly.

She narrowed her eyes.

No, not about that. Apparently he was the only one
brooding about that. Pretty fucking pathetic given that the
just sex thing had always been his own MO.

"This isn't about the other day."

He mentally hit rewind on the past few days. He'd flown
up north. Worked his ass off. Stayed in a hotel with Brady,
which had pissed off Melinda, but he hadn't wanted to be
with her. Not that he could explain why when she'd asked.
Hell, he couldn't even explain it to himself. Being with Melinda had always been great. Fun. Easy. No strings attached—
his favorite way to have sex.

But when she'd leaned into kiss him, he'd yearned for a

different set of arms and a touch that turned on his mind as well as his body. "Jade, you're going to have to give me a hint."

"Okay, you're spoiled and egotistical and annoying." She fisted her hands in his shirt. He figured she was going to shove him farther away but she hauled him back down over her. "And you're an orgasm hog."

He choked. "What—"

"Yeah. And I really, really, really want to hate you, but I can't. I'm going to settle for intense dislike."

He shook his head, trying to loosen some reason, because either he'd had his clock more royally cleaned by Adam than he'd thought, or she'd gone off the deep end. "I'll cop to the spoiled, egotistical, annoying accusations. But back to that orgasm thing—"

"God, you are such a . . . *guy*! That's all you heard, right? Orgasm? I mean you *just* slept with Melinda and you still—"

"Okay, whoa." He shook his head and laughed. In hindsight, that might have been a mistake because Jade turned wildcat beneath him. He actually nearly lost his grip on her because she and that damn effective knee nearly took out his entire future line of Connelly's. "What the fuck, Jade."

"You're the one who keeps telling me to hit the groin area. I've never had angry sex, but I want to have it now."

He shook his head, trying to both focus and hold her down at the same time. Not easy. Good to know he'd been successful at teaching her to fight. He might have taken pride in that except he was very busy trying to protect himself and not hurt her in the process. He shoved a leg between hers and she countered by wrapping one of hers around his waist to try to roll him. He could feel every inch of her plastered up against him. If he wasn't so confused, he'd be turned on as hell.

No, scratch that. Even with the confusion, he *was* turned on as hell. "You think I slept with Melinda . . ."

"I don't care." She was breathing heavy, still struggling beneath him. "You don't do relationships, so why should I care?" She nipped his jaw with her teeth, eyes hot and clearly pissed off, which for some sick reason really worked for him. "Jade—"

"Don't talk. There's no talking in angry sex."

Right. Because angry or not, this was just sex. But then she squeezed his ass at the same time she bit his lower lip, and his dick bypassed his brain, going instantly hard as a rock. "Jade, I'm all sweaty."

"Don't care about that, either."

He felt like he'd been clubbed over the head. Everything about her said Furious-but-Aroused Female and while he stared at her, suddenly so turned on himself he could hardly breathe, she hauled him down to her and kissed him, shutting down the rest of his remaining operating brain cells.

Eighteen

Jade hadn't come here for this, for Dell's amazing mouth on hers, his hands on her body, the rough rumble of a very sexy, very turned-on man as he tried to eat her alive.

Oh, wait. She totally had.

Maybe after three long days of stewing about some of the things they'd said, on top of months and months of denying her feelings for him, all while pretending that what was happening between them wasn't really happening, her body had taken over her brain.

And though she'd been the one to instigate the kiss, Dell had certainly taken over, capturing her lips in a long, deep sensual kiss that had melted all her bones. She was still flat on her back on the mat with him holding her down when she heard herself moan. He straightened his arms, pulling back an inch to stare at her.

She wasn't sure what she was looking for, but evidently he found it in her expression because then he was kissing her again; hot open-mouth kisses along her jaw to her neck.

She moaned again and gripped him tighter, shifting her

head to the side to give him better access, which he took, nibbling at the base of her throat before sucking the skin there into his mouth. It was as if he'd pulled a cord weaved through her very center and her hips thrust against his.

"Not here," he said, voice rough, his mouth never pausing in its quest, moving along her collarbone now. "Not on the mats. I need a shower, and we're going to take our time. *Not* here," he repeated.

"*Here*." Her fingers slid into his hair to direct his face back to hers. "Now. Right now, you . . . you—"

"Orgasm hog?" he offered.

"Why are you still talking?" she asked, tearing at his shirt. She could hear the need in her own voice and didn't care, didn't care about anything other than getting him inside of her.

He made a noise deep in his throat and came up on his knees to yank his shirt over his head, tossing it aside.

God, he had a beautiful body. While she was admiring it, he shoved her skirt up.

"My boots," she said.

"The boots stay." Still on his knees, he tugged the straps of her bra to her elbows and watched as her breasts popped out the top of her demibra. "You are the most beautiful thing I've ever seen," he murmured hoarsely, taking her in from messed up hair to boot-covered feet.

The words shouldn't have moved her. This was nothing more than a mutual satisfying of needs. Not emotion-based. *Need*-based. But she shivered with desire. "Why are you still talking?"

"I can multitask." He stroked a finger over her lace panties. "So demanding on the outside, so tough." He slid his finger beneath the lace, unerringly finding the exact spot to have her writhing beneath him. "So soft and creamy on the inside."

She made a sound that revealed her desperation, and he

lifted his intense gaze from what he was doing to look at her. "Be sure, Jade. Because once we get on this train, we're riding it home."

"Do I feel like I'm not sure?"

"Fuck, no. You feel ready for me. You feel amazing." Leaning over her, he kissed her hard and deep, then pulled back to look at her sprawled out beneath him, then swore reverently beneath his breath. His body was hard all over and she wanted him. Tired of thinking, she planted her feet on the floor, knees bent, and grinded shamelessly against him, drawing a groan from him.

Good. Rearing up, she licked her way over a pec, flicked at his nipple, and headed downward, nibbling at his six-pack abs. Loving how unsteadily he was breathing, she pulled at the drawstring of his shorts and dipped her hand inside.

She didn't have to reach very far to wrap her fingers around his silky hard length.

He groaned and she watched the muscles of his abs contract as she tightened her grip and stroked. Then she tugged the shorts to his thighs and leaned in to tease him with her tongue.

"Oh Christ," he gasped. "That's good." His hands went to her hair and tightened for a minute, his head falling back on his shoulders.

But then he pulled free.

In one smooth motion, he rose fluidly to his feet and grabbed her up in his arms.

She wrapped her legs around his waist and lifted her head for a kiss. Holding her up with a hand on her ass, the other still in her hair, he started moving.

Up the basement steps.

Through the kitchen.

Up another set of stairs.

Into a dark room and then . . .

A bathroom.

"Condoms," he said, and plopped her on the counter. He yanked open a drawer and then another, swearing as he rifled through them.

"Why aren't they by your bed?"

He glanced at her. "I told you, I don't bring women here. And while we're talking again, I didn't sleep with Melinda. Haven't in months. Haven't slept with anyone but you. So really, if anyone's been an orgasm hog, it's you. If you go by sheer ratio, anyway . . ."

She stared at his broad back as he tried his last drawer, swearing roughly as he emptied it out on the counter. Comb, deodorant, new toothpaste . . .

Box of condoms, unopened.

"Thank Christ," he said fervently and tore the box open. Grabbing one, he turned to her, reaching out as if to pick her up again, probably to take her to his bed.

She didn't want that. That would be personal. That would be lovemaking, and she'd come for sex.

Angry sex. Because she'd been so angry. Or hurt. Actually it was some terrible combination, but he kept defusing her without even trying. Dammit. Dammit, how was she supposed to hold on to her temper with him? And she *needed* to hold on to it, needed that badly because with angry sex, she couldn't mistake this for anything else. Or so she hoped. So she snatched the condom from him. Hands freed, he used them on her, gliding them up her torso to her breasts. Her nipples were still peeking out of the demibra, and he bent and kissed her right nipple, then drew it into his mouth, sucking until she clutched at him.

He kissed his way to her other breast.

Her head fell back against the mirror, her body humming with need. "Dell," she said, her boots clunking against the cabinet below.

He ran a hand down her leg to her ankle, lifting it so that the bottom of her boot rested on the countertop, effectively opening her to his gaze.

Stepping back, he looked his fill and groaned again, then grabbed her hips and rocked into her. At her needy whimper, he slid a hand across her belly and then beneath her panties, expertly stroking her with the calloused pad of his fingers before moving one into her. She heard herself cry out and bit her lip.

"No," he said. "I want to hear you." He scraped the lace to the side to watch as he teased her slippery folds until she writhed and cried out again.

"Yeah," he said. "Like that. More, Jade."

"In," she gasped. This wasn't like her. She didn't sit naked except for boots on counters with her legs spread, she didn't demand sex, she didn't talk dirty, but she couldn't stop herself. Not with Dell. "I need you inside me," she said. "I need you in me now."

But he wasn't done with her yet because first he drew the agonizing torture out until her toes curled, until sensations were flowing through her hot, heavy body, until she was an inch from bursting. Then he replaced his fingers with a most impressive erection, pushing into her body inch by delicious inch. When he finally began to move, she gave herself over to the pleasure.

God, the pleasure. "*Please.*"

"Anything, Jade. Anything you want."

"You." It was all she could manage as he changed the angle of his penetration, making her gasp and clutch at him. "Just you."

He began to move, one hand gripping her bottom, the other sliding between them, using his thumb to apply exquisite pressure on her swollen flesh.

It sent her skittering right off the edge, crying out his name, barely conscious of the fact that he followed her over, gripping her in his big hands as he came hard, grinding his hips to hers to savor the last of the pleasure.

When she came back to herself, she realized she'd snuggled into his arms, her face pressed to his throat. He was nuzzling her hair, his breathing as ragged as hers. "You okay?" he murmured.

Still unable to speak, she settled for nodding. But her head was spinning. Because that? That had been a hell of a lot more than angry sex. "I need some room."

"Why?"

"Because I'm still mad at you."

"You're still mad at me?" he repeated, clearly baffled by this.

She sighed. "You didn't sleep with Melinda," she explained.

Dell lifted his head and blinked once, slow as an owl. "So you were mad when you thought I slept with Melinda, and now you're mad because . . . I didn't?"

She hopped off the counter. "I have to go." She adjusted her bra and panties and looked around for her clothes, remembering she'd left them in the basement.

Great.

"Jade." He blocked her exit. "What the hell are we doing? Tell me what's going on."

Admit that she'd done the unforgettable and fallen for him? No thank you. "Move, please."

"No."

Fine. He wasn't going to let this go so she searched her brain for a plausible lie. "I wanted to give you your messages."

He looked at her. "Try that again, your left eye twitched."

"So?"

"It always twitches when you lie."

Dammit. She put her finger to her eye.

"Jade."

She blew out a breath. "You already know."

"Tell me, anyway."

"Fine, but it's not pretty. I thought you were having sex with Melinda. And . . . I turned a ridiculous, ugly shade of green."

He went brows up.

She tossed up her hands. "And even though I told myself that was great, that you could do whoever you wanted, I kept picturing it . . ." She closed her eyes. "And I got . . . I don't know."

"Green."

"Yeah." She covered her face. "Maybe."

He pulled her hands down. "Green looks good on you."

A terrible confusing combination of annoyed and amused, Jade walked out of the bathroom, cursing herself for having to make the walk of shame through his entire house for her clothes. She couldn't find her shirt fast enough, so she grabbed his.

"You don't have to go," he said as she shimmied back into her skirt.

"Yes, I do."

Because it was getting harder and harder to hold her heart from him. In fact, if she kept this up, she knew she wouldn't be able to do it at all.

"Jade."

Throat tight, eyes burning, she turned back, then gasped softly as he cupped her face and kissed her. If he'd kissed her long and deep, she might have been able to resist, but he was far more devious than that. His mouth was devastatingly gentle. Tender. A sweet good-night kiss.

But not a good-bye kiss.

Oh, damn, she thought when he pulled away and walked her out to her car. Damn. She was in big trouble.

The next day Jade got out of bed before dawn. Actually, to be exact, it was four thirty A.M. It wasn't a time she'd seen often and she yawned more than once on the drive.

She'd watched the calendar and told herself she was merely indulging her curiosity, but she knew it was more than that.

Much more.

She pulled back onto Dell's street less than seven hours after she'd left and saw that his truck was still there. Finding it unlocked, she sighed in relief and climbed in to wait. Ten minutes later his front door opened. It was still dark, but she could see his outline as he headed for his truck carrying what looked like grocery bags and his medical bag.

He stopped short, presumably at the sight of her car. Then he turned to his truck. She gave him a little wave.

He walked through the dark, foggy, chilly morning, stowed his stuff behind his seat, and angled in behind the wheel. "You didn't want to stay last night, so what's this?"

"You said I could ask you anything, that you're an open book."

"Yes," he said, with a great deal of wariness.

"Where are you going?"

He paused. "If you're asking, you must already know."

"All I know is that every Monday, you start about a half hour late. And until I got my hands on your laptop, I had no idea why. But you're going somewhere and providing your services to someone, a bunch of someones, who clearly mean a lot to you. I figure it can't be too close or you'd just have them come to Belle Haven. So I got here extra early just in case."

"Jade, why does this matter to you?"

Because you matter . . . "You said you wanted to get to know me. Maybe I feel the same."

He studied her a long moment, then shook his head but started his truck.

They drove for an hour straight out into the middle of nowhere before Dell turned off at some invisible landmark, because Jade sure as hell didn't see a sign. Or even a road. He switched into four-wheel drive and kept going.

"Getting nervous?" he asked when she white-knuckled the dash over a particular bad rut.

"It has occurred to me that out here would be a great

dump site for my body." The next rut nearly rattled her teeth right out of her head. "Probably I should stop watching *Criminal Minds* before bed, it makes me see a serial killer in everyone."

"I know something else you could do before bed . . ."

Yeah, yeah.

He flashed a grin in the rising dawn. "You know, you hopped into my truck. I didn't coerce you."

"My mistake."

After another ten minutes, they began to pass some signs of civilization. Mobile homes and trailers, each more run down than the last. He parked in front of a double-wide with bars on the windows and turned to her, smile gone. "You can wait here if you want."

"Are you going to tell me what this is about?"

"I told you. Pro bono work for people who can't afford pet care."

She knew there was more, it was in every line of his body, but he said nothing more, just grabbed his black medical bag and got out. He waited for her, and together they walked to the trailer.

It was that brief beat of time between dark and dawn. Purple and pink light hovered in the air, made evanescent by a low-lying fog.

The door to the trailer opened before Dell could knock, revealing a woman somewhere in her fifties. She had dark skin, dark eyes and dark hair streaked through with silver. She took a look at Dell, then Jade, and arched a brow.

The movement, the subtle, almost wry surprise, was so instantly recognizable to Jade that she almost gasped.

The woman was clearly related to Dell.

Stepping back, she allowed them access without a word.

Dell set his hand on the small of Jade's back and urged her into the trailer. He didn't introduce her to the woman. In fact, he pretty much dismissed both of them and walked through to the small living area.

There, lining a bench, sat a small crowd, each person with an animal.

Dell sat at a nearby table, opened his bag, and pulled out his laptop. This he thrust at Jade. Apparently, she was going to make herself useful.

The first patient was held by a ten-year-old girl with jet black hair and matching eyes. Clutched in her hands was a skinny, scrawny cat, both looking terrified.

The woman who'd answered the door smiled at the little girl, nodding encouragingly.

The girl shuffled closer.

"Hi, Lakota," Dell said to her. "How's Duncan doing?"

Lakota didn't speak, she just nodded. Dell gently took Duncan from her and gave him an exam. "He's asthmatic," Dell said in a low voice to Jade, gesturing that she needed to take notes. "Lakota found him a few months back. Note that there's still no weight gain. Heart rate, one eighty; respiratory rate, forty-eight breaths a minute. No heart murmurs and his abdomen palpates normally, but he's dehydrated." He looked at Lakota. "He needs to have more water. You need to make sure it's always available to him. You've been giving him his meds?"

When Lakota nodded, Dell rummaged through his bag and brought out a small pill bottle. "Here's what he'll need until next time."

"Dell," Jade said softly. He couldn't give a minor meds like that, he . . .

Once again the older woman stepped forward and put her hands on the girl's shoulders. And that's when Jade saw another resemblance—they were mother and daughter. Jade glanced at Dell, who was looking at her, eyes as dark and silent as his family's. Jade sat back, sorry she'd started to speak, even sorrier that she'd doubted him. Bowing over the laptop, she went back to note taking.

Two hours later, Dell had seen the last of the people

waiting and he was stuffing his instruments back into his black bag.

Jade shut the laptop and stood. On the walk outside to the truck, Dell shook his head. "I can't believe you Dell'd me."

She had. She totally had. "I'm sorry."

He shook his head. "Don't be. I'd give these people whatever they needed, legal or not."

She stared at him. He was utterly serious. Before she could ask him why, the door of the trailer opened behind them.

The woman, whom Jade now knew was named Nila, came out.

Nila's gaze met Jade's. "Thank you," she said.

Jade stopped, surprised. She glanced at Dell, who was still walking. He hadn't stopped. "For what?" she asked the woman.

"For coming out here, for giving back to people that most others have forgotten about."

Jade looked at Dell, who was at the truck now, then back to the woman. "I didn't do much. It's all Dr. Connelly's doing."

"Yes." The woman nodded, without looking at him. "But he won't take my thanks."

Jade nodded at her and got into the truck. They had an hour before their first patients at Belle Haven would arrive, and she figured they'd just make it. "You were amazing back there."

Dell put the truck into gear and began the considerably rough drive back without a word.

"That woman . . ." Jade turned in her seat to watch Dell's reaction. "Nila. She's related to you."

They hit a rut and she nearly kissed the windshield. Dell stopped the truck and turned to her, tightening her seatbelt.

They were on the move again before he answered. "Yes."

Jade drew a breath. "She's your mother."

"Birth mother."

Jade nodded. There was a difference, of course. A birth mother was exactly that. The giver of life but not necessarily the caregiver. "Why did you bring me?"

A very small smile came into his eyes. "You hijacked my truck."

"You could have told me to get out."

"Jade, has anyone ever successfully told you what to do?"

"No," she admitted.

They were quiet a long moment, then Dell let out a long breath. "You wanted to know me. I'm not sure why that means something to me, but it does. So I brought you." He glanced over at her. "I can count on one finger the number of people outside of Brady, Adam, and Lilah who have been inside my home, who have unlimited access to my computer, who know what I do every Monday morning for a woman I shouldn't give a shit about."

Her breath caught. "Me."

"You." The sun slanted in, blinding them. He put on his sunglasses. "You're in. As in as you can possibly be. Your turn, Jade."

Nineteen

Two days later, Jade had lunch with Lilah in town at the bakery, where they stuffed themselves with turkey and cheese croissants. Lilah was entertaining herself by turning her ring finger to and fro so that the sun coming in through the window hit the diamond just right and glared into Jade's eyes. "How do you get any work done if you're staring at that thing all day?" she asked, slipping on her sunglasses to keep from being blinded.

"It takes concentration, believe me." Lilah grinned. "Hard to believe, right? That Brady and I live together now—*and* I still love him."

Jade tried to fathom it. Living with a man. Letting him see the morning routine. Having to share closet space. Needing to consult someone when she ran out at midnight because she had to have ice cream.

"You ever done it?"

"Live with a man?" Jade shook her head. "Nope."

"Is there someone back home, waiting on you?"

"After a year and a half," Jade said lightly, "I'd have mentioned it, don't you think?"

Lilah shrugged. "You're pretty tight-lipped."

"There's no one."

Lilah tilted her head. "So you and Dell . . . ?"

"How did we get on this subject?" Jade asked. "We're talking about you, sharing your space with a man. And how does that even work, anyway? What happens if he leaves the toilet seat up? Drops his tighty-whities on the floor? Eats your emergency stash of ice cream?"

"Brady doesn't wear tighty-whities. Sometimes he doesn't wear any underwear at all."

There was a beat of silence as they both contemplated that image for a moment.

"And if he eats my ice cream—and he does—he buys more."

"Are you telling me he has no bad habits that drive you nuts?"

Lilah laughed. "Well, he's a man, isn't he? Of course he drives me nuts. He stubborn as a damn mule, he thinks he's always right, and he hogs the remote."

"So how are you going to live with that for the next sixty years?"

"Buy another TV."

Jade stared at Lilah. "I'm serious."

"So am I," Lilah said.

Jade must have looked confused because Lilah patted her hand. "You do realize that none of those things are deal breakers, right?"

"How do you know?" Jade asked. "Maybe a year from now, you'll—"

"What? Get tired of the way he looks at me as if I'm his entire life? Get over the fact that for the first time ever, someone wants me for me? That the man somehow actually enjoys making me happy?"

Jade stared at her. "The ice cream . . ."

"I'll buy a lifetime supply of ice cream. Hell, I'll even pretend he's right some of the time . . . it's worth it. He's worth it. And you know what? So am I." Lilah popped her last bite into her mouth and pointed at Jade. "And so are you." She pointed to Jade's plate, and the half of her croissant still sitting there. "Now see, that's why you look so hot in all those pretty clothes of yours. You have self-control. Too much even."

"I'm taking a line-dancing class. If you think I have too much control, you ought to see me on Wednesday nights."

"Yeah? Any cute guys in it?"

"Not that kind of lack of control. I didn't know how to dance before. So I'm pretty much winging it."

Lilah was looking at her with approval. "You're trying to learn how to have fun."

"Yes."

"Maybe you should take Dell with you."

"Dell doesn't need to learn how to have fun. He invented the word."

Lilah gave her a little smile. "You of all people shouldn't let his protective shell fool you. You're smarter than that."

Jade let out a breath. "You know he does pro bono vet work every Monday?"

"Yes, and I know he didn't tell you that. He doesn't tell anyone."

"I went with him."

Lilah's brows shot up so far they vanished into her hair. "You went with him?"

"I just showed up at his house in the morning and got into his truck. He had no choice."

Lilah laughed at that. "Honey, that man has all the choices in the world, and all the brawn. Believe me, if he didn't want you to go, you wouldn't have. He must have needed you there."

Now it was Jade's turn to laugh. "Need? Dell doesn't need anyone."

Lilah was shaking her head. "He might like to think it—all three of them do. But it's not true. Brady realized it with me. And someday Adam and Dell will know it."

"Know what?"

"That needing someone isn't the same as being weak. That they can still be big and bad and strong and still lean on someone. You're that someone for Dell."

Jade's heart stopped. "Lilah, I—"

"I know." Lilah covered Jade's hand with her own. "You're leaving. I don't want you to. I've been trying not to say that because you have to go back, I get it. But I'm sick over it, and if I feel that way, I can only imagine how Dell feels."

"I've got a temp service on standby and the front desk running like a charm. Anyone can take over, they'll be fine."

"You know damn well that's not what I'm talking about."

Brady walked through the door juggling two hot dogs and a large soda from the convenience store up the street, tailed by Dell and Adam. Dell was also armed with crap food, but Adam strode directly to the bakery's front counter.

Adam was the only one of the three who cared in the slightest about what he put into his body.

"He's going to order tea," Lilah murmured. "That man is hot, but he doesn't know much about how to eat."

Brady's gaze went directly to Lilah, and he gave her one of those smiles that told the whole world they'd very recently been naked together and were planning on getting that way again as soon as possible.

Dell was on his phone, but his eyes tracked to Jade in a way not all that different from Brady, and her pulse kicked up. Brady had already dragged a chair to the table and was kissing Lilah hello when Dell kicked another chair over. He glanced at Brady and Lilah kissing like their mouths were fused and something flickered in his gaze.

Jade wasn't sure what he was thinking, but she knew what she was thinking. That the intimacy between Brady and Lilah was so easy and real. Which stirred up a surprising twinge of envy.

A woman came into the bakery and saw Dell. "Finally," she said. "I catch up with you."

He looked up and gave her an easy smile. "Stacy."

Stacy was a petite, curvy brunette in jeans, boots, and a broad smile. "I wanted to tell you that Trickster's feeling so much better. We appreciate your house call the other night. I'm just sorry you had to leave so fast. Was everything okay with the emergency call?"

Brady and Lilah were preoccupied with something on Brady's iPhone. Jade tried to busy herself with her own cell phone, but her ears weren't on board with that plan and she eavesdropped shamelessly.

"Yes," Dell said. "It's handled."

"I was thinking maybe you could come back out tonight," Stacy said, hunkering at his side, giving him a nice view down her top. "My kitty needs a checkup."

Jade, who'd just taken an ill-timed drink of her water, choked.

Dell slid her a glance and she went back to studying her cell phone, like look at me, I'm just sitting here working . . .

"Tonight's not great," Dell said to Stacy.

"Oh. You working?"

"Teaching a self-defense class, actually," he replied, and this time didn't look at Jade at all.

"After, then."

Dell didn't say anything. Clearly taking that as agreement, Stacy leaned in even closer and whispered something in Dell's ear, and though Jade nearly fell out of her chair to try to catch it, she couldn't. Whatever it was, he had no reaction at all as Stacy sashayed out of the place, taking one last look over her shoulder at him.

Jade rolled her eyes and stuffed the rest of her croissant into her mouth in three bites, not even tasting it. Which meant that on top of being inexplicably irritated, she was also going to have to work out to lose the extra million calories she'd just consumed.

Lilah was helping herself to Brady's soda. "Was Lulu delivered to the kennels while I was gone?"

"Yes, and Dell had just come by to get me. She was very happy to see him, so happy that she ate one of his socks."

Dell pulled up the leg of his jeans. He had only one sock on.

"Sounds like she thinks she's a goat."

Brady leaned back in his chair, tilting it so that he was leaning against the wall as he grinned. "Turns out lambs don't recognize calm assertive. All they want is something to eat." He tugged a strand of Lilah's hair fondly. "Saw that new puppy you rescued. Cute little guy."

"Yeah, but I think I've given everyone in town a puppy by now. Not sure who I can get to take him."

"You've never given Jade a puppy," Brady said.

"That's because Dell's her puppy."

Brady cracked up. Dell kicked the leg of Brady's chair, almost toppling him over.

Brady dropped his chair back down and looked at the soda, which had spilled on his chest. "You do know I can still kick your ass, right?"

Dell leaned close to Jade, slipping his arm around her. "I have a kick-ass partner now. You can't take us both."

"I knew it!" Lilah grinned, pointing at them. "You're an 'us'!"

"Hey, man, this was a clean shirt," Brady grumbled, swiping his chest with napkins.

Lilah smacked him. "Did you not hear?"

Brady lifted his head. "Hear what?"

Lilah ignored him, looking between Dell and Jade. "So what is this? What does this mean?"

"It means that I can finally kick Brady's ass," Dell said. "With Jade helping me."

"And . . . ?"

"And we'll take Adam, too. Just on principle."

Lilah sighed. "One of these days you'll admit it."

Jade didn't look at Dell, because she knew better. She knew that while sometimes she and Dell were indeed an "us"'—like when they were working or possibly naked—most of the time there was no "us."

They both wanted it that way.

Besides, Dell wasn't interested in an us and even if he was . . .

You're leaving . . .

She kept forgetting that one pesky little thing. And maybe she kept forgetting because at some point she'd started thinking about not leaving . . .

Twenty

At ten o'clock that night, Jade answered her door to Dell. She had *The Notebook* on pause on the TV and a half-empty box of tissues on the coffee table. "Dell?"

He narrowed his eyes. "What's the matter?"

"Nothing."

He pushed past her and entered her place. "Well, come right on in," she murmured.

He turned back to face her. "I thought you'd come over for some gym time but you didn't show. And you've been crying."

"I'm watching *The Notebook*."

He looked confused so she filled him in. "A go-to sob movie."

"Why would you have a go-to sob movie?"

Clearly the man had never felt the need to just cry. "Never mind. And I didn't come over because I thought you'd be with Kalie."

He looked even more confused than before. "Who?"

"Kalie, Cara . . . whatever her face, from the bakery earlier."

He pinched the bridge of his nose and studied his shoes for a long moment but apparently no wisdom was forthcoming on how to deal with Crazy Females. "I'm not sleeping with Melinda."

"You've said."

"And I'm certainly not sleeping with Karen. There's only one woman in my bed." He stalked toward her and hauled her in against him so hard the air escaped her lungs. "Her name is Goddess Jade, and she's got my full attention."

Her heart stuttered in her chest and her hands slid up his chest.

"So now if we're clear on that," he said, forehead to hers, "let's move onto the next portion of the meeting."

Her heart, her traitorous heart, took a hard leap thinking maybe he was going to say that he'd changed his mind about relationships and he wanted one. With her. "Which is?"

"Your to-do list." He lifted her off her feet and started toward her bed. "I know I'm on it, I put myself there. Now I'm adding you—" He broke off because his phone was vibrating between them. With a low oath he stopped, read the text, then swore again. "It's Adam. One of his clients has a dog in labor. She's in trouble and on the way to the clinic. Adam's two hours out."

"So more angry sex is off the table?"

"I wasn't angry," he said.

"Then what kind of sex were you hoping for?" she asked, grabbing her coat and purse as they moved in tandem to the door.

"I was wide open," he said as they made their way down the stairs and into the night. "Maybe boss-and-naughty-secretary sex?"

"Seriously?"

Unembarrassed, he shrugged.

She was quiet a moment, considering as they walked to his truck. "There's always doctor and nurse," she heard herself say.

He slid her a wicked bad boy smile as he opened his passenger's door for her. "You want to play nurse?"

"Oh no. I get to be the doctor. *You'd* be the nurse."

He tipped his head back and laughed, and she found herself grinning. *Grinning.* "So that works for you?" she asked. "Being the nurse?"

"For you, Jade, I'd be anything you want."

If only that were true . . .

An hour later, Dell was sitting on the floor in the surgery suite next to a large open box. Inside was Rose, the laboring golden Lab with the bad timing. Adam was on his way in, but for now Dell's only assistant was Jade.

She sat on the other side of the box, stroking Rose's face.

Rose lay quiet, her sides rising and falling quickly with her restless panting, eyes closed. She was clearly having contractions, readying her body for the pushing. Dell was waiting for her to start licking herself, a sign that birth was imminent.

Rose's owner was Michelle Eisenburg—the woman whose son had inadvertently caused Jade's parking lot breakdown all those weeks ago now. Dell had promised he'd take care of Rose as if she were his own, and sent her home to relieve the babysitter.

"You know," Jade said. "I've been here a year and a half and I've never seen puppies delivered." She shook her head in the quiet room. "I've never even had a puppy."

"Ever?" Dell asked.

"My mother's allergic. I sneaked a puppy in once, kept her for a week before my nanny ratted me out. I was grounded for a month."

Dell ran his hand down Rose's side, gauging her breathing, her contractions, as always fascinated by these little peeks into Jade's childhood, which were like fairy tales compared to his growing up years.

"What about you?" she asked. "Tell me about your first dog."

"Bear." He closed his eyes, remembering. "Adam and I found him when he was nothing but a few days old, blind, starving." Just a tiny handful of skin and bones, he'd been filthy and mewling. Dell had taken one look at the newborn puppy and had one thought, that it was even more pathetic than him. "We were living with our dad, then," he said. "My dad said the thing would die that night, but it didn't." Bear hadn't died the next night, either. Dell had nursed him back to health. "He grew into this huge mutt who took up more of my bed than I did."

"Aw. You saved his life."

"Yes. And then he saved mine several times over, so we were quite the pair."

"He saved your life?"

Dell gave a mirthless smile. "I was a sickly, skinny ten-year-old, and far too dark-skinned for the very white neighborhood we lived in. Bear proclaimed himself a brother-in-arms. He once scared off three kids who tried to drag me into an alley."

She was smiling. "Good. Did Bear live to a ripe old age?"

Dell bent over Rose. "I don't know. We had to give him away when we went to the first foster home."

"Oh," she breathed with a world of empathy in her voice. She slid a hand to his back, and then she set her head on his shoulder. "I hate how bad things were for you, Dell. I hate how hard your life was."

"It's not hard now."

He felt her smile against him and wanted to turn and pull her in close.

"Dell?"

"Yeah?"

"Do you ever think about what would happen if I stayed?"

He went still, something kicking in his gut hard. And if he was being honest with himself, it was both hope and fear. "I didn't know that was an option."

She shrugged but was just as still as him, as if she was waiting for a certain reaction from him.

But which reaction exactly, he wasn't sure.

Then Rose whined and began to rustle frantically around, staring wide-eyed and terrified up at Dell. He rubbed her sides. "First one's coming."

Jade straightened but kept her face averted. Still, it didn't take a genius to tell that his nonreaction had been the wrong one. "How can you tell?" she asked.

Rose grunted, and the first puppy slid out.

"Well, that's a clue," she said.

Dell waited to see if Rose would lick and tear the amniotic sack off, but she seemed confused and unsure so Dell gently tore the membrane and allowed the fluid to be released. Rose dutifully took over bathing the newborn with her tongue while Dell tied off the cord and made sure the puppy was breathing.

Things moved quickly after that. Three more healthy puppies in a row, and then one that wasn't moving. Dell wrapped the puppy in a small warmed towel and dried it aggressively, trying to stimulate it so it would cry. Crying was the natural way to clear the mouth and trachea of amniotic fluid.

But the puppy didn't draw air.

"Oh no," Jade breathed, leaning over him. "Is she going to make it?"

Dell worked the puppy for over a half hour, but it was no good. There was no heartbeat. And when Rose started to push again, he set the wrapped stillborn down to help her.

Twenty minutes later, Dell had helped extract all the stragglers. One by one he and Jade dried the pups with sterile towels, cleared their mouths and set them back next to Rose to keep them warm. When Rose was alert and starting to nurse, Dell went to his office to call Michelle and fill her in.

By the time he finished and went back to check on Rose, it was nearly four in the morning. Not sure where Jade was, he picked up the stillborn and moved out the back door to sit on the top step with her, staring out into the black sky.

Adam showed up with a quiet greeting for Jade as he leaned over her and looked into the box. The corners of his mouth quirked at the blind, soggy puppies nuzzled up against Rose. His sharp, dark eyes counted them up. "Six."

"Seven. We lost one."

Adam let out a breath, barely discernible, but she was learning to read him now. Grief for the one they'd lost.

"Where's Dell?" he asked.

"He went to call Michelle."

Adam was quiet a moment, stroking Rose. "He takes it hard. Losing them. Always did."

"He feels things," Jade said. "Deeply."

"Deeper than the rest of us. Always did that, too. Along with the whole saying good-bye issue."

Jade met his gaze. "Good-bye issue?"

"Doesn't like 'em. In fact, he'll go out of his way to avoid them."

"Meaning?"

"Love isn't real, at least not the kind you get from people. Never get too close, leave 'em smiling . . ."

She inhaled. "But leave 'em."

He nodded. "So you do understand him."

All too well. But there was something in Adam's voice she'd never heard before.

Protectiveness.

Dell might be a grown man, but Adam was the older brother, if only by two years. "He has seen more than his fair share of good-byes," she said softly. He and Adam both had.

"And he makes sure to say them first if he can," Adam said. "But the animals are different. He'd never leave an animal first, never."

"He doesn't blame himself, does he?"

"Not for the animals, no."

Jade stood up and brushed off, wanting to go find him. "Are you saying he blames himself for all the human good-byes in his life? None of them were his fault."

Adam lifted a shoulder. "You know that self-blame isn't logical."

Yes, she knew. She knew exactly. She'd been blaming herself for a year and a half for the attack that hadn't been her fault.

"Our dad died in a car accident on the way to a job he hated with a passion but kept to provide a roof over our heads. Sol died while riding broncos on a day that Dell had missed his competition. Then I left him to go off to the National Guard because there was nothing other than jail in my future if I stayed. And you—"

"That's all ridiculous," she said. "Not a single one of those things were his fault. And me . . ." She wasn't sure she'd ever heard Adam string so many words together at once, but when he did, he packed a punch. "What about me?"

Adam didn't answer.

"He's not blaming himself for me leaving," she said slowly. "I was always going to go."

Adam just looked at her from those dark, dark eyes.

She stared at him some more, feeling her heart quicken as she took in everything that he wasn't putting to words. "I'm not abandoning him. We're not . . . He and I . . ."

One of the puppies mewled and Adam stroked a finger over the tiny body, whispering something softly to it until it stilled.

"I mean, it's not like we're . . ." Jade broke off.

"You're smart," Adam said in the same soothing voice he'd just used on the puppy. It was shockingly effective. "You'll catch up eventually."

Oh God. She was pretty sure she'd done that now. Just because she and Dell had never put a label on their relationship didn't mean that it didn't exist. Of course it did. True, it was different from any other relationship she'd ever had. It was also true that there'd never been a man in her life who could drive her crazy in one moment and then make her tremble in the next like he could. He was her best friend. Her lover.

And she was desperately afraid he had become much more than that.

But just because *she* understood that didn't mean he did. "He doesn't do relationships," she said. "You know that." And she was discovering something that she hadn't known about herself—she liked him too much to do anything less. Too bad she had no idea what to do with that.

"So you really are going."

"I always was." What she didn't say was that her own reservations about leaving were keeping her up at night. But given Dell's reaction—or lack of—to her trying to talk to him about it, it didn't matter all that much. "It's not like I'm suddenly abandoning him because we didn't work out. We did work out, as much as he allowed us to. We both knew this was coming." She stood up. "I'm going to go find him."

He wasn't in his office or anywhere that she could see, but the back door was ajar. She found Dell on the top step in the dark night, his big body hunched protectively over a small, still bundle in his hands.

Heart squeezing, she sat at his side. "Hey." She nudged him gently with her shoulder, and he nudged back but said nothing.

"Rose is okay," she said quietly.

"Good."

"And now I'm wondering about you. Are you okay, too?"

"I just always take a minute with them. Afterward." His voice low and a little raspy, like it hurt him physically to lose any animal, no matter how short a time he'd known them.

He hadn't taken his hands or his eyes off the carefully wrapped puppy, and Jade couldn't take her eyes off of him. Without being consciously aware of moving, she scooted closer, setting her head on his shoulder.

For a moment he didn't move, then slowly he shifted and leaned into her. She slipped her arm around his waist and he shifted even more, turning into her, pressing his face to the crook of her neck.

She went still as her heart squeezed. Always it'd been him offering her comfort, safety, whatever she needed, but now for the first time he was taking those things from her.

She didn't dare move, not even when her toes and fingers and nose and nipples got so cold she could no longer feel them. In fact, she wanted to never move again. She wanted to preserve this quiet closeness between them that felt almost more intimate than when they'd been naked.

But Dell pulled back and straightened. "You're frozen. Get back inside."

He was already regretting the brief moment of weakness. If she wasn't still so touched that he'd trusted her enough to see it, she'd have rolled her eyes at the utter manness of the move. "Dell—"

"I've just got to take care of him first, then I'll be right behind you." He stood and pulled her up.

"Need help?" she asked, knowing what he'd say even before he shook his head with a quiet thanks and vanished.

She went back inside, looking around at the animal center that was as much a part of him as any of his long, perfect limbs. It was a visceral reminder how much more than a good-time, funny, charming guy he was. He had this huge capacity to care, and something else, too.

He hadn't just picked a job for himself the way most people did. The way she had. He hadn't let other people's wants and goals guide him.

The way she had.

No, not Dell. He'd instead chosen a life that suited him to the core. One that gave him pleasure and was an innate part of him.

She hadn't done that. Not until she'd come here, to Sunshine. To Belle Haven. She went to her desk thinking she was here, she might as well get something done. She'd barely booted up in the semidark front room when Dell came back through.

"You're not working," he said.

"Well, I—"

He pulled her out of her chair. "You're going home to bed."

Back to being the alpha pack leader. "I'm okay, Dell. What we haven't established is if you're okay."

He didn't move but she felt him draw in a deep breath. "Why wouldn't I be?"

She wanted to say because he acted like he was all alone in charge of everyone and everything, when in reality, the people he had in his life wanted to take care of him every bit as much as he took care of them. She wanted to say how sorry she was for how he'd grown up, but that would go over about as well as hugging him right now would.

Screw it, she thought, and ran a hand up his arm, over his broad shoulder, over his throat to his jaw, which she brushed with her fingers.

Reaching up, he took her hand in his and squeezed her fingers gently, then brought them to his mouth and lightly brushed his lips over her palm. "I'm okay, Jade. I'm always okay. You don't have to worry about me."

She stepped into him, her breasts brushing his chest, their thighs touching. "Did you always know?" she asked quietly. "That you were meant for this?"

Bending his head, he lightly rubbed his lips to hers. "Kissing you?"

"Yes," she murmured. "No." She let out a low laugh and stepped back. "*No.*" God, he was good, too good, at distracting her. "At this. Your job. Being a vet."

"Actually, for most of my growing up years, I was pretty sure I was meant for nothing good."

She opened her mouth to vehemently oppose that but he kissed her again. "I'm lucky, Jade," he said against her mouth, his hands going to her hips to hold her against him. "I didn't get screwed up, at least not too bad. I might be commitment shy and not big on traditional relationships, but thanks to Sol, I got into college and figured my shit out and ended up with a skill that works for me."

"And it's a bonus that you love what you do."

"Yeah. A lot. I highly recommend it."

"Working with animals?"

"Loving what you do."

She lifted her head and looked at him as he stroked his fingers over her jaw and into her hair, which he tugged lightly so that she couldn't pull away. "You ever going to try it?" he asked, his mouth whispering over hers.

"Maybe I already have." She gripped him tight as her body reacted to his with hopeful little tremors. "How about you? Maybe it's time for you to try something new, too."

"Like?" he asked.

"Like . . ." She nipped at his lower lip, giving it a little tug until he hissed in a breath. Then she soothed the sting with a kiss. "Like . . ." *Needing me . . .*

Adam stuck his head in from the back. "Michelle just called, she's on her way in to pick up Rose and the puppies.

There's also a message on the phone from the Anderson ranch that they need you out there pronto."

Dell stayed still against Jade for one beat, and she thought maybe he'd ask Adam to handle something. Or let her help in some way.

But Dell never passed off responsibilities, and as he'd proven over and over, he sure as hell didn't need anyone to step in for him. He pulled away from Jade and looked at Adam. "I'll call Brady and have him get the Bell ready for flight. On your way into town to get your things, drop off Jade. I'll handle Rose and the Anderson ranch."

He was standing right there in front of Jade, right there, close enough to still touch, yet he was a thousand miles away on his own island. Dell Connelly Island. Where no one and nothing could touch him.

Twenty-one

B ecause she was a glutton for punishment, on Monday morning Jade was leaning against Dell's truck at four thirty A.M. when he came out of his house carrying two bags of what she now knew would be groceries and his medical bag slung over his shoulder.

This time he didn't look surprised to see her. He just shook his head, shrugged out of his jacket, and tossed it to her. "Are you nuts?" he asked. "It's forty degrees and you're in just a sweatshirt."

"I got hot in that trailer last time." But she gratefully slid into his jacket, inhaling his scent and greedily wrapping herself into it, trapping his body heat for herself. "And it's thirty-two."

"Winter's coming."

She nodded as he started the truck and shoved it into gear, taking them to the highway. He drove like he did everything else in his life, with apparent effortless ease. Without his jacket, he wore only a light blue button-down shirt, untucked over faded jeans that made his legs seem like they were a mile long. His sleeves were shoved up, revealing forearms corded with strength. He had one big hand on the wheel, the other shoving his still damp hair out of his face. The Dell version of hair combing.

"The next time I drive out here, you'll be gone," he said.

This was true.

"Friday's it, right?" he asked.

Next Monday was the first. In order to fulfill her promise to Sam and her parents, she'd have to start driving back to Chicago by Friday.

Four days. "Thursday," she whispered.

Silence greeted this.

"You won't hardly even miss me," she said. "I've taught Keith enough to maintain the front until you get a replacement. And the temp agency is on notice, by the way. I wish you'd let them send someone out this week, but either way you're going to be fine. You don't need me." She held her breath, hoping against hope that he would say that he *did* need her.

In some aspect of his life. In any aspect of his life.

But he didn't. He said nothing at all. And she wasn't going to bang her head up against the wall seeking something that hadn't been given to her freely.

Nila was waiting on them. Unlike her son, she looked very surprised to see Jade again. "Are you Dell's woman?"

"I'm my own woman."

There was a slight spark of what might have been humor in Nila's eyes. "You know what I'm asking."

Jade looked at Dell, who was suddenly engrossed in unpacking his bag. Gee, wasn't he a help. She was tempted to give his mother the same line she'd once given Leanne and tell her that they were engaged just to see him swallow his own tongue. "I'm just helping."

"Why?"

"Because I like to help."

Nila looked at Dell. Dell looked right back at her, not explaining himself. He wouldn't.

Even if Jade wished that for once he would.

They turned to their waiting patients. There was a cat in labor, another who needed dental work, and two dogs who'd been in a vicious fight and needed cleaning and stitching up, all of which Dell took care of with relative ease.

The last patient was a little girl sitting next to Lakota.

The little girl was clutching a dead rabbit. "You fix," she told Dell, and set the rabbit on the exam table.

Dell's gaze met Jade's and she gave a slight shake of her head, utterly unable to imagine how he was going to handle this one. He very sweetly and gently wrapped the rabbit up and took both girls outside. Jade watched through the window as they walked out into the open land until they were nothing but three tiny pinpricks on the horizon.

"He'll help them bury the rabbit and say good-bye."

Jade turned and faced Nila, who stood there, eyes dark and solemn, long braid hanging over her shoulder. "He doesn't like good-byes."

"And you think that's my fault."

Jade didn't want to go there. "It's not my place to judge."

Nila turned and poured two cups of coffee, handing one to Jade. "You're polite. Too polite to tell me what you really think. But it's true. I was a terrible mother for him and Adam. My only defense is that I was young. Too young."

As far as defenses went, it was a good one.

"He turned out to be a good man, in spite of me," Nila said quietly. "You make him happy."

"Oh. We're not—"

Nila shook her head. "I don't need your words to tell me what I can see with my own eyes. You're the first one in all this time to hold his heart. I hope you manage to take better care of it than I ever did."

In the pit of her stomach, Jade knew otherwise. That regardless of whether or not she held a special place in Dell's heart, she wasn't going to be the keeper of it.

He didn't want her to be.

Behind her, the trailer door slammed open with enough force that Jade nearly jumped out of her skin. A young man stood there, eyes narrow, teeth bared. He was in his late teens and built like a linebacker. He was obviously Native American, and spitting fury. "You told on me?" he grated out. "You told my parole officer that I cut classes?"

"Because you did," Nila said.

"You have to take it back!"

"I'm your teacher, Robby. You know I won't lie for you." Nila set her coffee into the sink and closed her fingers around a paring knife there, her gaze meeting Jade's with a clear message. Be aware.

Jade's heart leapt into her throat. With a growl, Robby pushed forward and crowded both Jade and Nila in the kitchen up against the sink. "Tell him you were lying," he said through his teeth, his face close. Too close. "If you don't, he's going to send me back to juvie."

"All you have to do is show up for classes," Nila said. "All of them, including your anger management class."

With a yell of frustration, Robby threw out another arm, this time swiping everything from the counter in one fell swoop, sending it all flying. A set of keys hit Jade in the face. Nila was sprayed with hot coffee from one of the mugs, but she still gripped the paring knife from the sink. "Stop. Robbie, stop."

Robby grabbed Nila's arm and twisted.

With a cry of pain, Nila dropped the knife and scrambled back against the counter, bumping into Jade, who was doing her best to be invisible.

Robby picked up the knife and stared at it as if transfixed before lifting his gaze to Nila.

Both Nila and Jade shrank back and down, hunkered together against the laminate wood behind them. Jade could feel something warm trickling down her temple and she swiped at it.

Blood.

She'd been cut by the keys. Nila was pulling her shirt away from her body, and Jade hoped that the coffee hadn't burned her too badly.

"You've ruined my life," Robby yelled. "Because of you, they'll try to make me go back. I won't go. I won't." He jabbed the knife in their direction for emphasis.

Jade's hand found Nila's, and they gripped each other for all they were worth, staring in horror up at the teen.

"This isn't going to help your cause," Nila told him, her voice admirably even. Dell had gotten that from her, his nerves of steel.

Jade wasn't feeling nerves of steel. She had nerves of Jell-O and they were jumbling around in her stomach.

You don't have to be a victim.

Dell's words. But Dell was outside, possibly out of screaming range. No one was going to get them out of this, they were on their own. Her purse had been on the counter but had hit the floor with everything else on the counter. It was right behind her, and gazing still warily on Robby, she slowly slid her hand into it, wrapping her fingers around the first thing she could.

A tampon.

That wasn't going to help.

She fumbled a bit and found what she'd hoped for. Her compact can of hair spray. God bless Adam and the hair spray lesson.

Robby was gripping the knife tight, looking beyond reason with some wild eyes and a menacing stance that did not bode well. "J-just put the knife down," Jade said softly.

Could she pull the can out fast enough to spray him in the eyes? And what then? She and Nila had to get to the door, which Robby was blocking.

Robby's eyes slid from Nila to her. They were black, his pupils fully dilated. He was sweating, panting with exertion.

He was on something. "There's no way out for me," he said solemnly.

"There is. There always is," Nila said.

Jade hadn't breathed in far too long. Panic had long ago blocked her throat. If Dell and those two little girls walked back into the trailer right now and startled Robby, it would go all bad. That terror outweighed the terror of taking action. "If you stop now and just leave," she said, "nothing terrible has happened. You don't have to take this any further."

"I have no way out," he said again, and lifting the knife, reached for Nila.

Dell had been right when he'd told Jade that adrenaline would kick in and everything would happen in slow motion. She pulled her hand out of her purse, hair spray in hand, and nailed Robby right in the eyes.

In slow motion.

Stopping short, Robby bellowed with rage, his hands going up to his face.

That's when Jade kicked him. She was lower than him, still crouched next to Nila so that her leverage was bad, but she got him. She got him right between the legs and he dropped like a stone.

Nila scrambled up, grabbed Jade by the hand and had them stumbling out of the trailer in the bright morning sun where they gulped air like they'd been running a marathon.

"Nice shot," Nila breathed, bent at the waist, hands on her thighs. "Good aim."

"I was aiming for his knee," Jade said. "I didn't mean to get him . . . there."

Dell and the two little girls came around the corner of the trailer, holding hands. Nila rushed toward Dell. "Need your phone," she gasped.

Dell pulled out his phone. "What's the matter?" His gaze was on Jade, and it narrowed in concern. "What happened?"

"Your woman-who-isn't-your-woman is one tough girl," Nila said, and called 911.

Twenty-two

When they got back to Sunshine, Dell pulled up to his house, where Jade's car was. He'd wanted her to take the rest of the day off but she wasn't having any of it.

"You have two stitches over your eye," he said, trying to reason with her, but really, he should have known better. There was no reasoning with a woman.

She wanted to work.

"Two stitches is nothing," she said. "The doctor said I wasn't concussed."

"He also said you were damn lucky."

"So were you. I was so afraid you were going to come back into the trailer and startle him and that he'd cut you and those little girls."

He stared at her. "So you were trying to protect me?"

"Well . . . yeah. And you should have seen me trying to do it with a tampon."

"What?"

"It's the first thing I grabbed in my purse."

He chuckled, even as his own ego bumped up against the

pride he felt for what she'd done. But every single time he looked at the bandage above her eye he flashed back to her and his mother stumbling out of the trailer like two drunken sailors, both looking like they'd just been in a bar brawl.

The reality of what had happened had been worse, though not nearly as bad as it could have been.

But she'd handled herself.

At the very small smile that crossed his lips, Jade cocked her head. "What?"

"You kicked his ass."

A small smile of her own crossed her lips. "Well, not quite his ass."

Dell let out a low laugh. "You did what you had to do."

"I did, didn't I?" She shook her head. "It seems like a dream now. I was terrified at the time. And pissed off. So pissed off. I mean if he'd waited a few minutes before he'd come in, you could have done all the ass kicking."

Reaching across the console, he stroked a finger above the bandage. "I'm proud of you, Jade."

Her eyes went a little shiny, and she took a moment to answer. When she did, her voice was soft and husky, telling him how much his words meant. "I'm a little proud of me, too. I faced my biggest nightmare and beat it down."

"You ever going to tell me about that nightmare?" he asked, tucking a strand of her hair behind her ear, ducking down a little to maintain eye contract when she tried to look away.

"It's over and done," she said. "It's all in the past."

"Not when you're still letting it affect you here and now, it's not."

She stared stubbornly out the window, the set of her jaw telling him she was done talking.

"Jade—"

"It doesn't matter now."

"Because you're leaving?"

That startled her into looking at him. "No." When he

lifted a brow, she sighed. "Maybe I'm just tired of it having such power over me."

"Then stop giving it that power," he said. "You've never told anyone about it. You're hoarding it, storing it up, letting it eat at you."

"Not today. Today I made Robby eat it."

"Yeah, and you did great. But—"

"Dell." She rubbed her temples. "I don't want to do this."

With him. Right. He nodded, trying not to react to that even though he felt kicked in the teeth. "Okay, let's get you back to your loft so you can rest, then." He unhooked his seat belt and got out of the truck, moving around to physically extract her from the car if he had to.

Adam came out of the house but Dell shook his head and Adam stopped on the porch. Dell opened the passenger door for Jade, reaching down to help her.

"I'm *fine.*"

"I need you to cooperate on this," he said.

"You *need* me to cooperate? Dell, you never need anything, and you don't need this. I'm *fine.*"

He drew a deep breath. She wasn't going to do as he asked. Of course not. Because if he looked her up in the dictionary, she'd be there under STUBBORN.

And he'd be right next to her. "I need you to rest. The doctor said—"

"Wow." She leaned back against his truck and crossed her arms. "Look at you throwing around that need word. The next thing you know, you'll be telling me how you *feel.*"

He stared at her incredulously. "You think I don't feel?"

"Dell, the only time I have even an inkling of what you're feeling is if your tongue is down my throat."

"What? That's crazy."

"Oh, really. It's crazy." She tossed up her hands. "Then tell me. Tell me right now. How do you feel?"

"About what?"

"Anything. You pick."

He narrowed his eyes. "Is this a trick?"

"Not even a little bit."

"Okay." He searched his brain. "I feel . . . angry over what happened to you. I should have been there, right there. I brought you and put you in danger—"

"We both know I pretty much forced you to bring me," she said dryly. "And please. Alpha male aside, I know damn well you must have other feelings than anger."

"Okay . . ." He tried to access one. "I'm hungry."

"You're what?"

"Hungry. I haven't eaten since last night and—"

Jade pushed off his truck and headed to her car.

Confused, he followed her, ignoring Adam's smirk. "See, it *was* a trap. You're mad because I didn't come up with whatever it is you wanted to hear."

Jade tossed her purse into the car before straightening and facing Dell. "Tell me one thing, Dell. The women you've dated. What's their biggest complaint about you?"

"That I don't . . ." He broke off.

She lifted a brow.

"Engage. I don't engage my emotions with them." He grimaced. "You wanted to know how I feel about you."

She didn't answer and he sighed. "Jade, I'm not good at this. It's why I don't do relationships."

"Getting that. Gotta go," she repeated.

Her eyes, Christ. They were suspiciously bright. The pulse at the base of her neck beat as frantic as a hummingbird. "I'm driving you," he said.

"Not necessary." She flashed him a forced smile, slid behind the wheel, and pulled out.

Adam came up to Dell. "She okay to drive?"

"Yes," Dell said, and it was true. She was okay. Much more okay than him.

Her car vanished down the street before Adam spoke again. "So you let her get attacked by some punk-ass with a knife? How the fuck did that happen?"

Dell shook his head. "Mom had the knife. The punk-ass took it from her."

"And Nila?" Adam didn't like to call Nila "Mom." He didn't like to call her anything. But he betrayed his concern when he asked, "She get hurt?"

"There was a scuffle. She got hit with a mug of hot coffee and suffered some second-degree burns on her stomach and chest, but she's okay."

"Jesus," Adam said.

"Yeah." Dell turned toward the truck, made a detour, and punched the closest tree.

Pain sang up his hand, wrist and arm.

"Well, that was stupid," Adam said. "You break it?"

"No." Dell opened and closed his hand carefully, and winced. Probably not, anyway . . .

"Feel better?" Adam asked.

"No."

"So she really schooled you on that feeling thing, huh?" Adam said.

Dell wished he hadn't punched the tree so he could punch Adam. "Shut up."

"Why? Because you know she's right?"

"Right about *what*?"

"That you don't do need. And you don't feel."

Fuck the fact that his hand hurt like a son of a bitch, he was going to hit Adam, anyway. "You know that's not true."

Adam nodded. "Yeah. But I'm just your sorry-ass brother. I don't give a shit if you show your feelings or not. She's the one who needs to know."

Dell stared at him. "What, are you Dr. Phil all of a sudden? You, who haven't looked at a woman since you got back from your last mission? What the fuck, man? Why don't you worry about your own love life, or lack thereof?"

Adam shrugged. "Fucking with you is more fun."

Dell stalked to his truck, shoulder-checking Adam hard as he did.

Adam let that go, which was just as well.

Because yeah, Dell had been schooled. Not only that, he was one hypocritical son of a bitch. All this time, all these months, he'd been so proud of himself for helping her. For giving her a job. For being there for her. For boosting the confidence that had grown inside her. For showing her how to face her demons and keeping her safe.

He'd actually thought that *he'd* been saving *her*.

Instead, he'd had it all ass-backward. *She'd* been there for *him*. She'd supported him, she'd made him look at himself differently, changing what he'd thought he'd wanted out of life. It used to be enough for him to have Belle Haven, to have just Adam, and Brady and Lilah. He didn't need more.

But that was no longer the case. Now when he went to sleep at night, he lay there wondering what Jade was doing and why she wasn't in his bed.

He didn't want to be alone anymore.

"Man, you're going to have to get over yourself," Adam said.

"You get over yourself."

Adam snorted. "That the best you've got? Why don't you just go after her, dumbass?"

"Thursday is her last day."

Adam rubbed a hand over his jaw. "Well, damned if that didn't sneak up on us."

Dell looked down the road where Jade's car had vanished. "Yeah."

That night on the drive home from work, Jade quickly realized the weather had taken a left turn directly into winter. She hadn't turned the heat on high enough and the loft had a chill when she entered. She fed Beans and went directly to her laptop and her things-to-do-when-upset list.

Bath.

Candles.

Ice cream.

She combined all three, stripping and sliding into the water.

Beans sat on the mat, well out of the reach of any possible stray water drops, cleaning behind her ears.

Jade was halfway through the ice cream when her cell phone rang.

Jade set her bowl on the edge of the tub and gingerly leaned over to the sink counter where her phone sat. It was Lilah. "Hey," she said. "I'm in the bath so—"

"You okay?"

Jade eyed the phone warily. "Why?"

"Just wondering."

Jade sighed. "Dell or Adam called and asked you to check up on me."

There was a guilty pause followed by a guilty laugh. "I know you said no good-bye party, but how about we go out for a drink?"

"Already there," Jade said. She'd added a glass of wine to her pity party and it was nearly gone. Someone knocked at her door and she went still. "Wait—are you here?"

"No, but I can be."

"Lilah, I'm fine." She stood in the tub and accidentally splashed Beans, who sent her a reproachful look. "Which of them called you, Lilah?"

"Oh God. Don't make me tell you that."

"I just want to know who's knocking at my door at"— she looked at her watch, also on the counter—"ten o'clock at night."

"Honey, you don't need me to tell you who's on your doorstep."

Jade's stomach clenched. Too much ice cream. "It could be Adam."

Lilah laughed. "And the Tooth Fairy is coming by later, too. Look, we both know who's at the door. Answer it. Talk to him. He's worried about you."

"I'm in the bath."

"Naked?"

"Well, that is my usual preference for bathing."

"One of us has to see you tonight, Jade," Lilah said. "It might as well be the one of us who's falling in love with you."

Jade went still, then jerked at the second knock on her front door. More water splashed over the sides of the tub and Beans trotted out of the room in self-defense this time.

"Jade?" Lilah asked. "You still there?"

"Dell's not falling for anyone, Lilah. He's a serial dater and doesn't believe in relationships."

"He hasn't had a real date in months. And don't look now, but he's got plenty of relationships in his life. Adam, Brady, me, his mother—though he'd deny that to his dying day, the stubborn ass—and . . . you."

There was a third knock, not nearly as patient as the first two. "Dammit, I gotta go. I'll deal with you later." Still dripping wet, she wrapped herself up in her bathrobe and gave herself the quick once-over in the mirror. No makeup, hair a mess—hell, who was she kidding? Her entire being was a mess. With a sigh, she moved through the loft to the door. Maybe he'd left, maybe . . .

"Jade, open up."

"I'm fine. I told you I was fine."

"Okay. Great. I'm not."

Letting out a breath, she undid the security chain, unbolted the door, then pulled it open.

Dell's hands were braced high on the doorjamb. His head was bowed, and when he lifted it, his eyes trailed up from her bare feet and legs to the robe that clung to her, heating her skin inch by slow inch. By the time his gaze met hers, his eyes were dark, filled with an emotion somewhere between possession, protection, and lust. "Invite me in, Jade."

He wasn't even going to try to sweet-talk his way in. He wanted her to invite him.

And that wasn't all he wanted. He wanted some answers, too. She knew this. Just as she knew she hadn't been able to give anyone those answers in all this time. But maybe . . . maybe that was the problem. God knew, keeping it in wasn't working for her.

Maybe it *was* time to try something new.

So she drew in some air and stepped back. He didn't move, just stayed in that position, arms up, eyes stark, expression bare.

Waiting.

"I want you to come in," she said.

He dropped his arms and ignored the space she'd made, stepping into her, pushing them both into her place and shutting the door behind him.

Twenty-three

Dell followed Jade into her kitchen, trying like hell not to notice that her white fluffy robe was sticking to her obviously wet body. Water dripped from her hair and her legs, and her feet squeaked on the tile floor. He was here for a reason, but that reason was fuzzy now that he had her in sight, all dewy fresh, no makeup, smelling like some complicated mix of sweet, sexy woman. "Jade."

She turned back with a bottle of wine, which she poured into a glass before handing over to him.

"I've already had mine," she said. "You might want to catch up."

She didn't look completely toasted so he tossed back some wine.

"You want to talk," she said.

Actually, he wanted to strip off that robe and lift her up to the counter so he could have his merry way with her. But first things first. "I want *you* to talk."

"About?"

"Come on now, Jade. This has gone on too long. It's time."

She played with the tie of her robe a moment before lifting her gaze to his. "As you know, before I came here, I ran a large medical center." She paused. "One night we were held up in the Urgent Care for drugs. I was the one who let the intruders into the lockup to get those drugs."

Dell set down his wine, thinking he probably needed something stronger for this, much stronger.

"The following week," she went on, "against my family's and doctor's wishes, I got into my car and drove west for a few days and ended up in Sunshine."

Dell took a careful breath but otherwise didn't react. He didn't want her to stop talking. "Doctor?"

"I needed something to eat," she said. "So I went into the bakery on Main and heard the woman behind the counter talking to another woman about Belle Haven. It was Lilah, and she was saying how the animal center needed a receptionist to man the desk and answer the phones because your old receptionist had left to have a baby and you guys were trying to do it on your own. I didn't need a job, but I *needed* a job, you know?"

No. No he didn't know. "Jade, the robbery. Previously, you'd said you were attacked. How badly were you—"

"After Lilah paid and left, I asked the lady behind the counter how to find the animal center. And then I drove out there. Got lost twice. Adam found me in the middle of the road trying to get my GPS to work, and he led me to Belle Haven. You were sitting in the middle of the waiting room floor wearing scrubs and a doctor's coat, playing with Mrs. Nelson's eight-week-old pug puppies. They were climbing all over you, and the phone was ringing and your computer was frozen, and you were just sitting there, calm as can be. Laughing. You were laughing at the puppy trying to climb up your chest to lick your face."

Dell remembered that. Adam had opened the door for her and she'd walked in, eyes hidden behind her big mirrored sunglasses, wearing white jeans and an aneurysminducing pink fuzzy sweater that somehow went with her red hair, looking as if she'd walked off a movie set.

He'd been a little dazzled.

And more than a little head over heels in lust.

But then she'd dropped to her knees and had loved up one of the puppies, letting it crawl all over her fancy clothes, not caring about hair or slobber.

She'd wanted to sit behind his desk and answer his phones, and he'd had to change gears because he'd needed someone to do those things. He'd conducted a real interview, and they'd hit their first problem—in spite of the intelligence and wit blaring from those green eyes, she couldn't provide references. Or proof she could indeed handle the job.

He'd known she wasn't from Sunshine, or anywhere close. That was obvious. Everything about her, from her clothes to her speech to her mannerisms, spoke of a big city and big money.

"Belle Haven was so . . ." Jade searched for the words. "Warm. Open. Inviting. Not at all like the uptight medical center I'd come from. There was no tension, no angry, sick, frustrated people waiting for hours, no harried office staff fighting insurance companies for approval. Just you. And you looked so easygoing," she said softly. "So . . . laid-back. Fun. I wanted to work for you."

"So you did," he said. "And it's been great. But Jade, you've got to tell me. Tell me what happened to you."

"It was late." She let out a long breath. "I'd stayed because it was month's end and the accounts payable and receivable clerks had gotten behind, not sending me their reports until the very end of the day. We were closed and I was just leaving, walking through the parking lot when someone ran at me. It looked like a teenager in a hoodie, so I stopped. I thought he was hurt, but"—here she squeezed her eyes shut—"he lifted his head and straightened. He wasn't a teen. He was a full-grown man, wearing a Halloween mask."

Dell heard the sound escape him, a low murmur of regret and horror for her, remembering how she'd fallen apart in the parking lot at Belle Haven when she'd faced yet another Halloween mask.

"Before I could react," she went on, "he'd shoved me and I fell to the asphalt. And then . . ." She cut herself off and shook her head.

"Jade." Dell pulled her close and wrapped her arms around him. "Stay with me."

"I am." But she burrowed in, pressing her face into his neck. "He had a gun. He pulled me up and yanked me close, holding his arm over my windpipe so I couldn't breathe. I could feel blood running down from hands and knees where I'd gotten scraped, and he kept tightening his grip and . . . and I couldn't breathe."

With another low sound of empathy and fury mixed, Dell pulled her in even tighter, as if he could fight her eighteen-month-old demons for her.

"He made me unlock the front door and dragged me through the reception area, demanding to know where the meds were kept. He wanted OxyContin, Vicodin, morphine, whatever we had. He needed a fix, he was shaking bad. I should have—I should have . . ."

"You did what you had to," Dell said, stroking a hand up and down her back to remind her that she was here, safe. "And you survived." Her robe and body were damp, and she was trembling. He tried to wrap himself around her to give her his body heat. "That's all that matters now."

Face still pressed to his throat, she shook her head. "That's just it, I didn't do all I could. I did nothing."

"Jade—"

"No, it's true. When I was on the ground, I could have kicked at him standing over me. I could have tried to fight back and I didn't."

"He had a fucking gun," Dell said, hating that she'd ever

felt so helpless. "You didn't have the tools to fight back. It wasn't your fault."

"But what happened next was." She gulped in more air. "I wouldn't tell him where the meds were, so he dragged me through to the back. Karen was still there, one of our nurses. She was working late, too, cleaning up. She came out of the small kitchen area and he—"

Dell was already hating this story. Hating it with everything he had. "He what, Jade?"

"He pointed the gun at her and said if I didn't tell him where the meds were, he'd shoot her."

Dell closed his eyes and rested his cheek on the top of her head, wishing he could take it all away.

"I told him," Jade said. "I told him what he wanted to know, but he hit her, anyway, in the face with his gun. He made me tie her up to a chair and then dragged me down the hall. I fell and nearly took him down with me, which really pissed him off. He kicked me in the ribs and I couldn't breathe again. I still couldn't breathe when we got to lockup. Corey was in the room, we surprised him."

"Corey?"

"A lab tech. He was studying for his exams. We startled him. When he saw me, all the blood startled him. I looked much worse than I was."

"Jade." Dell could barely speak. "God, Jade."

"Corey jumped up and . . ." She tightened her grip on him, both hands at his chest, grabbing his shirt and a few chest hairs to boot. "He shot him," she whispered. "In the thigh. I screamed, and he shoved me up against the meds lockup and demanded the key or he was going to shoot Corey again. But the key wasn't on my ring, I didn't have it there because it's too dangerous. But when I refused to get it, he—"

God, he didn't want to hear this. "Jade."

"He touched me. With his gun. He rubbed it over my breast and when my nipple got hard, he laughed and said we

were going to have fun after. Corey yelled at him from the
floor where he was bleeding like crazy, told him to leave
me alone, and I could hear Karen screaming for help from
the kitchen . . . and you know what I did?"

Dell shook his head.

"Nothing. I did nothing."

"You were scared, Jade."

"I was useless."

"You were in shock."

"So was Corey," she said. "So was Karen. They were
both hurt—"

"So were you."

"Not like them."

She blamed herself, he realized, for not suffering as
much as they had.

"I wasn't hurt like they were," she said again. "And yet
they never stopped fighting. I never started." Galvanized
into action by her own words, she shoved him away and
grabbed the wine, tossing back a healthy long pull right
from the bottle. Gently he took it from her.

"I let him into the meds lockup," she said, not looking at
him, swiping her mouth with her arm. "I let him take whatever he wanted as I begged him not to hurt me." She looked
away. "After . . . I figured there had to be something funda-
mentally wrong with me that I hadn't been strong and brave."

"No," he said fiercely. "There's nothing wrong with you.
Jade, tell me he didn't hurt you."

"The police came. Someone in the next building over
heard Karen screaming. The guy who had me, he had an ac-
complice. He was in the getaway car, but he came in to shut
Karen up. The police burst in just in time. We were saved. No
thanks to me."

"You weren't . . ."

"No. He intended to rape me, he told me several times."
She shuddered. "In graphic detail. But he didn't get to it."
She closed her eyes. "I grew up hearing how strong I was.

How I was meant for big things, how I could do anything I wanted. That I'd been born for running the family show, so to speak. But I wasn't strong. I was weak."

What she'd been raised hearing from her family sounded more like a major contradiction to him—do what you want, but make damn sure that what you want is to do our bidding . . . "You're human, Jade. That doesn't mean you're weak."

She turned from him and shrugged. "Everything I knew about myself was wrong. Nothing felt right. I couldn't find my footing."

"Anyone would have felt that way."

"It was my own doing."

"The holdup wasn't your fault."

She rolled her head on her neck, like her muscles hurt. Since she was tense enough to shatter, it was no wonder. He put his hands on her shoulders. Her muscles were bunched and tight as rocks. He dug his fingers in a little and she exhaled, dropped her head back to his chest.

"When I left Chicago," she murmured, "I wanted to find myself again, but I couldn't. I think it's because I was trying to be someone who no longer existed."

He dug in on a particularly tightly knotted muscle and she hissed in a breath. "God, that feels good." She tilted her head to give him more room to work. "I think working at Belle Haven was supposed to be a statement, like look at me further sabotaging myself . . . but the joke ended up on me. I like it here. I like who I became here. And I liked to think I brought some things to the job that no one else has before."

"Hell yeah, you did," he said. "And you became an important, integral part of the place." He turned her to face him. "You know that, right?"

She gave a little smile. "Turns out I have mad skills no matter what type of an office it is."

"Turns out," he said, smiling back. God. She looked so

beautiful bare of makeup, bare of the clothes, of any of her usual shields. Just Jade. "But that's just the job," he said. "Did you figure out who you are outside of work?"

"Not a line dancer."

He smiled. "Okay. Anything else?" When she didn't say anything, he did. "You're a good friend."

She choked out a half laugh, and then another. And then as if her legs were weak, she slid down until she was sitting on the floor, her back to the cabinet. "Dell, I was here for a year and a half before I even let any of you come over here. Lilah—"

"Loves you. Adam loves you." He hunkered beside her. "We all—"

She covered his mouth with her hand. He gently kissed her palm and pulled it away. "You give something to each of us. Hell, you give something to perfect strangers, like when you paid the rest of Nick's bill from your own money."

"You saw that?"

"I see lots of things." He kissed her palm again, and held it in his. "I see the real you, Jade."

She stared at him. "Do you think you can tell me who that is?"

He dropped all the way to the floor next to her and hauled her into his lap. "The real you is the woman who gets to work early to make my day easier because she cares. The real you is the woman who goes to lunch with Lilah even though for the fifth time that week she's going to ask you if Lulu should be allowed at the reception, and even though you likely want to strangle her, you still smile and suggest that probably it's not a good idea to allow lambs at the wedding reception. The real you is the woman who can make both of my big, badass ex–military brothers smile." He lowered his voice and put his mouth to her ear. "The real you is the woman who, when you're naked in my arms, gives me absolutely everything you have."

She closed her eyes. "How do you know?"

"Because I've never seen you give anything less, in everything you do."

"You helped me."

Maybe. She'd come to Sunshine seeking confidence and inner strength, looking to find herself. He'd done his best to give her whatever she needed but in the process he'd helped her become strong enough to go back. "So why are you going back now?"

"My dad's ill. He has Parkinson's and hasn't been able to run the business for a long time. I was doing it for him, and when I left, they temporarily promoted a family friend to my position. Sandy's good, really good actually, but . . ."

"But she's not you?"

A small smile crossed her lips. "She doesn't want the job long-term. She wants to get back to part-time so she can spend more time with her young kids."

"They could promote someone else."

"I promised. And I always did really mean to go back. I love my job with you and love the friends I've made . . . I'll never forget any of it. But I pretty much ran away from home, you know? I can't just . . . keep running. Without a compelling reason to stay, it's time for me to go."

He looked into her eyes and saw regret, and he wondered if it was as painful as the regret swelling in his chest cavity. "So stay for a compelling reason."

What might have been a brief flash of humor came and went in her eyes. "Like more naked-friends sex?"

He nearly said, *Stay and you can have any kind of sex you want, as long as it's only from me,* but that would sound an awful lot like begging. "As hot as naked-friends sex would be," he said slowly, "you need to know, this isn't anywhere near as casual as that. Not for me."

"But . . . but casual is your thing. It's your signature. It's what you do."

"No, actually," he said. "My usual thing is even less than casual. But that went out the window with you eighteen months ago."

She shook her head. "Don't do this to me," she whispered.

"Do what? Tell you how I feel? You asked, remember? And yeah, you're leaving. I've heard the news flash. But we can . . . visit."

"Visit."

"Yes," he said firmly. It would suck but it was better than nothing. "The occasional holiday, weekends, whatever."

She stared at him as if he'd lost his mind. "Dell, it's seventeen hundred miles. We can't casually date from seventeen hundred miles away."

"It's a flight." He shrugged casually, even as his heart was pounding, pounding, pounding.

Her eyes hadn't left his. "I didn't know you'd want that."

Okay, that hurt more than it probably should. "Even casual friends would visit, Jade. And as we've already established, we're more than that."

"I'd have to think about that," she said very softly, cutting out his heart. "Keeping this up once I leave."

Because he didn't trust his voice, he nodded. He had not seen that one coming. He started to get up, but she grabbed his wrist and he looked down at her hand on his arm. Pale. Small. Deceptively fragile-looking.

"I'd have to think about it," she repeated. "Because I don't know about my ability to keep this up with someone I care so much about *and* keep it as light as our distance will dictate."

Dell wanted to point out that the distance part was her own doing, but she moved into him, pressing that warm, curvy body against him until his ability to talk, much less think, became impaired.

She brushed her mouth to his ear. "Dell?"

He let out a shaky breath. "Yeah?"

"Ever had good-bye sex?"

He made the fatal mistake of meeting her gaze. Her eyes were soft, solemn, as she rose up on her knees and gently touched her lips to his. "Jade—" He gripped her hips as his entire body reacted to that slight, almost chaste kiss. "I—"

She outlined his lips with her tongue and he groaned, sucking it into his mouth. God, he loved the taste of her, the feel of her. He couldn't seem to get enough. He was starting to wonder if he'd ever get enough when her hands slid under the hem of his shirt and over his abs.

"Mmm," she said in response to the feel of him, like maybe she couldn't get enough of him, either. "Off." Then she shoved the shirt up. When he took over the task, pulling it off, she straddled him, a knee on either side of his hips. Bending low, she licked his nipple.

He sucked in a breath, which made him realize his mouth was open to speak, but whatever he'd been about to say was gone since all the blood had drained out of his now poor, dehydrated, useless brain.

"I want you," she said against his lips, pinning him to the cabinet at his back. "God, I want you. Please, Dell."

He made a noise deep in his throat and kissed her long and deep. Not enough, not nearly enough, he thought. He had to touch her. "Stand up."

"What?"

He went for the belt of her robe. "What do you have on under here?"

"Um. Me."

He groaned again and tugged it open. She was right, nothing but warm, damp, sexy, curvy woman. His hands looked so dark against her pale skin and turned him on even more than he already was. "Stand up," he said again, then without waiting for her, lifted her by the hips so that she was standing, still straddling him.

Perfect.

Leaning in, he nuzzled at her belly button, then lower. Then lower still. Above him she made a low sound of hunger that went straight through him, then repeated it when he slid his hands up the backs of her legs and grabbed her ass, urging her a little closer so that she had no choice but to lean over him and slap her hands on the kitchen counter.

"I've been *aching* to do this," he said, and gently ran his thumb over her glistening folds, opening her before leaning in to stroke her with his tongue, sampling different spots, loving her reaction to each. A murmur, a gasp. His name torn from her throat. She was quivering in minutes, her breath choppy, her hips rocking into him, and he couldn't get enough. "You taste good, Jade."

"Oh God. Oh God, *there*—"

If he hadn't already known exactly her "oh God, there" spot, the way her fingers tightened in his hair would have been a big clue. Loving the sexy sounds being ripped from her throat, and the way she looked above him, damp and trembling and gorgeous, he gave her exactly what she wanted, building her orgasm until she shattered.

Her knees collapsed and she slumped against his chest. Stroking a hand down her back, he pulled her close and kissed her neck.

"Please tell me you have a condom," she said.

In his wallet, which contrary to what she probably thought, he'd put in there with her in mind. "Jade—"

She clapped a hand on either side of his face. "Yes or no."

"Yes, but—"

"Get it. For the love of God get it now."

He reached into his back pocket for his wallet, not easy with her straddling his lap and very busy with her own agenda—unzipping his jeans. She freed him, then she tore the packet open with her teeth, laughing when she spit out the corner of the wrapper over her shoulder. "Always wanted to do that," she murmured, and sheathed him, leaving him panting and sweating by the time she was done.

"Now," she whispered, demanding, sure of herself, the sexiest thing he'd ever seen. She wrapped her hand around him, lifted herself up a little, and took him deep.

"Oh, fuck," he managed.

"Yes, please."

He choked out a laugh and closed his eyes, thunking his head back against the cabinet, hissing in a breath when she bent over him and nipped at his exposed throat. Banding his arms tight around her, he opened his eyes and met hers as they began to move in tandem. Faster. Harder. She was moaning and whimpering for more, and he gave it, feeling . . . so much, lost, found . . . completely undone.

When she sucked his earlobe into her mouth and flicked it with her tongue, he knew he was an inch from losing it. "Jesus," he breathed, trying to slow her down. "Jesus, Jade. Wait—"

No good, she was too far gone, grinding on him, making those sweet noises that told him how good he was making her feel, that she was as gone as him, and he nearly went off on that knowledge alone.

"I need you, Dell," she murmured softly, her hands in his hair, her eyes on his. "Need me back."

"I do."

"No. No, I mean—"

He stroked a hand up her thigh, rasping his thumb over ground zero, and she sobbed out his name and arched into him. "Come," he urged her, wanting to watch her fly before he did. "Come for me, Jade."

And with a soft cry, she did.

He joined her, a kaleidoscope of colors bursting behind his eyes. For a moment he actually thought he was having a stroke, but it couldn't possibly feel this good to stroke out.

From the dim recesses of his mind he realized that there was an odd ache in his chest that both hurt and felt right at the same time. He knew the reason, but it could wait until she was gone. Until he was alone again. Alone, which had always worked out so well for him.

Too bad he suddenly—or maybe not so suddenly at all—no longer really believed that.

Twenty-four

Jade opened her eyes some time later. Dell had moved them to her bed and they'd fallen asleep. He was warm and she snuggled closer, kissing his shoulder, wishing . . .

That this was real. That she could figure out a way to make it real that worked for everyone.

Dell's breathing changed, and she knew he was awake. "Hey," he murmured, voice low and sleep rough. "What's wrong?" When she said nothing, he ran his fingers over her skin, and finally she sighed. "I had a dream. About my family."

"About going back?"

He never said home. Sunshine was home. For him, Sunshine had been the first place to ever feel like home. So she nodded again.

Brushing his mouth over her temple, he skimmed his way to her jaw. "You're conflicted."

It wasn't a question, but she answered anyway. "Yes."

"You have choices, Jade. You always have choices." His mouth moved along her throat, making her shiver.

"Like?" she asked, clutching at him.

"Like staying."

Her heart took a hard, hopeful leap. "If I took you up on that, you'd regret it," she said, a little breathless. She needed to drop this conversation now, while she still could.

"You don't know what I want."

A truer statement had never been uttered. "So tell me."

His tongue teased her skin, and she began to lose grip of her thoughts. "You," he said. "I want you."

Want, not need. She arched up against him as his hands ran over her body. "You have me, Dell." Wrapping her legs around his hips, she pulled him to her, locking eyes with him. "All of me."

"For now," he said.

Confused, she opened her mouth, but he used that to his advantage, kissing her hungrily, pushing closer, his body covering hers. The sheet tangled between them, not hiding a thing, not that he was big and hard. *Very* hard.

Dell yanked the sheet away and then he was on her, warm skin in place of the cool cotton.

Her eyes slid shut as his lips moved over hers. She'd learned he loved to kiss, to explore, and she loved to let him. It made her feel . . . wanted. Cherished. Sexy. He'd seen it all before, of course, every inch of her, and yet each time he kissed the small scar on her knee from a long-ago childhood mishap, or ran his tongue over the curve of her breast or the length of her hip with such appreciation, it sent tingles through her. Like now. Her fingers tightened in his hair and brought his mouth back to hers. "Again?"

"Yes," he breathed against her lips. "And then again. Because as it turns out, I don't think I can get enough of you."

"I have no self-discipline when it comes to you," Jade said much later.

Dell didn't open his eyes, but he did let out a low, rough sounding laugh.

"I'm not sure how that's funny," she said.

Dell lifted his head, his hair tousled from her fingers, his expression one hundred percent pure sated male. "You expect to be disciplined during sex?"

"I—"

He laughed again and she elbowed him.

Ignoring that, he reached for her, but she shoved him. "No. Oh no. We've had enough."

He was still laughing when he easily pulled her in close and nuzzled his face in her hair. "Speak for yourself. I'm not sure I could ever get enough."

Running her hand down his beautiful back, she closed her eyes and wished she were brave enough to believe it.

When she woke up, Dell was gone. She ignored the little ping of disappointment and glanced at Beans.

"Mew," Beans said, a knowing look in her sharp eyes.

"No, I am *not* wishing he was still here. Sheesh, what do you take me for, a sex addict?"

"Mew."

With a sigh, Jade showered, dressed and grabbed Beans and got to the office at the same time as usual, but unlike the usual, she wasn't the first one in.

On her desk sat a hot coffee and a bag from the bakery. An egg and turkey bacon croissant, which she dove into as if she'd spent all night running a marathon.

Or being made love to for hours on end . . .

The croissant was so good she moaned as she ate it. Forget having sex all night long. She wanted to have this croissant all night long.

"Mmm," came Dell's low, sexy voice in her ear as his arms encircled her from behind. He nipped at the side of her throat. "That sound you make. It drives me crazy, especially when I'm buried in you and—"

Her cell phone rang.

Drawing a shaky breath, she pushed Dell away and grabbed it.

"The first is Monday," Sam said. "You on track to be here?"

Jade's gaze met Dell's. She knew he could hear Sam. "Yes. I'm leaving in two days."

Sam's relieved expulsion of air sounded in her ear. "I'll fly out and drive back with you."

"No. No, I want to do it alone," she said, still holding Dell's unwavering stare. "I'll be okay."

She hung up and sighed. "Dell—"

"I know. You . . . promised."

He understood promises, he understood loyalty, and he was very good at hiding his thoughts when he wanted to. For a long moment, he continued to look at her as if he wanted to say something, but he didn't. He simply nodded. "Do you need any help?"

She felt her heart crack right up the center. No matter what she needed, he was there for her, sometimes even before she knew what that might be. Yes, he was obstinate, way too sure of himself, couldn't put real words to an emotion to save his life, and yet . . . and yet he had her back in a way no one ever had before. "I really wanted to train someone for you."

"I'm not replacing you, Jade. No one could."

"Dell—"

"I'm going to be fine. Don't worry about me." And then he was gone, the door to his office shutting quietly.

Okay. Good. He was going to be fine. And if he wasn't . . . well, no one would ever know because that's how he operated.

That's how they both operated.

* * *

On Jade's last day, Belle Haven had a record number of patients. This was due more to people wanting to see Jade before she left than any of Dell's skills, and he knew it.

But he couldn't blame anyone. He felt the same. He wanted as many last looks at her as he could get.

They met at Crystal's that night, he, Adam, Brady, Lilah. And Jade.

They shared two pitchers of beer and stories. Lilah brought a cake. "Not homemade," she said. "Because we all know I can't cook worth shit." She hugged Jade hard. "Dammit, I'm testing this waterproof mascara tonight." She sniffed. "I'm really going to miss watching you keep Dell off balance."

Dell would have argued, but it was hard to argue the truth. Jade had been keeping him on his toes since the day she'd walked into his life.

They all walked out to the parking lot together and Lilah hugged her again. And then again, until Brady pried her loose. "She's coming back to visit," he assured Lilah, and looked at Jade. "Right?"

Jade, eyes shimmering brilliantly with unshed tears, nodded. Brady pulled her in close, whispered something Dell couldn't catch, and when he pulled back, Adam moved in. He didn't speak, just hugged her, then tugged lightly on her hair, his eyes solemn but affectionate.

Dell waited until everyone pulled out and it was just him and Jade in the parking lot.

"It's late," she said, voice thick. "And I want to leave before dawn."

He nodded. She didn't want him to follow her home. Message received. "Jade—"

"I don't know how to do this," she whispered. "I don't know how to say good-bye to you."

"So don't."

"Dell—"

He put a finger to her lips. "I just mean that I'll come see you."

She closed her eyes, then nodded. Then she stepped into him and hugged him hard, eyes fierce. "Make sure that you do."

He stood in the lot and watched her drive away. He got into his truck and turned toward home.

Except he went right instead of left, and let his heart steer him to where it thought home was.

Jade's.

She opened the door, eyes and nose red. "This is a bad idea," she said shakily.

"Spectacularly," he agreed, and shut the door behind him. Then he found himself pushed up against it and she kissed him, all hot, confusing desperation, which unleashed his own.

"We shouldn't do this," she said against his mouth when they came up for air.

"No." Look at him, all agreeable, as if his heart weren't breaking in fucking two. Her body heat was seeping into him, warming the core of him with the very essence of her. Then she made a sound in the back of her throat and cuddled in, soft and pliant and willing. God, so willing.

They dove at each other. Apparently, they were doing this.

Lacing his fingers into her hair, Dell took her mouth in a drugging kiss, holding her face in one hand, sliding his other down her back to cup her ass, squeezing until she moaned. He worked his way down her body, divesting her of clothing as he went. She moaned again when he flicked his tongue over her puckered nipple and arched into him with a gasp when he dropped to his knees, pinned her hips to the door and kissed his way lower. By the time he made his way to her center she was writhing beneath his hands, the little whimpers coming from her the sexiest sounds he'd ever heard.

"Dell," she panted. "Now. God, please. Now."

Her face was upturned, lips parted, her eyes closed, her fingers digging into his shoulders. He'd never seen anything hotter. "Come first," he said. "I love to watch you come."

"Oh God. I . . . Don't stop. Don't ever stop."

She came on his fingers, and then on his tongue, and then again when he surged upright, magically produced a condom and entered her right there, taking her against the door.

"Oh," she cried, her fingers digging into his back. "We need to—"

"Yes." They needed to do this. Now. He did his best to move slow, to build up the pressure for her, trying to show her a patience he didn't feel. But she bit his neck and then sucked a patch of skin into her mouth, flicking her tongue over it, and slow went out the window. "Jade—" He wanted to tell her to relax, that this was it, their final time and he wanted—*needed*—to make it last.

But she wasn't feeling the same need. She grinded against him and he closed his eyes. No, that made it even worse.

Or better . . .

Her hands were everywhere, grasping ahold of anything she could brace herself with, and though he tried to keep the pace steady, she wasn't helping, moaning his name, arching against him, trying to climb inside his body. He felt her body tighten around him as she burst and he opened his eyes to watch, but that proved to be his undoing and he came with her, hard. When his knees gave out, he slid to the floor, barely managing to keep a grip on her. Not that she noticed. She was limp, content, and clearly sated, and for once he felt the same. Breathing hard, he braced them against the wall and held her close.

"Gonna miss that," she said hoarsely against his chest.

Yeah. Big-time.

"Are we going to get up?"

No. He wanted to stay here, right here, still inside her body, in her life. "I'm not ready to let go of you."

With a soft little hum of agreement, she cuddled in tight.

Twenty-five

Nearly a week later, Dell shut himself in his office after a long day and sank exhausted to his chair. He'd caved and called the temp agency (emphasis on *temp*) on the second day. He'd told Jade he wasn't going to replace her and he wasn't. The agency had sent a perfectly nice twenty-two-year-old receptionist from Boise, who was interested in wintering in Sunshine to ski on the weekends.

That was the same excuse Jade had given him when she'd come to Sunshine and it hadn't escaped him, and as he thought of her, as he had for five straight days now, he felt a stab of pain in his chest.

Of course that might just be the fresh scratch from pec to pec, courtesy of one pissed-off feline from an earlier patient visit.

His day had sucked.

His life sucked.

Leaning back in his chair, he closed his eyes, wanting to snap at whoever had just opened his door and let themselves in. "It's called a knock."

Ignoring his scowl, Lilah sat on the corner of his desk. "You okay?"

As if he were too busy to talk, he stared at his computer—which wasn't even booted up. "Yeah."

"You working?"

"Yep," he said, without taking his eyes off his blank screen.

She came around the desk and stood behind him, staring at the blank screen along with him. "Dell—"

"Look," he said. "I know you think you're trying to help with the phone calls, the texts, the lunches you keep bringing by, but I want to be left alone."

"Really? Because when *I* was hurting, you never left me alone. You badgered, bullied, and pretty much shoved me back to the life of the living."

"I'm not you," he said, closing his eyes.

The next sound he heard was that of his office door shutting quietly. He dropped his head to his desk, pounding it a few times because he was a complete asshole.

When the door opened again, he didn't lift his head. "I'm sorry. I just want to be alone."

"Got that loud and clear. And nice job on kicking the puppy, you asshole."

Adam. He sighed. "I meant for you *all* to go away."

"Aw, and here I wanted to join your pity party."

"Fuck you."

Adam came around Dell's desk and kicked Dell's chair back from it. "You sent her away and now you're punishing everyone that's left. What the hell's that?"

"I didn't send her away. She left all on her own."

"So ask her to come back."

Dell shoved Adam away and stood up, stalking to the window.

"It's unlike you to hole up and hide out."

"I'm not."

"Bullshit you're not. How many women have you dated this year?"

Dell craned his neck and narrowed his eyes at his brother.

"Yeah," Adam said. "I can't count, either. You've never even looked back. But you're looking back now. Why don't you just man up, tell her how you feel, and work it out?"

"We're *not* talking about this."

"Okay. Except we are." Adam took the desk chair and made himself comfortable, leaning back, folding his fingers together over his abs. "Because I've been voted to kick your ass into gear."

"Look, she was needed back at home, so she went. It's not that far. We're going to visit."

Adam nodded.

"And anyway, I should be relieved. It's a forced slowing-down period, right? Things . . . they were getting a little out of hand."

"Out of hand?" Adam repeated. "Is that what you kids call falling in love these days?"

Dell turned to face Adam, his ass resting against the window sill because his legs felt a little wobbly. "Who said anything about love?"

"Oh, that's right. You only love four-legged furry creatures."

"Fuck you."

"Aw, you're repeating yourself again." Adam stood. "Listen. What happened to us when we were kids, that was . . . fucked up."

Not wanting to hear this, or anything else for that matter, Dell gave Adam a push toward the door.

Adam took a step back but held his ground. "But we still managed to make something of ourselves."

"Adam—"

"That was all you, man. Brady and I kept our heads on straight because we had you to look after. And then later on when the both of us lost it, *you* kept your head on straight. You give everything you have to us, to this place, to the animals that come to you in it. So why can't you give everything you have to the one woman who's ever made you happy?"

"Look, I told you, we'll be okay. I'll see her whenever I'm in Chicago, and—"

"You're in Chicago never."

Dell gave Adam another push to the door.

"Good talk," Adam said, just before Dell slammed the door in his face.

It took three days for Jade to get back to Chicago. The drive was easy enough, smooth weather, no car problems. Her phone rang steadily. Lilah, checking in with traffic reports, wanting Jade to know about the cow reportedly on the highway in Wyoming, and the detour in Nebraska, and that Lilah had already planned a Chicago trip.

Jade had hung up each time smiling.

Then tearing up.

She missed Lilah already.

Brady called, letting her know he'd changed her oil the night before she'd left and also put on new windshield wipers.

Adam called several times as well, asking about work and scheduling. Things they both knew that he already knew.

No pressure to come back, not from any of them. They wanted what was best for her.

They wanted her to be happy . . .

Dell didn't call. She didn't expect him to. But she picked up her phone often and thumbed to his contact info, then set her phone down.

Back in Chicago, she went straight to her town house. There were no surprises. Well, except that when she set

Beans's carrier down and opened the door, the cat didn't want to come out.

Jade coaxed her with some treats, but after she ate them she went right back into her carrier with a low growl that Jade would have sworn said, *This is not home.*

Jade's mother had sent people in to clean periodically and Sam had long ago adopted her few plants, so she shouldn't have been surprised to find everything in order and in its place, smelling slightly of lemon cleaner.

It was bigger than she remembered. More open.

More empty.

She'd spent her first day alone, not having told anyone she was back, but by day two Sam had sniffed her out.

He let himself in with his key and called to her from the front door. "Jade?" Before she could blink, he'd crossed the living room, hauled her off the couch and was hugging her. "Jesus, are you a sight for sore eyes." Pulling back, he stared down into her face and smiled.

When she didn't return it, his slowly faded. "You okay?"

"Of course," she said. "Just tired from the drive."

"How tired? Because your mother's expecting you for dinner."

"I know. I'll go get that over with and then come back here and crash, I think. Catch up on some sleep. Three solid days of driving is pretty exhausting."

"Is that all it is?" Sam asked quietly, still holding on to her. "Trip exhaustion?"

Pulling free, she moved around, running a finger on some of the pictures on the walls, pictures of her and her family over the years.

Friends.

Old friends that had easily vanished from her life when she'd left here. There'd been a few token efforts to keep up, from both sides, but that had petered out with shocking ease.

Now she looked at the pictures and realized her real friends were seventeen hundred miles away in Sunshine, Idaho.

And possibly her heart.

"Jade?"

Throat burning, she turned to face Sam, forcing a smile that totally crumpled when he just looked at her and said her name.

"I'm just really tired," she whispered, and swiped angrily at the sole tear that escaped. "That's all."

And utterly belying these words, she burst into tears.

His face softened and he gathered her in, stroking her hair. "Oh, Jade. It's going to be okay."

She nodded and tried not to snot on his shirt, hoping he was right. That somehow it was going to be okay.

Sam drove to Jade's parents' house, which worked for Jade. She was too nervous. Unsettled.

Heartsick.

She stirred when Sam got off the freeway two exits early.

"What are you doing?" Jade asked.

"Need to go by the center and pick up some files to read tonight."

Panic slithered through Jade. "No."

Sam slid a look at her, then did a double take, his easy smile fading into worry. "Jade."

"I'm not doing this now."

"They're expecting you tomorrow, you know that, right? I thought it'd be easier for you if we went there now, tonight. When there's no one there. You can walk through, get your bearings."

Her pulse was up to stroke level and her palms were sweating. "I'm not going back for the first time at night."

Again Sam sent her a questing, concerned look but he

didn't press. He simply executed a U-turn and got back on the freeway without another word.

"Thanks," she said quietly.

"I just got you back." He reached for her hand to give it a gentle squeeze. "I'm sure as hell not risking chasing you out of here."

Ten minutes later, they pulled up to her family home, which was a large Colonial with a circular driveway lined with oak trees and strategically placed flowerpots to give a sedate but elegant glow of color.

Growing up, she'd run across the grass, picked flowers for the neighbors, and climbed the trees. Despite the place's sophistication, it had been a warm, family home.

There were cars in the driveway, too many, which made her stomach jangle uncomfortably. Never in her life had a crowd bothered her, certainly not a crowd of what was sure to be people she knew and knew well, but as they got out of Sam's car, she held on to the door a little too long.

Sam came around for her and took her hand. "Ready?"

"As I'll ever be." But at the front door she hesitated again. It hadn't been that long, she'd flown home for a long weekend for her father's birthday. And then over Memorial Day for another quick trip when her cousin had had a baby.

"Jade," Sam said softly.

"Give me a minute." Or another year and a half.

But then the matter was taken out of her hands when the door whipped open and her mother stood there.

"Well goodness, darling. You're standing out there like a delivery person waiting for a tip." Lucinda Bennett had given up practicing medicine five years ago now to dedicate her time to Jade's father, but she hadn't given up a single concession to looking good. She was in a black Prada cocktail dress, her carefully maintained red hair twisted up out of her face. She was as beautiful as ever as she gestured for

Sam to come in, giving him a hug that she had to reach up for since Sam was a foot taller than her.

Sam dutifully bent and kissed his aunt on the cheek, gently squeezed Jade's shoulder, and moved into the house out of sight.

Lucinda took Jade's hands into her own and held tight. "So you don't escape."

"Mom."

"What, you ran off once. I am not risking it again." She looked Jade over. "Your hair's getting long."

"Yes." Jade resisted patting at it self-consciously. "Mom, I—"

"And you haven't been wearing sunscreen religiously like I taught you—you have a tan. Darling, your skin is your age meter."

Jade let out a low laugh. "I know, Mom."

"And what is that you're wearing . . . *jeans*?"

"Yes."

Her mother's eyes lifted to Jade's and filled. "And the cashmere sweater I sent you for your birthday." She tightened her grip on Jade's hands. "Oh, baby. Are you really here?"

"Yeah, I'm really here."

Lucinda pulled her in for a warm hug, then stepped back, searching her pockets for a tissue, which she used to dab precisely at her eyes. There was never an excuse for running mascara.

"Where's Dad?" Jade asked.

"Right here, pumpkin." William Bennett rolled into the foyer. Even in his motorized wheelchair, he still cut an imposing figure. He had straight shoulders and thick gray hair that gave an impression of great knowledge and power. He held out his arms and Jade crouched at his side and hugged him.

"Thought I was going to have to come get you myself," he said with affection in his voice.

"I promised, didn't I?" Jade said, some of her joy at see-ing him diminished by the feel of him in her arms. Thinner. He'd lost weight.

A line appeared between his brows. "Honey, I don't give a fig about a promise. I thought you were back because you wanted to be."

"Of course she wants to be," Lucinda said. "Chicago's her home, we're her family."

William cupped Jade's face and looked into her eyes. "You're really okay?"

"I'm okay." When he didn't relax, just kept looking at her, into her, she sighed. "Do you want me to promise?"

"No more promises," he said softly, for her ears alone. "Family isn't solely about obligation."

Jade didn't have words for that, so she hugged him again.

"Stop making me cry," Lucinda said behind them. "I don't want to be blotchy for pictures."

Jade's stomach shifted. "Pictures?"

"We're having a welcome-home party."

"Now?"

"Well, when else?" Her mom pulled Jade through the foyer toward the grand living room. "I sent Sam for you to make sure you showed up."

Oh, for the love of—

"Surprise!" yelled a bunch of voices as people popped up from the furniture and out of the woodwork—friends and family she hadn't seen in far too long.

Jade's gaze sought out a guilty-looking Sam's.

Sorry, he mouthed. But before she could do anything— and killing him seemed to top her personal wish list—she was surrounded.

Twenty-six

Dell was as good at denial as the next guy, but even he was going to need some good distractions to get through Jade's being gone.

Turned out, he got plenty of distractions.

He was called into Belle Haven at five A.M. A five-month-old golden retriever had consumed a kitchen towel and gotten deathly ill.

Dell met them at the center and confirmed his suspicions—the dog's intestines were blocked by towel shreds. He operated and was back in his office by seven, leaning back in his chair studying the ceiling.

His eyes felt gritty. He was exhausted, but every time he closed his eyes he saw Jade. He could feel her touch, hear her laugh, taste her tears in their last kiss.

Closing his eyes, he took a deep breath. He'd been such a cocky son of a bitch. He'd actually convinced himself that Jade being the one to walk away was a good thing. He wouldn't have to break her heart.

And then he'd gotten his broken. He had definitely not seen that one coming . . .

His door opened. "Mrs. Mason's Chinese Shar-Pei puppy is in exam one," Keith said. "Star was wounded in a scuffle with a housemate."

The twelve-week-old Star weighed all of ten pounds dripping wet. Her "housemate" was a twenty-pound Siamese cat with the disposition of Scrooge. Shit. Well, he'd needed more distractions . . .

It was easy enough to busy himself. He'd already fucked up his neat, organized office. That had happened the day Jade had left. He was back to his old ways. If she wanted to fix it, she'd have to get her sweet ass back here.

Only that wasn't going to happen.

If he wanted her sweet ass back here, he was going to have to go get it. He was going to have to figure his shit out, figure out how to give her what she wanted and get what he wanted at the same time.

The next day Jade got up, showered, dressed, and drove into work. She parked in the lot, grabbed her purse, and reached into the backseat for Beans's carrier.

Which wasn't there, of course.

Jade had left the cat in the town house. The medical center was no place for her.

Beans had taken this as the final insult. After a three-day drive and being thrust into yet another new environment, she'd revolted, retreating to beneath Jade's bed, and no coaxing or bribing could get her to come out.

Jade had been forced to leave her there or be late for work, but she felt like shit, like she'd let down the one friend she had in the same state as her. She locked her car and hurried out of the lot into the biting November cold. Her hand was in her purse, fingers wrapped around her can of hair spray.

Adam would be proud, she thought, not allowing herself to think of Dell because thinking of Dell brought a rush of emotions that made her knees weak and threatened her mascara.

And everyone knew, a Bennett never let her mascara run.

It was bright daylight and there was no danger now, not like there'd been that night, but unreasonable fears always trumped logic. She practically ran up the steps and then stopped, hand on the door.

The point of no return. Sandy was supposedly perfectly happy with going back to managing the Urgent Care Department of the center, but still, Jade didn't like the idea of pushing her out.

Jade, Jade, Jade. What you don't like is the idea of being back . . .

She took her hand off the door handle. A woman and a man walked up the steps behind her. The woman smiled politely and said, "Excuse me," gesturing that Jade was in her way.

Jade backed up. The building was a large glass and concrete beauty, surrounded by other equally impressive buildings. Her father loved architecture.

Belle Haven wasn't an architectural marvel, but the country exterior surrounded by the majestic, rustic Bitterroot Mountains had felt infinitely more warm and accepting and inviting.

Home . . .

She shook her head. The parking lot behind her was as busy as the streets, and so was the front door. People were entering and exiting around her. Between each, Jade stared at the door but never quite managed to walk through it. After a few minutes, the door opened and Sam came out. He was in a doctor's coat with a stethoscope around his neck, his badge pinned to a pec pocket: DR. SAM BENNETT.

Clearly he'd been working but had either looked out one

of the windows or been alerted to her presence. Who knew what she'd drawn him away from. "I'm sorry, Sam."

"Jade—" He put his hands on her arms. "You're shaking. Come inside, we'll get some coffee and—"

"No." She pulled free, taking one of his hands in hers and staring up into his handsome, caring face. "Sam, listen to me."

"I'm all ears for you. You know that. Talk to me."

"You remember how this used to be so exciting that we'd show up for work early? That everything we accomplished here was a thrill?" She could see in his eyes he knew exactly what she meant, that he still felt that way. She swallowed the lump in her throat. "I don't feel that way anymore."

He shook his head but she squeezed his hand. She needed to say this. He needed to hear it. "Being here isn't the same for me. The very things that fueled me, working with people, living in a big city—it all paralyzes me now."

"Jade," he said, sounding raw and devastated. "You can talk to someone about that—"

"It's not the attack." She pressed the heels of her hands to her eyes, then dropped them. "Okay, that's what started it. But that's not what it is now. I'm not afraid, I just don't want to be here. I've changed, Sam. This place isn't for me anymore. And to be honest, I don't think it ever really was."

"What are you talking about? All your life you were groomed for this."

"Exactly. I was groomed. I never made the choice. I'll take responsibility for that, but it's time, past time, for me to do what's right for me." Going up on tiptoe, she brushed a kiss to his jaw. "I love you. Please believe me when I tell you that I wanted to do this for you, for all of you. But I can't." She hugged him and felt the vibration of his cell phone furiously going off in his pocket. "You're needed inside."

He squeezed her hard. "You're going back."

Yeah. She was going back. She knew it as she crossed the lot and got into her car. She didn't want to run a big empire. She wanted to sit at the front desk of Belle Haven and run that world. She wanted to see friendly faces, she wanted to play poker with her friends, she wanted to listen to Lilah wax poetic about Brady, she wanted to watch Adam play his tough guy while melting over the puppies he bred.

She wanted . . . Dell.

No, he hadn't asked her to stay. He wouldn't. It had been her decision to make and he'd trusted and expected her to make the right decision for herself.

She'd screwed up there.

She'd screwed up a lot. But she was hoping she was smart enough to learn from her mistakes.

Back at her town house, she stuck her key in the lock, figuring she'd pull Beans out from beneath the bed and load her things, which she'd never unpacked.

That should have been a sign.

She had no idea exactly what the plan was. Just get in her car and drive? Show up in Sunshine and hope that the relationships she'd forged there were as real as they felt?

Count on Dell being happy to see her?

But all those thoughts were derailed when she realized her alarm was decoded. Her dad was in his chair in her living room, Beans in his lap, eyes closed in bliss, purring.

Jade stared at her. "Are you kidding me?"

Her dad smiled. "She's a sweet thing."

Hmmm. Jade gave Beans a long look, then crouched at her father's side. "Sam called you."

He nodded. "Sam called me. I had my driver bring me here, I hope you don't mind." His tremors were slight but more noticeable than the last time she'd seen him. "He's waiting outside for me."

"Dad." She had to find a way to explain it all to him, why she couldn't do this, why she couldn't stay, how she never meant to hurt him, but she had to do this for herself. "Dad, I—"

He covered her hand with his, and when she looked up and met his gaze, his eyes were full of something she hadn't expected.

Understanding. "It's okay, Jade," he said. "Whatever it is, just tell me."

"You always said I could do whatever I wanted," she said softly, and her voice caught. Dammit. Dammit, she was already too close to tears.

"Yes," he said. "Whatever suited you."

"The thing is, I never really knew what that was."

He ran a thumb over her knuckles. "Now, see, I was under the impression you did."

"I wanted to make you happy," she said.

"Oh, Jade." He closed his eyes, then opened them, a world of emotion there. "You've always made me happy."

"Because I lived here and ran your medical center. I was your Jade."

"You're still my Jade."

She shook her head. "No, I'm—"

"You're also your own version of Jade. That's new," he said, his voice carrying a tremor, too, she realized.

Her eyes filled. "Yes. Dad, I'm not . . . I can't . . ."

"You aren't staying," he said.

God. God, this was hard. "No, I'm not staying. I'm so sorry."

"Oh, honey. Don't ever be sorry for being who you are. Most of us go our whole lives not really getting it right, just settling." He tugged a strand of her hair. "Do you have any idea the strength it takes to *not* settle? To keep pushing and seeking for what works?"

It was like a huge weight lifted off her chest. She could breathe again, and when her dad was gone, Jade looked for Beans.

Who was once again beneath the bed. "We're going

back," she told the cat, bending low to look into her eyes. "Home."

Beans just stared at her.

"To Sunshine."

Beans paused, just long enough to make it clear that this was Beans's decision and no one else's, and then she walked out from beneath the bed, head high.

They were going back. Not running from something this time. But running to . . .

An hour later, Jade was staring at her spreadsheets. She was leaving tomorrow and she'd made a list of lists to keep organized. She had a things-to-do-before-selling-the-condo list. And a buy-for-the-trip list. A who-to-call list. And she was working on a places-not-to-stop-at list, which would include that rest stop in Nebraska that never had toilet paper. Her tummy rumbled, reminding her she hadn't eaten since . . . She couldn't remember. She scoured the kitchen and came up with a box of graham crackers, a candy bar, and a bag of marshmallows.

S'mores supplies from two years ago when she'd had a party. She eyeballed Beans. "Dinner's on me tonight." She stepped onto her front porch and looked at the small little hibachi barbecue that also hadn't been used in far too long. There was frost on it.

She went back inside and searched for something for kindling. The only thing she could come up with was her business cards. She put on a wool coat, hat and gloves, and using her business cards, built a very nice little bonfire, if she said so herself.

She figured she had maybe half an hour before someone reported her to the association and they complained. They could all take a flying leap, she was out of here in the morning.

She was putting the finishing touches on her first s'more when a car drove up. Damn, that was fast. She peeked, then went still, certain her eyes were deceiving her.

Because it was a cab, and she recognized the dark silhouette getting out of it. Dell, with a duffel bag slung over his shoulder.

Her mouth fell open.

It stayed open as he paid the cab and headed up the walk toward her.

His eyes tracked to hers and locked on, and she felt a surge of warmth spread through her. God, he was a sight for sore eyes in jeans and a down jacket, hair tousled, eyes tired—though they sparked at the sight of her.

She sparked, too. In her good parts, certainly, but most of all in her heart.

He'd come here.

All the way here.

Why?

He took the steps two at a time with his long legs, and then he was standing right in front of her. "Hey."

She tilted her head back and tried for cool but couldn't access any cool. "Hey," she whispered.

He dropped the duffel bag and hunkered at her side. "You did say we could have the occasional weekend. Too soon?"

The lump in her throat was back, but she swallowed it and smiled, so damn happy to see him she could hardly put words together. "So you flew out here to go on a date?"

His lips curved, and something happened inside her chest. It filled with . . . hunger. Longing.

Need.

"A date sounds good," he said. "We never really did much of that, did we?"

"No." She crumpled up a few more spreadsheets and tossed them into the dying flames. "But that was okay with me. You didn't keep any of the women you dated. And even if you had, I didn't want to be one of your . . . gaggle." She handed him a stick and a marshmallow. "S'more?"

"Gaggle?"

"A family of noisy geese. Or in your case, all the single women in all the land."

His smiled widened, but he took the stick and snatched three additional marshmallows. "You aren't part of my gaggle, Jade. You never were." He eyed the small stack of business cards she had left but was smart enough not to mention them. Instead, he concentrated on carefully constructing a s'more with the same precision he used in surgery.

Jade could hardly believe he was here. She wanted to throw herself at him. Instead, she stuffed her face with her own delicious s'more, then licked chocolate off her fingers. "I'm surprised to see you," she said as casually as she could. "Given your whole no-relationship decree."

He took his time creating another s'more. "If you think about it," he finally said, "we already have a relationship."

This admission caught her by surprise. She'd known. She just hadn't realized he had as well.

"It sort of sneaked up on me," he said softly, reaching past her for more chocolate. "Tripped me up some, I'll give you that. But it's true. We're friends. Maybe even best friends. Unfortunately, it's not enough for me."

She stopped breathing.

"Is it enough for you, Jade?"

She opened her mouth, but before she could answer he hedged his bet by lowering his head and gently kissing her. "You asked why I'm here," he said against her lips. "It's because you're a part of my life, you're a part of *me*, Jade, the most important part, actually, and have been since the day you walked into Sunshine."

She stared at him while her heart slowly rolled over in her chest and exposed its tender, vulnerable belly.

He stood, tugging her up with him and wrapping his arms around her. "You should know that my office is a mess. I fucked up the computer system. And the printer won't work."

"Hmm." She hung on, snaking her hands beneath his jacket and shirt just to touch his warm, smooth skin. "It's only been five days."

He tightened his grip on her. "Five and a half."

Her hands settled on his chest, where she could feel his heart beating under her fingers. Strong and steady. Sure. "Dell."

"Yeah?"

"I've missed you, too."

"Good." He lowered his head and kissed her, his lips promising everything his words never did.

Twenty-seven

Somehow they moved inside, mouths still fused. From a distance, Jade could hear ringing, but she didn't want to take her mouth off of Dell's to figure it out. If she stopped kissing him, it might turn out to be a dream.

"Your phone," he said against her lips, then pulled reluctantly back.

She walked into her den, which she'd always used as an office. It was her fax machine, and as the papers started to spit out, she smiled, knowing she'd made the right decision.

Dell had followed her in, removing his jacket. "What?" he asked.

She held up the list of painters her mother had sent over. "I'm going to put this place up for sale."

He went still, his eyes guarded, so carefully guarded they pierced her heart. "What does that mean?"

"It means," she said, "that the next time you want to pick me up for a date, it'll take you a whole hell of a lot less time to get me."

He didn't smile. He took the fax out of her hand and set

it on the desk. He pulled her to him and looked into her eyes, his own expression dialed to his surgery face, the one that gave nothing away. He looked utterly impenetrable, but she knew him now, and she knew that he was at his most vulnerable when he felt he had to hide his thoughts. She knew that her leaving Sunshine must have brought some of his deep-seated abandonment issues to the surface, yet he'd done his best to deal with that while still stepping back and letting her make her own decisions. Bringing her hands up, she cupped his face. "You remember what I told you about my grandmother?"

He didn't blink at the subject change. "Yes. You were named for her."

"Yes, so I'd have her strength. I never even questioned it. I willingly followed the path she'd started. I let myself be an empty mold. No one meant to hurt me, but all my life I allowed others to make my path for me. After the attack, I lost that path. I lost me. Do you know how I found myself?"

He gave a slow shake of his head.

"It was you, Dell. Your belief in me, to make me strong enough to say good-bye to a life I wasn't really living, to get my own life, to choose who I am, to build that person. To be strong. Like you."

"Jade." His voice was thick. Clearly he was stunned and deeply affected to hear that he'd so impacted her life. "It was all you."

"I know what you did that day you first had me organize your desk and then let me look at your accounting. And then again when you showed me how to break out of that hold. If it wasn't for you, I'd never have discovered who I really was. Or the fact that I am not defined by the worst day of my life."

His eyes softened. "I just wanted you to never be afraid again. To believe in yourself. And then, when that started happening, when you started gaining confidence, I realized the truth. It was happening, exactly what I wanted—you were learning to live without fear and getting strong . . . so that you could leave. I was helping you leave." Letting out a low laugh, he pressed his forehead to hers. "Christ, that sucked." He tilted his head and kissed her gently, eyes open, locked on hers. "I love you," he breathed. "I love you so goddamn much it hurts."

Her heart swelled. A single moment of terror had led to her running from everyone and everything she'd ever known, but she could no longer regret or resent it.

Not when it'd all led to this, to the best moment of her life.

She pressed her hand to his chest. "I love you, too, Dell. With all my heart. And I want my job back."

The corners of his mouth tilted up in a slow, intimate smile. "I was hoping you would."

"You should know, I gave up my lease on that loft in Sunshine. I'll have to find something else."

"I know a place."

"Yeah?"

"Yeah," he said. "It's not too far from work."

"Tell me about it."

"It's a house. Airy rooms, wide-open space. There's ice cream in the freezer at all times. Pizza on speed-dial. Cats are welcome. And there's a gym. Comes with a personal trainer. Interested?"

Her heart caught. He'd been serial dating for years and had never even brought a woman home with him. Not once.

Until her. "More than you can imagine."

"Good." He kissed her, not gently this time. "There's only one thing left, then."

"What's that?"

"The terms."

She turned, and he unzipped her dress so that the bodice fell from her breasts to the crook of her arms. Stepping close, he pressed himself against her. She could feel him hard against the cleft of her buttocks as he dipped his head and nipped at the nape of her neck. "T-terms?" she managed.

"Are you a bed hog?"

"I—" One of his hands slid up to cup her breast, his fingers teasing her nipple until she moaned and ground into him. "You already know that I am."

"That'll have to go on the spreadsheet." He ran his lips down her throat to her shoulder. Her knees buckled, but he had her.

"S-spreadsheet?" She sounded like Peanut.

"Yes. We'll need a spreadsheet to keep track of things. We don't want any hard or hurt feelings. I'm a hot-water hog. That'll go in my column. I'll have to make retribution for that . . ." He pushed her dress over her hips so that it dropped to the floor, leaving her in her lace bra and matching thong, which pulled a rough groan from deep in his throat as he stroked the curve of her breast.

A rush seared through her so strong it was almost painful. She held her breath and waited, for it to relent, for it to lessen into a normal level of desire, but there was nothing normal here, nothing in her realm of understanding.

She'd never felt like this with anyone else before. "Will we share the cooking?"

"Or dialing for takeout."

She started to laugh but choked on it when he pressed a hand low on her spine, urging her to bend over the desk slightly. "I dreamed about you last night," he said, voice rough.

"You did?" She flattened her hands on the wood as he slid a hand up her thigh and let his fingers brush the front of her lace thong. "You dreamed about doing this, here, with me?"

"Yes." His tongue traced the shell of her ear. "I dreamed of you, like this." He thrust two fingers into her in one long, smooth movement. She gasped. With no effort, and without relenting the rhythm of his fingers, he rearranged her to suit him, spreading her legs a little, bending her over more so that he could continue to drive her mad.

Or make her beg.

"What else?" she whispered. "What else was in your dream?"

He produced a condom and protected them both. "Taking you like this."

Wriggling back against him, she reached back and grasped his thigh. He ran a finger down her ass and she wriggled some more. "Please," she murmured.

"Yes. But this first." He whipped her around and set her on the desk. "I want to see you. Watch you as you come, my name on your lips." Her thong vanished, and a second later he was poised at her entrance.

Teasing.

"Dell." He was there, right there and every part of her body was trembling, on fire, so ready that each breath brought a new wave of desire and need for him. She lifted her hips, hoping to tempt him as she tried to angle herself but he held her still.

She moaned and arched against him, her breasts pressing into his chest. He slid into her in one thrust, filling her, somehow touching every part of her, giving her the connection she'd been craving, needing. She let her head fall back on her shoulders and closed her eyes. "What else? What else did you dream?"

"Open your eyes," he said, voice rough as he thrust again, deeper.

Farther.

Filling her more than she'd thought possible.

She struggled to open her eyes, and found his hot and intense on her. "This, Jade. I dreamed of this. The way you're looking at me, how you feel beneath me, all of it. Every night. Every minute." His hand slid between them, unerringly finding her so that she arched into him, meeting his thrusts, clinging to him as the sensations swept over her body, building, heating, until she exploded. Somehow she managed to keep her eyes open, letting him watch as everything within her tightened and burst.

That was all it took. His control snapped, and he thrust into her hard, fast, and then stilled, groaning her name as he came.

It took her a while to come down, and even then the tremors still spiraled through her, giving her little aftershocks. "Jesus," Dell breathed, shaking his head like he was dazed.

"How is that even possible?" she asked. "How come that's still so . . . amazing, every single time?"

He was still inside her, and getting hard again. "Animal attraction."

"So you're saying . . ."

"It's not going away."

"That's what I was afraid of." But she wasn't afraid. Not of this, not of him. She was exhilarated.

Bending low, he breathed the words against her mouth. "I'll never get enough of you, Jade. Never. Now kiss me. Kiss me and seal our deal."

And that's just what she did.

Turn the page for a preview of
Jill Shalvis's next novel

RUMOR HAS IT

Coming in November 2013
from Berkley Books

One

⌒

Kate Evans would've sold her soul for a stress-free morning, but either her soul wasn't worth much or whoever was in charge of granting wishes was taking a nap. With her phone vibrating from incoming texts—which she was doing her best to ignore—she shoved her car into park and ran across the lot and into the convenience store. "Duct tape?" she called out to Meg, the clerk behind the counter.

Meg had pink and purple dyed hair, enough piercings to ensure certain drowning if she ever went swimming, and was in the middle of a heated debate on the latest *The Voice* knockout rounds with another customer. But she stabbed a finger in the direction of aisle three.

Kate snatched a roll of duct tape, some twine, and then, because she was also weak, a rack of chocolate mini donuts for later. Halfway to the checkout, a bin of fruit tugged at her good sense so she grabbed an apple. Dumping everything on the counter, she fumbled through her pockets for cash.

Meg rang her up and bagged her order. "You're not going to murder someone, are you?"

Kate choked out a laugh. "What?"

"Well . . ." Meg took in Kate's appearance. "Librarian outfit. Duct tape. Twine. I know you're the math whiz around here, but it all adds up to a *Criminal Minds* episode to me."

Kate was wearing a cardigan, skirt, leggings, and—because she'd been in a hurry and they'd been by the front door—snow boots. She supposed with her glasses and her hair piled up on her head she might resemble the second-grade teacher that she was, and okay, maybe the snow boots in May were a little suspect. "You watch too much TV," Kate said. "It's going to fry your brain."

"You know what fries your brain? Not enough sex." Meg pointed to her phone. "Got that little tidbit right off the Internet on my last break."

"Well, then it must be true," Kate said.

Meg laughed. "That's all I'm saying."

Kate laughed along with her, grabbed her change and her bag, and hurried to the door. She was late. As the grease that ran her family's wheel, she needed to get to her dad's house to help prepare her little brother, Tommy, for school, and then coax the Evil Teen into even going to school. The duct tape run wasn't to facilitate that, or to kill anyone, but to make a camel, of all things—part of the drama project Tommy had forgotten to mention was due today.

Kate stepped outside and got slapped around by the wind. The month of May had burst onto the scene like a PMS-ing Mother Nature, leaving the beautiful, rugged Bitterroot Mountains looming high overhead, dusted with last week's surprise snow. Here on the valley floor there wasn't any snow. Just lots of wet muck.

Spring in Sunshine, Idaho was MIA.

As she watched her step on the wet, slippery asphalt, she pulled out her once again vibrating phone just to make sure no one was dying. It was a text from her dad and read: Hurry, it's awake.

It being her sister. The other texts were from Ashley herself, upset because she couldn't find her cheerleading top, and also did Kate know that Tommy was talking to his invisible friend in the bathroom again?

Kate sighed and closed her eyes for the briefest second, which was all it took for her snow boots to slip. She went down like a sack of cement, her phone flying one way, her bag the other as she hit the ground butt-first with teeth-jarring impact.

"Dammit!" She took a second for inventory—no massive injuries. That this was in thanks to not having lost those five pounds of winter brownie blues didn't make her feel any better. The cold ground seeped into her tights and abraded the bare skin of her palms. Rolling to her hands and knees, she reached for her keys just as a set of denim-clad legs came into her field of vision.

The owner of the legs crouched down, easily balancing on the balls of his feet. A hand appeared, her keys centered in the big palm. Tilting her head up, she froze.

Her polite stranger wore a baseball cap low over his eyes, shadowing most of his face and dark hair, but she'd know those gunmetal gray eyes anywhere. And then there was the rest of him. Six foot two and built for trouble in Army camo cargoes, a black sweatshirt, and his usual bad-ass attitude, the one that tended to have men backing off and women checking for drool, there was no mistaking Griffin Reid, the first guy she'd ever fallen for. Of course she'd been ten at the time . . .

"That was a pretty spectacular fall," he said, blocking her from getting up. "Make sure you're okay."

Keep your cool, she told herself. *Don't speak, just nod.* But her mouth didn't get the memo. "No worries, a man's forty-seven percent more likely to die from a fall than a woman." The minute the words escaped her mouth, she bit her tongue, but of course it was too late. When she got nervous, she spouted inane science facts.

And Griffin Reid made her very nervous.

"I'm going to ask you again," he said, not moving his tall, linebacker's body an inch as he pinned her in place with nothing more than his steady gaze. "Are you okay?"

Actually, no, she wasn't. Not even close. Her pride was cracked, and quite possibly her butt as well, but that wasn't what had her sitting there on the ground in stunned shock. "You're . . . home."

He smiled grimly. "I was ordered back by threat of bodily harm if I was late to the wedding."

He was kidding. No one ordered the tough, stoic, badass Griffin to do anything, except maybe Uncle Sam. He was some secret Army demolitions expert who'd been in Afghanistan for three straight tours. But his sister Holly was getting married this weekend. And if there was anyone more bossy or determined than Griffin, it was his baby sister. Only Holly could get her reticent brother halfway around the world for her vows.

Kate had told herself that as Holly's best friend and maid of honor, she would absolutely not drool over Griffin if he showed up. And she would especially not make a fool of herself.

Too late, on both counts.

Again, she attempted to get up but Griffin put a big, tanned, work-roughened hand on her thigh and she felt herself tingle.

Well damn. Meg was right—too little sex fried the brain.

Clearly misunderstanding her body's response, Griffin squeezed gently as if trying to soothe her, which of course had the opposite effect, making things worse. Embarrassed, she tried to pull free, but he still held her effortlessly. Griffin's steely grey eyes remained steady on hers.

"Take stock first," he said, voice low but commanding. "What hurts? Let me see."

Since the only thing that hurt besides her pride was a

part of her anatomy that she considered no-man's-land, hell would freeze over before she'd *let him see*.

"I'm fine. Really," she said.

Griffin took her hand and easily hoisted her up, studying her in that assessing way of his. Then he started to turn her around, presumably to get a three-hundred-and-sixty-degree view, but she stood firm. "Seriously," she said, backing away, "I'm good." And if she wasn't, if she'd actually broken her butt, she'd die before admitting it, so it didn't matter. Bending to gather up her belongings, she carefully sucked in a grimace of pain.

"I've got it," Griffin said, and scooped up the duct tape and donuts. He looked like maybe he was going to say something about the donuts, but at the odd vibrating noise behind them, he turned. "Your phone's having a seizure," he said.

Panicked siblings, no doubt. After all, there was a camel to create out of thin air, and a cheerleading top to locate, and God only knew what disaster her father was coming up with for breakfast.

Griffin offered her the cell phone and Kate stared down at it thinking how much easier her day would go if it would have smashed to pieces when it hit the ground.

"Want me to step on it a few times?" he asked, sounding amused. "Kick it around?"

Startled that he'd read her so easily, she snatched the phone. When her fingers brushed his, an electric current sang up her arm and went straight to her happy spots without passing go. Ignoring them, she turned to her fallen purse. Of course the contents had scattered. And of course the things that had fallen out were a tampon and condom.

It was how her day was going.

She began cramming things back into the purse; the phone, the donuts, the duct tape, the condom, and the tampon.

The condom fell back out.

"I've got it." Griffin's mouth twitched as he tossed it into her purse for her. "Duct tape and a Trojan," he said. "Big plans for the day?"

"The Trojans built protective walls around their city," she said. "Like condoms. That's where the name Trojan comes from."

His mouth twitched. "Gotta love those Trojans. Do you carry the condom around just to give people a history lesson?"

"No. I—" He was laughing at her. Why was she acting like such an idiot? She was a teacher, a good one, who bossed around seven- and eight-year-olds all day long. She was in charge, and she ran her entire world with happy confidence.

Except for this, with Griffin. Except for anything with Griffin.

"Look at you," he said. "Little Katie Evans, all grown up and carrying condoms."

"One," she said. "Only one condom." It was her emergency, wishful thinking condom. "And I go by Kate now."

He knew damn well she went by Kate, and had ever since she'd hit her teens. He just enjoyed saying *Little Katie Evans* like it was all one word, as if she was still that silly girl who'd tattled on him for taking frogs to one of his mom's elegant luncheons, getting him grounded for a month.

Or the girl who, along with his nosy sister Holly, had found his porn stash under his bed at the ranch house and gotten him grounded for two months.

"Kate," he said as if testing it out on his tongue, and she had no business melting at his voice. None. Her only excuse was that she hadn't seen him much in the past few years. There'd been a few short visits, a little Facebook interaction, and the occasional Skype conversation if she'd happened to be with Holly when he'd called home. Those had always been with him in uniform, looking big, bad, and distracted on Holly's computer.

He wasn't in uniform now but she could check off the

big, bad, and distracted. The early gray light wasn't doing her any favors, but he could look good under any circumstances. Even with his baseball hat, she could see that his dark hair was growing out of a short military cut, emphasizing his stone-colored eyes and hard jaw covered in a five o'clock shadow. To say that he looked good was like saying the sun might be a tad bit warm at its surface. How she'd forgotten the physical impact he exuded in person was beyond her. He was solid, sexy male to the core.

His gaze took her in as well, her now windblown hair and mud-spattered leggings stuffed into snow boots. She wasn't exactly at her best this morning. When he stepped back to go, embarrassment squeezed deep in her gut. "Yeah," she said, gesturing over her shoulder in the vague direction of her car. "I've gotta go too—"

But Grif wasn't leaving, he was bending over and picking up some change. "From your purse," he said, and dropped it into her hand.

She looked down at the two quarters and a dime, and then into his face. She'd dreamed of that face. Fantasized about it. "There's 293 ways to make change for a dollar," she said before she could bite her tongue. Dammit. She collected bachelor of science degrees. She was smart. She was good at her job. She was happy.

And she was ridiculously male-challenged . . .

Griffin gave a playful tug on an escaped strand of her hair. "You never disappoint," he said.

And then he was gone.

Two

F ive minutes later Kate pulled up to her dad's place. One glance in the rearview mirror at her still-flushed cheeks and bright eyes told her that she hadn't gotten over her tumble in the parking lot.

Or the run-in with Griffin.

"You're ridiculous," she told her reflection. "You are not still crushing on him."

But she so was.

With a sigh, she reached for the stack of casserole dishes she'd made to get her family through the week without anyone having to actually be In Charge. She got out of her car, leaving the keys in it for Ashley, who'd drive it to her private high school just outside of town.

Tommy stood in the doorway, waiting. He wore a green hoodie and had a fake bow and arrow set slung over his chest and shoulder.

"Why are you all red in the face?" he asked. "Are you sick?"

She touched her still-burning cheeks. The Griffin Reid Effect, she supposed. "It's cold out here this morning."

The seven-year-old accepted this without question. "Did you get the tape?"

"I did," she said. "Tommy—"

"I'm not Tommy. I'm the Green Arrow."

She nodded. "Green Arrow. Yes, I got the tape, Green Arrow."

"I still don't see how duct tape is going to help us make a camel," he said, trailing her into the mudroom.

She refrained from telling him the biggest aid in making a camel for the school play would've been to give her more warning than a panicked five A.M. phone call. Instead she set down the casserole dishes on the bench to shrug out of her sweater as she eyed him. She could tell he'd done as she'd asked and taken a shower, because his dark hair was wet and flattened to his head, emphasizing his huge brown eyes and pale face. "Did you use soap and shampoo?"

He grimaced and turned to presumably rectify the situation, dragging his feet like she'd sent him to the guillotine.

Kate caught him by the back of his sweatshirt. "Tonight'll do," she said, picking the casseroles back up and stepping into the living room.

Evidence of the second-grade boy and the high-school-junior girl living here were all over the place. Abandoned shoes were scattered on the floor, sweatshirts and books and various sporting equipment lay on furniture.

Her dad was in the midst of the chaos, sitting on the couch squinting at his laptop. Eddie Evans was rumpled, his glasses perched on top of his head. His khakis were worn and frayed at the edges. His feet were bare. He looked like Harry Potter at age fifty. "Stock's down again," he said, and sighed.

Since he said the same thing every morning, Kate ignored him and moved into the kitchen. No breakfast. She went straight to the coffee maker and got that going. Ten minutes later her dad wandered in. "You hid them again," he said.

She handed him a cup of coffee and a plate of scrambled egg whites and wheat toast before going back to wielding the duct tape to create the damn camel. "You know what the doctor said. You can't have them."

His mouth tightened. "I need them."

"Dad, I know it's hard," she said softly, "but you've been so strong. And we need you around here for a long time to come yet."

He shoved his fingers through his hair, which only succeeded in making it stand up on end. "You've got that backward, don't you?"

"Aw. Now you're just kissing up." She hugged him. "You're doing great, you know. The doc said your cholesterol's coming down already and you've only been off potato chips for a month."

He muttered something about where his cholesterol could shove it, but sat down to eat his eggs. "What is that?" he asked, gesturing to the lump on the table in front of him.

"A camel." It'd taken her two pillows, a brown faux pashmina, and a couple of stuffed animals tied together with twine, but she actually had what she thought was a passable camel-shaped lump.

Ashley burst into the kitchen wearing a way-too-short skirt, a skimpy camisole top, and enough makeup to qualify as a pole dancer. In direct opposition to this image, she was sweetly carrying Channing Tatum, the bedraggled black-and-white stray kitty she'd recently adopted from the animal center, where she volunteered after school. Contradiction, meet thy queen.

Channing took one look at the "camel" and hissed.

"What the hell is that?" Ashley asked of the makeshift prop, looking horrified as she cuddled Channing.

"Don't swear," Kate said. "And it's a camel. And also, you're going out in that outfit over my dead body."

Ashley looked down at herself. "What's wrong with it?"

"First of all, you'll get hypothermia. And second of all, no way in hell."

Ashley narrowed her overdone eyes. "Why do you get to swear and I don't?"

"Because I earned the right with age and wisdom."

"You're twenty-eight," Ashley said, and shrugged. "Yeah, you're right. You're old. Did you find my cheerleading top?"

Kate tossed it to her.

Ashley snubbed her nose at the scrambled eggs, though she fed Channing a piece of turkey bacon before thrusting a sheet of paper at Kate. "You can sign it or I can forge dad's signature."

"Hey," Eddie said from the table. He pushed his glasses further up on his nose. "I'm right here."

Kate grabbed the paper from Ashley and skimmed it. Permission slip to . . . skip state testing. "No." Skipping testing was the last thing the too-smart, underachieving, overly dramatic teen needed to do.

"Dad," Ashley said, going for an appeal.

"Whatever Kate says," Eddie said.

"You can't skip testing," Kate said. "Consider it practice for your SATs for college. You want to get the heck out of here and far away from all of us, right? This is step one."

Ashley rolled her eyes so hard that Kate was surprised they didn't roll right out of her head.

Tommy bounced into the room. He took one look at the camel and hugged it close. "It's perfect," he declared. Then he promptly inhaled every crumb on his plate. He smiled at Kate as he pushed his little black-rimmed glasses farther up on his nose, looking so much like a younger, happier version of their dad that it tightened her throat.

A car horn sounded from out front. Kate glanced at the clock and rushed Tommy and Ashley out the door. Ashley got into Kate's car and turned left, heading toward her high school. Tommy and Kate got into the waiting car, where they turned right to head to the elementary school.

Their driver was Ryan Stafford, Kate's second best friend and the principal of the elementary school.

And her ex.

He must have had a district meeting scheduled because he was in a suit today, complete with tie, which she knew he hated. With his dark blond hair, dark brown eyes, and lingering tan from his last fishing getaway, he looked like Barbie's Ken, the boardroom version. He watched as Kate got herself situated and handed him a to-go mug of coffee.

"What?" she said when he just continued to look at her.

"You know what." He gestured a chin toward the cup she'd handed him. "You're adding me to your little kingdom again."

"My kingdom? You wish. And the coffee's a thanks for the ride, not an 'I don't think you can take care of yourself,'" she said.

Ryan glanced at Tommy in the rearview mirror. "Hey, Green Arrow. Seatbelt on, right?"

"Right," Tommy said, and put on his headphones. He was listening to an Avenger's audio book for what had to be the hundredth time, his lips moving along with the narrator.

Ryan looked at Kate. "Thought you were going to talk to him."

She and Ryan had dated for four months, during which time they'd decided that if they didn't go back to being just friends they'd have to kill each other. Since Kate was opposed to wearing an orange jumpsuit, this arrangement had suited her. "I did talk to him," she said. "I told him reading was a good thing."

"How about talking to himself and dressing like superheroes?"

Kate looked at Tommy. He was slouched in the seat, still mouthing along to his book, paying them no mind whatsoever. "He's fine." She took back Ryan's coffee, unscrewed the top on the mug, blew away the escaping steam, and handed it back to him.

"You going to drink it for me, too?" he asked, then laughed. "Just admit it. You can't help yourself."

"Maybe I like taking care of all of you. You ever think of that?"

"Tell me this then—when was the last time you did something for yourself, something entirely selfish?"

"Ryan, I barely have time to go to the bathroom by myself."

"Exactly," he said.

"Exactly what?"

Now she laughed. Ryan shook his head and kept driving. They passed the lake just before the bridge into town. The water was still and flat in the low light. On the far side was the dam that held back the snow melt, controlling the volume feeding into the river so that Sunshine didn't flood. Along the very top of the dam was a trail, which Kate sometimes ran on the days that she wanted to be able to fit into her skinny jeans. Up there, at the highest lay, was an old fallen Jeffrey Pine. On its side, battered smooth by the elements, it made a perfect bench.

It was her spot.

She went there to think, or when she needed a time-out from the rest of the world, which happened a lot.

"You get a date for the wedding yet?" Ryan asked.

No. She'd put that particular task off, and now, with the wedding only two days away, there was only one man who'd made her even think about dating. But tall, dark, and far-too-hot Griffin Reid was way out of her league. In fact, he was so far out of her league, she couldn't even see the league. "Working on it."

Ryan made a sound of annoyance. "You've been saying

that for months." He glanced at her over the top of his sunglasses. "Tell me it's not going to be me."

"Hey, I'm not that bad of a date."

He slid her another look. "You going to put out afterward?"

Kate whipped around to look at Tommy, but the kid was still listening intently to his book. "No," she hissed, and smacked him. "You know I'm not going to put out. We didn't . . . suit that way."

"Well, I'm hoping to . . . 'suit' with one of the bridesmaids." He glanced at her again. "You ought to try it."

"Sorry. The bridesmaids don't do it for me."

He smiled.

"Stop picturing it!"

Ryan's smile widened, the big male jerk, and she smacked him again.

"All I'm saying," he said, "is that you should stop treading water and try for some fun. Live a little."

"You think I have no life."

Ryan blew out a sigh. They'd been down this road before. "You know what I think. I think you do everything for everyone except yourself. Look at your track record. You've had exactly one boyfriend in five years and you're still making him coffee every morning."

"And you're still driving me to work so I can fill you in on the school gossip without you having to actually pay attention in the staff room," Kate said more mildly than she felt. Maybe because she heard the underlying worry in Ryan's voice, and she didn't want anyone to worry about her. She was fine. She was great. "We use each other. And we're both fine with that."

Ryan reached over and pulled the fancy, thick, white envelope with the gold embossing sticking out of her purse. "Fourteen more days."

"Hey," she said, trying to grab it back.

He waved it under her nose. "Treading water, Kate. And

the proof's right here. Just like it was at this same time last year. And the year before that."

Again she tried to grab back the envelope.

"Why do you carry the nomination around with you when you know damn well you aren't going to go?"

She wanted to go. But . . . "It means a whole year away from here."

"And?"

She blew out a breath.

"It's a dream come true for you," he said quietly.

It was. Being nominated for a full-ride scholarship to the graduate program of science education at the University of San Diego—a world away from Sunshine, Idaho—was exactly her dream. It would take a year to accomplish, an entire, glorious, science-filled year. With the degree, and the grant that Ryan promised to get her if she finished, she could bring a new and exciting science program to the county's school district. It was something she'd wanted for a long time. Some women wanted a spa week. Kate wanted to go dissect calves and work with scientists whose work she'd admired for a long time. Yes, it would be great for the school, but the truth was that Kate wanted it for her.

Badly.

"I was thinking maybe I'd accept and go this time," she said.

"But?" he asked.

"But," she said. "Next year is crucial for Ashley. We have colleges to decide on . . ."

"Uh-huh," Ryan said. "And last year it was Tommy's health."

"He had pneumonia." Snatching back the envelope, she shoved it in her purse.

They didn't speak again for the rest of the ride.

She never wanted a hero...

NEW YORK TIMES BESTSELLING AUTHOR

JILL SHALVIS

RESCUE
MY HEART

An Animal Magnetism Novel

After a tragic stint in the National Guard, Adam Connelly returns to Idaho and to Belle Haven, the animal shelter he owns with his brothers. All Adam wants is to be alone. Then he opens the door to the past—the woman whose heart he once broke. Still gorgeous, still tough-as-nails, but this time, unusually vulnerable.

Holly learned the hard way to never depend on a man for anything. Of all men, Adam is the last one she wants to see, and the only one she needs. Her father has gone missing in the Bitterroot Mountains and she could use someone with tracking skills to help find him.

For Holly and Adam, each with their own ghosts, a trek this desperate, this unpredictable, and this intimate will have its share of risks—including opening their hearts one more time...

**"Shalvis makes me laugh, makes me cry,
makes me sigh with pure pleasure."**
—Susan Andersen, *New York Times* bestselling author

"Jill Shalvis sizzles!"
—JoAnn Ross, *New York Times* bestselling author

jillshalvis.com
facebook.com/JillShalvis
facebook.com/LoveAlwaysBooks
penguin.com

M1285T0313